Gone for a Burton

Dave Cox

Gone for a Burton

Matador
9 De Montfort Mews
Leicester LE1 7FW, UK
Tel: (+44) 116 255 9311 / 9312
Email: books@troubador.co.uk
Web: www.troubador.co.uk/matador

ISBN 10: 1 905886 17-9
ISBN 13: 978-1-905886-17-3

All characters and events contained in this book are fictional, and are solely
the product of the Author's imagination.

Typeset in 11pt Stempel Garamond by Troubador Publishing Ltd, Leicester, UK
Printed in the UK by The Cromwell Press Ltd, Trowbridge, Wilts, UK

Matador is an imprint of Troubador Publishing Ltd

To Lynne and Angharad

CHAPTER ONE

'Points of Order'

"Finbar O'Driscoll's pert young buttocks quivered in nervous anticipation at the sight of m'lady's riding crop."

He put down his pen and stared at the page. He liked the first line, but what to write next? It suddenly dawned on him that it would be quite difficult to write the million-selling blockbuster that was going to catapult him from a dead-end job as a clerk in Llatadoogon Borough Council and into a world of Caribbean tropical islands, ownership of a Premiership football club, as much drink as he could cope with and so many women that he could have his way with that wanking would be as distant a memory as Farley's rusks and as about as appealing.

Turpin Thrust was a committee clerk in Llatadoogon Borough Council whose job was to write down the words uttered by Councillors in every meeting they attended, and to keep a 'proper record' of the proceedings. Llatadoogon Council had been formed in one of the numerous local government re-organisations that seemed to happen every so often, and was the council that covered the town of Port Talbot, the steelworks town that nestled between the mountains and the sea on the coast of South Wales. The Council covered towns and valleys that had no obvious relationship to one another, and indeed often had considerable antipathy, bordering on hatred for one another which generally manifested itself on the rugby field.

The name of the Council had obviously been dreamed up by a civil servant with a sense of humour, who ostensibly

1

naming it after a small centrally placed hamlet called Llan Cadwgan, decided to anglicise it as Llatadoogon, which appropriately spelt backwards said 'No good at all'. How they must have laughed at that one in Whitehall. Anyway the locals were stuck with it until the next re-organisation, though some felt it was great, in an ironic, post modern way.

Turpin had a traditional sturdy Welsh rugby player build with dark short hair. He was also fairly bright, and had gone to university when it was an achievement to have gone to one. However his aversion to hard work, decision making and responsibility had led him quite naturally to a career in local government. Now in his mid thirties, he had become totally disillusioned with the buttoned-up claustrophobic and inert world that he found himself trapped in, and, lacking the drive to change career or obtain promotion, sought to change his life by writing a blockbuster novel or becoming a media personality, or even, in his wildest dreams, both.

He had provisionally entitled the book 'Lesbian Bitch Vixens of Tongwynlais' and he now needed to flesh out the story of a bisexual nymphoniac dominatrix who shagged a swathe through the pubs, clubs and housing estates of the South Wales Valleys (starting with the aforementioned, naïve and innocent Irish labourer). He was certain that they'd soon be cashing their giros like billyo in Merthyr to read it, and in his mind it was a dead cert for a Welsh Language TV production, albeit toned down for domestic consumption.

The publication of the book, would give him financial security, and also allow him to fully develop his undoubted latent talents and give him the time, money and status to launch into his long cherished project, a musical based on the life of Dic Penderyn, the great Welsh working class hero, entitled 'No grass shall grow on my grave', which would then be followed by a Celto-African fusion rock opera set in the Zulu War of 1879 culminating in an 'all singing, all dancing' re-enactment of the battle of Rorke's Drift on stage performed by midgets in full battle dress.

His mind often wandered off in idle moments (and there were plenty at the Council) into alternative careers, book titles, rock operas, and anything else he could think of in order to transform his mundane existence. He would obviously have to change his name before embarking on a career as a novelist / media personality.

He'd often thought about his rather strange name. There had been Thrusts in Port Talbot for centuries and the name came from his forefathers who worked in the mines erecting wooden beams and joists—trawst being the Welsh for beam— and, to be fair, he felt it was a pretty dynamic, by definition assertive, no nonsense name. If he'd been called Brett, or Vince, he would probably have been happy with his name. However, of all names he'd been christened Turpin. He was particularly depressed that his parents had called him Turpin, a name that just didn't go very well with Thrust. He once asked his father why he had been given such an unusual first name. His father explained that Turpin's grandfather had hero-worshipped the famous highwayman, Dick Turpin, and had asked on his deathbed, that if he had a grandson, he be named in his honour. On the grandfather's death, Turpin's parents decided to go along with the old man's wish. In fact his parents only had some limited room for manoeuvre, and agonised over what to call their newly born son. They eventually ruled out 'Dick' for obvious reasons, and he was therefore christened 'Turpin Thrust'. Life could be so cruel thought Turpin.

Anyway—whatever—he had resolved that his name had to go. He would adopt a nom de plume, or even change it by deed poll—something masculine, snappy, sexy … Grant Hampton, or Melville Cairns, or ….

Suddenly the phone rang and interrupted his grand plans for a literary career and a new name. Reality thudded into him like a rugby tackle. He picked up the phone.

'Hello, Committee Section', Turpin Thrust here, what can I do for you?

He hated being nice to people on the phone, but as part of the councils commitment to 'Best Value' a mystery customer could phone up at any time to see if you were 'user friendly', and he could do without being hauled before the 'Customer Care Committee' to answer for any breach of this rule.

A voice he knew well slithered down the line.

"Thrust, get down here now; these minutes are totally unacceptable."

It was Caradog Owen-Jones, the Council Solicitor, who was as usual re-reading the minutes of the Entertainment and Leisure Committee, and who again as usual, wanted to show Thrust that he was in charge.

Thrust picked up the Committee papers and his note book, and trudged out of his office down the corridor to Owen-Jones' room. He despised Owen-Jones with all his heart, as did 99% of the councils' staff. Owen-Jones was a thin, balding, egotistical Welsh-speaking solicitor from a small village in mid Wales who had given a whole new meaning to the word 'mediocrity'. He had reached the giddy heights of Solicitor to Llatadoogon Borough Council at the age of 32 by a combination of toadying, membership of the Masons and always doing what he was told to do, the last trait culminating in a particularly degrading and painful afternoon submitting to a host of indignities at the hands of the gay sado-masochistic Chair of the Personnel Committee. However, this was as far as he'd got partly due to his unwillingness to submit to the ministrations of the Chair of the Personnel Committee again and partly due to his total lack of ability. Twenty years later he was now using his position, such as it was, to inflict suffering on others to lessen the pain of his thwarted, mundane career.

Thrust knocked at the door, and went into the small ante room to Owen-Jones' Office occupied by Owen-Jones Secretary Gloria 'Full-Kit' Lewis. He immediately cheered up at the sight of Gloria sitting, legs crossed, typing away with nonchalant abandon. Gloria was in her mid 20's and had consistently been in the top 10 shaggable women in the Council for the last 7 or 8 years (democratically achieving this accolade by virtue of a traditional secret poll organised prior to the Xmas dance by the boys in the Engineering Department).

Her long blonde hair was tied up, and she wore cute black rimmed glasses. Her cleavage was pushed up like a tidal wave about to burst on Aberavon beach, and her short skirt rode up to hint at the source of her nick name, the ever present 'full-kit' of a seamed stockings and suspenders that she always wore, even, so it was said, when she had trousers on doing the gardening or, even more bizarrely sitting in the bath. Thrust often said that the only reason he'd swap lives or jobs with

Owen-Jones was to have full-kit Gloria as his secretary. The thought caused him to shudder with anticipation at the prospect of seeing her every day, ready and eager, so he imagined to do his every bidding. The council and its Legal Department could spontaneously combust for all he cared, if only Gloria was his secretary.

There was much more to Gloria than what met the eye though. Turpin had known her through her brothers, and had seen her grow from a pony tailed young girl into a beautiful woman. She had always been a bright girl, but as often the case in the Town, she had turned her back on academic life to concentrate on a social life, and a succession of useless but rich boy friends and had ended up in the Council by default.

He was sure she felt they were a potential passport out of the drudgery of her job in the Council. He knew she had an interest in literature and poetry by the depth and quality of the books she kept on her desk for the odd spot of reading when not typing Owen-Jones' latest diatribe, and he had heard a rumour that she had enrolled on an Open University Course in English.

He was sure that if he was really able to get to know her they'd have a lot in common (in addition to their mutual hatred of Owen-Jones). If only he had the nerve to ask her out, he thought—though as she seemed to have a penchant for flash wealthy men he was sure any attempt would be deemed to failure—especially as his month's pay wouldn't pay the insurance on her boy friends car.

"Hello, Turpin, how are 'ew," cooed Gloria. "I didn't see you in Bryns last Saturday, got lost did 'ew?" Gloria spoke in a broad Port Talbot accent, and smiled a smile that would provoke a priest to chew the pages out of a Bible.

Bryns was the local nightclub, a cross between the London Dungeon, the Moulin Rouge and the Star Wars Bar. Its nicknames ranged from 'Crufts' to 'The Serengeti' to 'Siff City', and it was the only late night drinking place in Port Talbot. Gloria went there often, sometimes with her friends, sometimes with her boyfriend Finlay Quench, a local young doctor, who was incidentally one of the most hated men in the town.

5

Thrust used to go there in order to maintain his high level of alcohol consumption, to ogle the few decent girls that ventured there, and, once in every blue(ish) moon to get a shag. However, last Saturday he'd been too hung over from Friday and gone home straight from the pub.

"No, to tell the truth I had a better offer see," he lied, smiling his most winning smile, "but if I'd known you were there, I'd have told Pamela Anderson to bugger off," he replied.

"Never mind, might see you there on Saturday, Finlay said he's away with the rugby, and me and the girls fancy a bit of a night out," said Gloria, with a hint of 'don't bullshit me with that one good boy' in her slightly crooked smile.

The strings in Thrust's heart and groin both twanged with this news, but before he could make any further progress Owen-Jones' voice came through the door, summoning him in. With a resigned hunch and a weak smile, he walked past Gloria, and went into Owen-Jones' room, known to everyone in the Council as 'The Brothel'. It got its name not from any of the romantic or otherwise dalliances that went on there, but because basically it looked exactly like a cheap Parisienne boudoir, and you invariably came out of it feeling like you'd caught the pox.

Everything in the room was pink, purple or some variation of these colours, and the décor was even more puke inducing—China dogs, dolls and pictures of purple flowers lay everywhere interspersed with pictures of stern Victorians (presumably Owen-Jones' forefathers) and embroidered cloth pictures with biblical phrases on them in Welsh and English saying things like 'God is my Judge', 'Damned are the Damned' and 'Help me smite the wicked with thy powerful rod'.

No wonder Owen-Jones had been thrown out of his chapel for frightening the ladies with his sermon on the perils of Sunday Trading. He now practised his lay preaching from a mobile pulpit broadly modelled on the 'Popemobile' which was basically a specially modified Reliant Robin with an electronic cross that came out of the boot, when he lodged the gear stick at a particular angle.

Owen-Jones peered at Thrust over the rim of his half moon glasses like the Carry On veteran Kenneth Williams examining an edition of *Playboy*—a mixture of curiosity, loathing and contempt. He hated the fact that Thrust had some form of life, laughed a lot, flirted with Gloria and was not in any way intimidated by Owen-Jones' feeble attempts at bullying. Thrust was also good at his job, when he wanted to be, and this irritated the shit out of Owen-Jones. On this particular day, Owen-Jones was in a really bad mood, as his piles had been giving him agony all weekend, and his sermon on the 'wages of fornication' outside the workingman's club in the Port Talbot suburb of Sandfields had resulted in him being locked in his car by the darts team which was then set on fire by the men coming out from the lunch time strip show. His life was only saved by the pigeon breeder section of club members leaping onto the roof and bonnet and peeing through the open sunroof onto both him, and the raging fire. These events, coupled with him having to do a presentation to the Drainage Committee on an EU Directive on Waste recycling had put him into a foul mood, and the opportunity to bollock Thrust over anything was about the only thing he had to look forward to.

"These minutes are rubbish Turpin. I've had to change them all" said Owen-Jones in what he considered to be his sternest voice. "Why don't you pay attention in Committee— we pay you to make accurate contemporaneous notes, not this drivel that you turn out. If you don't sharpen up your act, I'll be forced to take things further."

"Yeah yeah" thought Thrust—Jones was too lazy to put together the paperwork to do a disciplinary, and in any event no-one been sacked by the Council for 30 years—members refused to sack even the laziest most useless staff. Thrust could be caught red handed shagging full-kit Gloria in the Council Chamber during a debate singing 'Tomorrow belongs to me', in an SS uniform, and they wouldn't sack him, especially if Jones brought the charge.

Thrust decided to play dumb and think up an outrageous story, in order to piss Jones off even more, rather than just try to argue back to prove his Head of Department wrong—it would be quicker and probably more fun.

"I'm really sorry, Mr Owen-Jones, but my girlfriend's mother's sex change operation's been cancelled again, and she's off work with worry. I'm afraid it stopped me concentrating at the Committee. I'm sorry" spluttered Thrust feigning anguish and contrition. (His theatrical training at the Port Talbot Little Theatre paying unexpected dividends).

Owen-Jones guessed that the story was a pack of lies but there was little he could do. He was intrigued by the sex change story, though—he was eternally fascinated by the degenerate goings on of the locals and was also tempted to see if there was a glimmer of truth in the story—in Port Talbot anything could happen.

"Her mother's sex change operation'? Isn't that a bit unusual?" queried Owen-Jones fishing for more details as his lips quivered like a prodded waterbed.

"No, it's all the rage in Cwmavon—anyway she only wants it in order to be more able to satisfy her new live in lover, a bisexual hermaphrodite Latvian sailor called Nobby."

Thrust nearly laughed at this embellishment but he knew that Owen-Jones revulsion at sexual deviation would win over against his curiosity of how deep human depravity could sink. Just in case however, Thrust threw in a legal issue to block any possible further questioning by Owen-Jones—if anything frightened Owen-Jones more than sex, it was the threat of legal action (an unusual but refreshing trait in a lawyer).

"I'd be happy to tell you more, but I'm sure we'd be in trouble if we breached Patient confidentiality—and there's possible liability under the European Convention on Human Rights, as I'm sure you know" stated Thrust with a knowing nod. Owen-Jones drew back and swivelled his eyes back and fore like extra in a Spaghetti Western—his cowardice in the face of legal action was legendary.

"Yes, oh yes, we'd better stop there—I'd anticipated those issues, and I'll let the matter drop. But try to put these matters to one side when you take the minutes next time. There is no more important job in the Council than being a minute taker Thrust. Well—get back to your office, I've got an important presentation to prepare for you know." Owen-Jones pulled a half open file in front of him, and started to peruse it with all the intensity he could muster.

"Thank you, Mr Owen-Jones. I'll try to put it all behind me. You're a real help" lied Thrust, turning away.

As Thrust closed the door Owen-Jones reached down to his right hand desk drawer and pulled out a copy of *Health and Efficiency* from the 1960's that he'd found in a skip in his back lane ten years ago. It gave him some consolation from not exploring Thrust's story further. The tattered magazine had certainly received a battering and now resembled an extract from the *Dead Sea Scrolls*. Nevertheless looking at its collection of scantily clad and nude dollybirds yet again cheered him up, and true to form, it was now in for a further vigorous examination.

"Miserable sod—his piles are playing him up, are they?" said Thrust to Gloria as he walked passed her desk.

"Yes, he's been in a foul mood all week" said Gloria crossing her legs flitatiously. "They played hell with him in Sandfields on Sunday when they peed through his sunroof to put out the fire in his car, and, his mothers 98th birthday party was a terrible flop. Two of the guests died of shock after the party poppers he bought fell into the fire. Poor dab leads a terrible life."

"Good enough for him—he's a fart-breathing toss bag, who makes my piss boil with revulsion. I'd rather bite the balls off a sleeping wildcat than help Owen-Jones do anything," said Thrust in a pent up explosion of anger, tempered by lust.

"Don't like 'im do 'ew? Funny that, no-one seems to" said Gloria in a splendid moment of reflection. "Never mind, working here pays the bills, don't it," she said and smiled sweetly before returning diligently to her work yet again.

Turpin smiled and stood dreaming of how he would whisk Gloria away from all this when his literary career took off, as it surely would.

"You going out this weekend Turpin?," she asked after a few minutes.

Turpin came back to earth with a jolt. "May do—it's Friday, pay day has just gone, and after a week in this place I definitely need a drink" said Thrust. "We're all meeting up tomorrow, and will probably end up at Bryns."

"Well I might see you there—as I said the girls are out on Saturday" said Gloria with a large wink of one of her beautiful blue eyes.

"Aye Aye—might see you there then," said Thrust coughing nervously.

"Turpin," said Gloria, "One thing before you go."

"What's that?" said Thrust, intrigued.

"Well—you know that voice you use—you know—the voice..." she stuttered.

"I don't know what you mean," smiled Thrust.

"You know, the sexy one—the Richard Burton one. Please say something to me before you go—a nice romantic poem," said Gloria, her eyes locked onto his in sugary admiration.

"Ok. Just for you Gloria. I don't do it for all the girls you know." He swallowed and adjusted his tie.

"Had we but world enough, and time, this coyness lady were no crime,

we would sit down and talk which way to walk, and spend our long loves day....."

Thrust recited a substantial edited version of Andrew Marvell's 'To his Coy Mistress' in his best Richard Burton voice, deepening and rolling the vowels like a mountain stream plunging into a dark pool. He knew it had a tremendous effect on Gloria, and indeed other women. An English degree at Aberystwyth University, and many hours of practice had enabled him to quote reams of poetry in a passable imitation of probably one of the most memorable voices ever heard on stage or screen.

"Oh Turpin, that was fantastic especially reciting Marvell—he's got to be one of my favourites, though I personally feel 'the garden' was a better poem. I could listen to you all day" said Gloria with a wistful sigh.

"Or night?" He winked at her, "Anything for you Gloria, anything."

Things might be looking up, thought Thrust as he trudged back to his room. Gloria's out tomorrow and only 4 hours until I can clock out and, not only has she heard of, but actually likes, Andrew Marvell. He was really surprised that Gloria had heard of Andrew Marvell. Most of the women he knew hadn't even heard of Captain Marvell. There was certainly more to Gloria than met the eye he concluded. I've really got to get to know her better. Suddenly his drinking gene kicked in. The weekend starts here!

The only trouble was that he had to clerk the 'General Activities and Leisure Committee' that afternoon. He hated his job generally, but particularly hated Committees. Never mind, but as Gloria always said 'it paid the bills'. However, listening to the Councillors drone on and on about pointless bilge made him even more determined to write his book and get out of the council.

He got his notebook from his room and made his way down the corridor. He sat in the stuffy Committee Room and prepared to take notes of the proceedings. It was 2.30 on a Friday afternoon and was not happy at the thought of having to sit through a tedious Committee meeting. The concepts of work and Friday afternoon rarely coincided in the Council, but in a fit of spite Owen-Jones had timetabled the Committee for this slot in a deliberate attempt to make Thrust's life more miserable.

However as it was Friday afternoon, it was unlikely that the Committee would go on long as most of the members, including the Chair would be aiming to get to the pub by at least 4 pm.

The Chairman of the Committee, Alderman Caractacus Pugh, was a typical example of the council. Male, elderly, a lifelong Labour Party Member, he had worked in the local steelworks all his life, and in so doing became a Trade Union activist. He was also a keen Aberavon rugby supporter, a pigeon breeder, a covert brothel habitue' and a freemason though rarely all at once. He had little formal education, but possessed an immense and irrational belief in his powers of intellect and an even greater irrational belief in his powers of oratory. These delusions, coupled with a deep seated hatred of council Officers (particularly those with professional qualifications and or degrees) made him the living psychological embodiment of the average councillor. There were a few women councillors, the odd youngish sociology graduate, and lurking in the shadows even one or two opposition members, but generally the entire council was made up of Labour, male, elderly former manual workers, exemplified by Caractacus Pugh.

However, in one way Pugh was slightly out of kilter with his colleagues in that he wore a wig. Thrust had noted that a significant proportion of councillors were bald, and on a hot day in council the benches often resembled rows of steaming boiled eggs. Some, in vain attempts to hide their baldness, combed or pasted a few strands of hair, like rats tails across their heads. This pointless activity often meant that their partings started millimetres above their ears. Spurning this retro fashion craze however, Caractacus Pugh chose to wear a splendid wig.

The fact that it was too small, the wrong colour, and was made out of some man made fibre that bore no resemblance to hair, did not seem to bother him one bit. It did however provide a source of light relief to the officers and members who attended his committees as it would often move from side to side during debates, coming to rest or lodging at bizarre and unbelievable angles.

His unfortunate nervous tick, and habit of 'gurning' at, to him, complex points on the agenda, would also move the wig forward to reveal a substantial uncovered area at the back of his head. Often bets were taken as to the amount of skin that would be revealed at the end of the meeting—usually in direct proportion to the difficulty of the matter being discussed.

There appeared to be little prospect of much wig movement today however, as the only item on the agenda was the utilisation of EU grant monies to build a public urinal in the town. If they all played their cards right, they'd be out in half an hour thought Turpin.

Caractacus Pugh called the meeting to order and the debate opened with the usual gaffes and malapropisms from some of the councillors.

The mover of the motion on the siting of the urinal (no pun intended) who went by the splendid name of Nimrod Squibbs, opened by saying 'we need to speculate to capitulate in spending this grant funding' whilst another indicated that he would like to see its walls covered in 'nice Muriels'. Turpin was saddened that no-one laughed at this traditional local government malapropism. In fact he was amazed to see that some of the members nodded in appreciation at the sagacity and breeding of their colleague in suggesting such a thing.

A few of the more sensible councillors then brought the debate on track with pertinent observations concerning the grant funding and construction costs, and Thrust, whilst writing down the essential points of their comments, began, as he often did to drift off into the strange world of his imagination.

He looked around the Leisure Committee room. It was adorned with photographs of some of the famous products of the Town who had gone on to achieve fame and fortune in the world of entertainment, culture and sport.

There were quite a number of Rugby and Football internationals, a few cricketers and athletics stars, some going back to the 19th Century. There were also fading photographs of hymn writers and composers together with winners of Eisteddfod singing and poetry prizes. However in pride of place were photographs of the towns great movie stars, Richard Burton and Anthony Hopkins.

How such a small insignificant town had produced one internationally famous Hollywood actor was a miracle, but to have produced two was beyond belief. Some said it was something in the polluted air or water—for which the Town was infamous—that was responsible for stimulating obscure glands and brain cells in the residents which turned ordinary people into esteemed thespians. Others said it was basic Darwinian evolutionary theory, which drove people to extraordinary lengths of dedication just to get away from such a miserable, dispiriting place. Whatever it was, the town was justifiably proud of its two great acting sons.

Turpin studied their faces, as he had done on numerous previous occasions, and weighed up their respective qualities, their acting careers, their contribution to life generally and inevitably, their shortcomings.

Thrust had collected most of their films on video, and also had many audio recordings—particularly of Burton. He'd also read almost all the published works on them, and, as a local boy, had talked to hundreds of people who had known them as they were growing up in the area. If anyone was able to critically evaluate the merits of the two, it was Turpin Thrust.

Nevertheless, he always came down in favour of Burton. Whilst both had immense talent, charisma and a prodigious appetite for life, in a number of key areas Thrust concluded that Burton had the edge over Hopkins.

Even though Hopkins had won an Oscar, when Burton hadn't, Thrust considered Burton to be the better actor—even though he'd probably made many poorer films than Hopkins. What probably clinched it for Thrust was the fact that Burton was from a poorer background than Hopkins (who had gone to Grammar School) could speak Welsh (Thrust always envied Welsh Speakers, though his knowledge of the language was minimal) and the clincher, played rugby with some distinction. This, capped by phenomenal hellraising, and a record of shagging some of the world's most beautiful women, tipped the balance in Thrust's consideration firmly in favour of Burton as Port Talbot's greatest son.

The only fly in the ointment of the hero worship that Thrust bestowed upon Burton, (and indeed on Hopkins) was that they'd both left their home town, and Wales, to go elsewhere, and indeed, not even to live in England, (which was bad enough, but tolerable) but to live abroad. Neither had really seemed to care about the Town after leaving—no scholarship, no memorial theatre, nothing, and this had really pissed Thrust off. The final insult, in Burton's case, was that he hadn't even been buried in the Town.

Thrust often considered the iniquity of this and in his mind composed impassioned speeches to Parliament, or whatever Swiss Canton was responsible for Burton's final resting place, to bring him back. If only someone could do something about it. If only.....

'Richard Burton'....

Thrust's mind suddenly snapped back to the proceedings of the Committee at the mention of that name.

The debate had now moved on to the siting and naming of the toilets, and one of the councillors, who had known Burton, was moving that they be named 'The Richard Burton Memorial Urinals'.

This provoked heated debate in the Chamber, as proponents of Anthony Hopkins, and even Ivor Emmanuel (the singing soldier in the film *Zulu*) advanced the causes of their favourite choice. A few wider thinkers threw in the name of Dic Penderyn, the local man who was unjustly hanged for his part in the 19th Century Merthyr Riots, and who was, as the speakers were keen to point out, at least buried in the Town—unlike Burton.

This provoked howls of opposition from the Burton camp, but immense support from others. The debate now swung into the merits of Hopkin's and Burton's stance in living, and in Burton's case, being buried, abroad. The obvious irony of calling a urinal after a man with the name of 'Dick' was lost in the furore that erupted.

The debate raged back and forth with some eulogising the actors to high heaven, whilst others condemned them as traitors, quitters and in one phrase that the speaker obviously meant as representing the worst insult possible, said that they'd behaved like Englishmen.

Time flew by as each member of the Committee spoke at length on the merits of the proposals. What Thrust thought was going to be a swift meeting was now turning into a very long deliberation indeed.

The room went silent when Glyndwr Meredith Griffiths, the only Welsh Nationalist on the council, got up to speak.

Griffiths was a fiery, committed Welsh speaker who lived alone in a hill farm in the darkest reaches of the Borough, and he was well known for his thoughtful, yet often provocative interventions in debate.

He started to speak in Welsh. Sadly, most of the councillors couldn't understand what he was saying, and complained to the Chair, Caractacus Pugh.

Glyndwr Meredith Griffiths insisted in both Welsh and helpfully English, he had the right, under the Welsh Language Act, to speak in his mother tongue at a public meeting such as this.

Caractacus Pugh initially ruled against him, but Glyndwr Meredith Griffiths insisted on a legal ruling on the point, and

Owen-Jones was summoned from his room to advise the Committee.

Owen-Jones crept into the Committee room, flushed purple after being interrupted in his over-vigorous examination of the battered *Health and Efficiency* magazine. He was shocked and shaken to be asked to rule on an important legal issue, but was particularly frightened of Glyndwr Meredith Griffiths and after pointedly and laboriously consulting the law books that he had managed to bring with him agreed in a display of rare decisiveness with the councillor.

Glyndwr Meredith Griffiths then spoke for half an hour, in Welsh, on where the urinals should be sited, and on what it should be called. The already volatile meeting simmered in anger as most of the members, who by now wanted to end the meeting, and go to the pub, had to listen to Glyndwr Meredith Griffiths address them in a language they didn't understand. The grainy unease was fuelled by a sneaking suspicion, often shared by English speakers, that Glyndwr Meredith Griffiths was using the language to insult them.

This perceived ongoing insult to themselves, and one of the Senior Labour councillors, caused growing resentment in the Labour ranks, but thge meeting finally flew into uproar, when, on finishing the speech, Meredith Griffiths turned on the rest of the members and accused them in English of not being Welsh for being unable to understand him. He announces that he held them, the meeting, and the council in total contempt for their lack of support for the Welsh language, and in a final gesture of defiance, strode over to Caractacus Pugh's chair and pulled his wig, which was nearly over his eyes by now, off, and after biting a chunk out of it, threw it across the Chamber like a frisbee.

This action caused uproar, and the meeting erupted into a free-for-all as Glynfwr Meredith Griffiths and his few supporters battled with the other councillors in and over the Chamber in a bizarre microcosm of Welsh history.

Caractacus Pugh tried vainly to maintain order before wading into the melée to find his half-eaten wig.

Owen-Jones hid under the Chairman's table reciting the Lord's Prayer, whilst Thrust simply recorderd 'Meeting adjourned' and sat watching and laughing at the chaos around him.

The security guards eventually arrived together with the police, and eventually order was restored. Unfortunately, statements were needed and Thrust, as the official minute-taker, was detained until quite late.

In true council tradition the matter was neverr resolved, and as far as Thrust was aware, the council never got around to naming the grant funded urinal!

However, what Turpin did know was that his Friday afternoon, and much of his Friday evening had been wasted. He was more certain than ever that his life had to change, and he knew he had to do something about it soon.

CHAPTER TWO

'Dirty Old Town'

Thrust walked out of the council building at the frighteningly late time of 8.30 and strolled home through the murky streets of Port Talbot.

Someone had once called it the arsehole of Wales, but that was being unfair to arseholes. The analogy was apt though, as the next town to it was incredibly called Pyle.

'Why do I stay here'? he thought as he looked at the rows of derelict frontages and charity shops. The town was an old one, yet the council had managed without any apparent challenge or protest, to knock everything of any age, or architectural merit down in the 1970s and had replaced it with a huge faceless concrete shopping mall. It was rumoured that someone had once discovered a large early Industrial Revolution vaulted cellar under the main street of considerable historical and architectural value, but the council had filled it with 300 tons of concrete before anyone could look at it or do anything about it. If they found Bodicea's tomb in Port Talbot it would be a car park before you could say 'Time Team'.

In Thrust's view, the council had waged relentless war against any historical edifice in the area, and fading black and white photographs of stately homes, castles and thatched cottages hung in mute testimony to the council's handiwork in the corridors of the Town Hall. Heritage was something you travelled to see if you lived in Port Talbot, the concept of such a thing existing in the town was alien to most of its inhabitants, as it had been systematically rooted out of the town, and its peoples consciousness by concentrated municipal vandalism.

Thrust fondly remembered his grandparents telling him of the rolling sand dunes and wide, sandy beaches that stretched for mile after mile, where thousands of day trippers would come to enjoy whatever good weather was to be had. It was strange how his grandparents insisted that there was always good weather when they were young. Perhaps it came with age—though Thrust's recollection of his youth was of wet, windy grimy tedium—Was it really like that? Or had the town made him think like that? Had he been worn down and bleached of happy memories by the grey gloominess of his surroundings? One thing was certain—no-one would shoot a Persil advert in Port Talbot.

To be fair to the council, though he didn't like to be, the town had been transformed for good, and ill, by the massive steelworks that were built between and after the wars, and which enveloped it like an unwelcome suitor, and which had ruined the famous mile after mile of golden sands and sand dunes. The works had belched fumes and smoke over the area for so long that it had grained the town in steel dust and rust. The only good thing about the steel works were that they had brought jobs and money, and in the 50s, 60s and 70s Port Talbot had been a kind of Welsh Boom Town—it's many pubs and restaurants (at that time) thronging with some of the best paid workers in the UK, over 20,000 of them, all intent on having a good time.

Sadly he recalled that it had all gone wrong when the old town centre, with its pubs, hotels and restaurants and closely packed streets was knocked down. By the time the new centre was built (replacing forty plus pubs with two!) the workers had gone to Swansea or Cardiff to enjoy themselves and before they could get used to the splendours of the new centre, the steel strike of the early 80s decimated the workforce. Since then it had been downhill all the way and the plant now only employed 3000 workers. It was rumoured that it too would soon close leaving the town with a derelict scrap yard ruining whatever natural assets this part of South Wales once had.

As if to compound the town's already large problems, the local authority had managed to site a huge council estate along the length of the remaining beach, and, to top and tail things, put a chemical works at the other end. Throw in a deep sea harbour with giant ore carriers coming in and out, coupled with unrestricted offshore sand dredging, which had turned the beaches into oil coated moonscapes, and you could see why its Tourist trade was only marginally better than that of Beirut's.

Thrust asked himself a question he'd wrestled with for most of his adult life: Why didn't he get away from this? He was sure he could get jobs in other councils—Swansea, Cardiff or even in England—yet he felt this fatalistic, yet defiant need to stay. His parents were still here, he had good friends, and he also felt a need to put something back, or put something right in his hometown.

In his wilder fantasies he would see himself acclaimed as Chief Executive by a cheering throng of councillors who had finally realised the need for a charismatic leader. His first act would be to sack Owen-Jones—publicly, with maximum humiliation, involving the revelation of his porn collection, swiftly followed by the promotion of Gloria to be his PA. He would then set out his vision for a new town—a total deregulation of liquor and licensing laws, coupled with active promotion of lap dancing which would turn it into UK's answer to Las Vegas. The money raised in business rates would then be used to turn the probably by now vacant steel works site into an interactive movieworld, where film buffs from all over the world could come and re-enact, or even live scenes from their favourite films—including sets out of *Casablanca, Zulu, Star Wars*—these would all rise out of the steelworks ashes. As a final gesture he would re-create the old town centre from scratch—not only to piss off any remaining councillors who'd originally acquiesced in it being knocked down, but also to give the town its old soul back.

He would then use the council's bursting coffers to do something that the town had shamefully totally failed to do, and which, in his view had blighted the town for decades—put up a fitting memorial to its greatest son—the man who took the name of Port Talbot to the furthest corners of the globe and who'd look anyone in the world in the eye and say 'I am from Port Talbot' and dare them with impunity to say anything disparaging about it—Richard Burton.

20

He thought back to the charade in the council committee that day. The fuss over naming a public toilet. Morons, all of them he thought. In Thrust's mind Burton was not only the greatest person to come from Port Talbot, he was also the greatest from Wales, indeed Britain, probably Europe and possibly the world. Ok, Port Talbot had produced some fine actors—obviously Anthony Hopkins, Michael Sheen, Ivor Emmanuel, whilst Catherine Zeta Jones had come from across the bay in Swansea. However, the best by a mile was Richard Burton, born up the valley in Pontrhydyfen, but raised in the grime and warmth of Taibach, a small area of Port Talbot nestling in the bosom of the steelworks, reknowned for its hard drinking and boisterous good humour. Burton was sometimes claimed by the neighbouring town of Neath. You can keep Ray Milland good boys—Dickie is ours, he thought!

Get a life!

Yes—a fitting memorial would be built, a huge bronze statue of Burton in his prime, arms out, declaring heroic stanzas on a plinth inscribed with his greatest speeches with the adoring women in life, Cybil, Susie, Sally and of course Liz, gazing up at him from the four corners of the plinth. This would replace the epileptic Dalek that now stood outside the council building—allegedly symbolising Steel and Coal, but more like a tribute to an exploding pin ball machine. Only a council as inept as this could fail to erect a statue to such a character—no-one would come to look at the existing monstrosity—yet thousands, nay millions would visit a statute to 'our Rich'.

In his mind's eye the statue would be accompanied by the obligatory interactive Burton centre showing his films non-stop, with a mini railway to take you through his life—Port Talbot, Oxford, London, Hollywood. The centre would be stacked to the brim with real or not so real memorabilia—quiff wigs and stick on spots, Burton Whisky (to be distilled locally) Aberavon Jerseys circa 1950 (he'd played a few games for the once famous local Rugby Club). There would also be stacks of *War of the Worlds* CDs and videos of all his films, and of course the books, including one Thrust was also going to write, entitled 'Where Burton walked as a boy'—an illustrated Pub / Mountain walk with quotes from his films to be read out at appropriate stopping points. Next door to the centre would be 'Burton's Hotel' where guests could stay in rooms themed on 'Where Eagles Dare', 'Taming of the Shrew', and, quite radically, in Thrust's mind 'Equus' and '1984'.

The piéce de resistance would be, obviously 'Burtons Pub', where the tormented inner soul of his hero could be fully and fittingly communed with by devoted fans. The pub would be packed with more memorabilia, with spoken extracts from *War of the Worlds* and *Zulu* continually playing on the juke box, whilst the bar would be festooned with the raunchiest barmaids money could buy serving every drink known to man, and a few invented for effect (by Thrust, of course).

There would be a grand opening by, who else, Anthony Hopkins (who would naturally donate his services for free and who would make a speech in his finest Burton voice available on a specially priced CD). To seal the undoubted orgasmic jollity of the occasion Sir Anthony would donate five million pounds to Aberavon Rugby Club (matched by a similar donation from Liz Taylor) to help it in its undoubted climb to European and World Rugby domination. Thrust was on a roll. However his dreams were rudely interrupted.

"Oy—knob rot—wakey wakey—dreaming of full kit Gloria are ew?" said a voice from the gloom.

Thrust's vision of a glorious new Port Talbot blossoming under his benign leadership was shattered by the words of his friend Vic Snipe booming in at him through the descending darkness.

"Uh—no, no, given that up for Lent. Just thinking of the ways in which I could murder Owen-Jones—nothing unusual. Tends to get me thinking though," said Thrust with a wry smile.

"Bollocks—you were in too deep for that" said Vic. "It'd have to be Gloria, or some stupid scheme to make money, or even make this town a better place—you've got an unhealthy obsession with that you know. Bit late to be leaving work. Any problems?"

"Yeah, huge row in council over naming a public toilet. Most of the councillors were arrested. It'll make a great story. Give me a bell tomorrow and I'll tell you all about it."

Snipe had been a friend of Turpin's for many years—they'd been in school together, and he was a reporter in the local paper. He was quite thin, with fairly long blonde hair. His journalistic career mainly consisted of accounts of punch-ups in the local Indian, speeding drivers or civic prize giving, though he had achieved national recognition with his scoops on the 'Neurotic Knicker Nicker from Neath' and the 'Suntanned Gnomes of Sandfields'. He had also interviewed the local young actress Catherine Zeta Jones and whilst drawing on his cigarette to look cool, accidentally swallowed it and phlegmed a combination of spit, tobacco and tick tacks over her blouse. Luckily she was only 17 at the time or his career could have been brought to an immediate but premature end.

His journalistic triumphs were way past him now and his work mainly consisted of regurgitating stories from other newspapers or hardy perennials like the sightings of strange cats or even UFOs in the hills above the town. His main interests in life were now masturbation, drinking and watching Aberavon, generally in that order, though it was a mighty close call between the first and second. Thankfully the topic he had in mind that evening was the second.

"Ok, sounds interesting. People like to know that their futures are safe in the hands of our wonderful council" said Vic with all the irony he could muster. "You going to Bryns tonight?"

"Don't know," said Thrust. "Probably not tonight—I'm knackered. But I'm definitely up for it tomorrow." (He knew he wanted to try to catch Gloria in there.)

"I'm going tonight—there's an offer on—Bow down to £1 a pint" said Vic with an involuntary lick of his lips.

"Yeah—but it's a real shit hole," said Turpin. "Hardly any women, the ones who are there look like skinned meercats, and its full of pissed, gormless farting men hoping for a shag, looking for a fight, who then litter the way home collapsing after a double or triple Indian meal."

"Nah—tonight's going to be different—I've been reliably informed there's a bus load of nurses going there tonight," said Vic.

Not the old 'busload of nurses story', thought Thrust. Every time they have any uncertainty about going to a pub (generally a rare occurrence) one of the boys would say 'there's a busload of nurses going' and in the vain hope there may be one, we all dutifully turn up. There never is, never will be he thought but ironically it always seemed to work. We men are fools.

"Really?" said Thrust.

"Yeah" said Vic. "It's one of the sister's leaving do's and they've decided to make it fancy dress, Ron, the hospital porter told me they're going as a gang of St Trinian's schoolgirls. Should be lively, they haven't been out for ages—well up for anything, as you'd expect from nurses."

"Balls—I don't believe you" said Thrust, desperately trying to fight off the lascivious expectations conjured up by Vic's words.

"Oh well, please yourself, but there's nothing else on tonight, so I may just stay in the pub. Anyway Stan and Archie are out tomorrow, so it should be a good night then especially if you've charged your batteries by staying in tonight. We're meeting up in the Penderyn at seven tomorrow, but I'm going straight to the pub tonight."

God, he liked his beer, thought Turpin. "Well I might pop along tonight" said Thrust, "I'll just have to phone Liz Hurley and tell her to wait until Sunday."

"Yeah, and you can have a couples night out with me and Nicole Kidman if you like," said Vic joining in the mutual bout of sarcasm.

"Sounds good. May see you in the Penderyn later, if not sometime tomorrow. After the ructions in council I just want to lie down," said Turpin.

Snipe walked off down the main street. Thrust watched him dodging the grey miserable people trooping home past the cracked paint shopfronts and 'To Let' signs. He could almost imagine tumbleweed blowing towards him.

"Something's got to change" he thought. Just like my pants, he mused. He was often prone to lateral thinking. Gloria will be out tomorrow, I may even buy a new pair. Where there's life there's hope! His fantasies began to run away with

24

him. Suddenly a gust of cold, dust laden air cut across his face and he returned to grim reality. He looked around him. Another work/life crisis. He had to do something. He felt he knew what to do, but couldn't quite put his finger on it. Something had to be done to change him, the Town, Wales, everything. But what?

He whistled optimistically and continued dreaming up his madcap schemes, as he walked home in the gathering gloom of the dirty grimey steelworks town which he thought he hated, but which deep down he knew he loved.

CHAPTER THREE

'Who Ate All The Pies?'

Exhausted by his exertions of the week, Thrust took the radical step of staying in on Friday night, and spent the rest of it demolishing a bottle of wine, whilst watching *Villain*, one of his favourite Richard Burton films. He fell into a deep and well deserved sleep.

The next morning, after a long lie in he went up town to do some shopping, which included buying a new pair of pants, before meeting Vic in their local, where he gave him chapter and verse on the events at the committee on Friday. They then went to his local rugby club, Brynglyn, to watch the second team play a team from Swansea. He would normally have played in the fixture himself, but had received a bang on the knee the week before and decided to watch instead. He only had a few pints in the clubhouse after the game as he was saving himself for what he expected to be a lively night.

After a shower and a change, Thrust walked into the Penderyn dead on seven. As he looked around him, he thought that if this was not the maddest pub in the world he could not conceive of anything madder, on a good night it often resembled the bastard offspring of a love tryst between a Breughel painting and a Hogarth print, with a bit of a Marvel Comic thrown in for luck.

The pub was one of the few left in Port Talbot that had not been knocked down by the council in the 1970's and even though it was now in the nineties, the décor remained mid 1960's.

The pub was peopled by some of the weirdest, baddest and saddest beings this side of TV pop-star auditions, and the icing on this particular human cake was the landlord, 'Glyn Jenkins, know to all in the area as 'Glyn, Glyn the human bin'.

He'd achieved this dubious accolade as a result of his drinking contests, one of which was downing, in his prime, a plastic bin full of beer. (This bin had been painted gold, and now stood proudly in the corner of the pub.) He would regularly challenge visitors to drinking contests, when he would strip to his waist, exposing a stomach that resembled a slightly punctured barrage balloon, and then, sitting upon his favourite chair, would psyche himself up into a frenzy of drink-lust, egged on by his regulars and cronies who would slap and massage his huge stomach whilst chanting 'Glyn, Glyn, the human bin, what comes out, must go in!'.

He would then bolt down whatever quantity of beer was before him before standing over his challenger leering and defying him to match his exploit. He never failed to win, and once the unfortunate challenger was led away dribbling and incoherent, Glyn would go to his gold plated bin, and with a bellow of exhalation chuck his entire gut contents up into the bin, cheered on by his over appreciative cronies.

Glyn had allegedly won the football pools in the 1980s and fulfilling his boyhood dream, bought a pub. He was also an avid *Star Trek* fan, and attended all their conventions and against all odds had learned Klingon. Justifiably proud of this achievement, he reputedly used to greet strangers, especially North Walians in classic Klingon.

."..just to piss them off 'cos I can't speak fucking Welsh," said Glyn. He would usually then go on to ask them in word perfect Klingon, the name of their favourite sheep, and whether they truly loved it.

His additional wealth enabled him to indulge in fantasies and japes that were far beyond the reach of most publicans, but which certainly made the Penderyn an entertaining pub to visit. His favourites included an elaborate CCTV system, linked to the toilets which enabled him to record the sights and sounds of persons conducting their ablutions.

These would then be played back to his cronies, who would then play a game known as 'match the crap', where videos of visitors would be played, then frozen, with the sound of the resultant visit to the toilet being relayed over the pub. Bets were taken on the various sounds made, and the winners would successfully match the visitor with the 'sound of the crap'.

The sounds themselves were often uproariously funny, ranging from high pitched whines like rockets on a bonfire night, or naval pipes greeting an Admiral, through to churning thunderclaps resembling the opening barrage of the Somme.

The greatest fun was had in trying to match some of the dreadful sounds in the ladies toilets to their demur and petite originators.

Many a return visitor to the Penderyn was puzzled at the outburst of hilarity on them re-entering a pub they had visited months before. Little did they know that their previous visit had often been replayed and bet over many times to the delight of the regulars.

Thrust admitted to himself that he found Glyn's antics funny, and even though he despised the vulgar depths to which Glyn often sank, he kept on coming back, not only for the laughs, but also to hear some of the bizarre conversation in the pub, and to have some decent beer (rare in Port Talbot) in one of its few non brewery chain pubs.

"Pint of woosh Glyn" (woosh was the local term for bitter).

"Boys in tonight then Turpin?"

Thank God he wasn't speaking Klingon thought Thrust. "Aye, a few beers, then probably of to Bryns, may have a curry to round the night off. You know what it's like," said Turpin.

"Cutting down are you—must be getting older—time was you'd have been here 5 or 6 o'clock then done 6 or 7 pubs, had a chinese, then gone to Bryns and then had an Indian—gone soft eh?" said Glyn laughing.

"Aye, old age, old age" said Thrust with a smile. Glyn was right, he thought—not so long ago he would have done that on a Friday, and played rugby the next day. He now realised that 10 pints and a curry before going to a nightclub didn't exactly enhance your chances of getting off with a woman, though obviously a balance had to be struck—going into Bryns sober would stop you getting off with one as well—they were all so ugly.

"Any celebrities in tonight Glyn?" asked Thrust.

"Nah, not really, only the usual suspects—Bomber, Will Dong, Mal, Nobby and the card boys. No fandango—too early," said Glyn.

"Fair enough. I'll wait for the boys—they won't be long. I'll sit in the corner. Might put the Jukey on" said Turpin as he turned from the bar and looked around the pub.

Turpin decided to sit in the near right hand corner—it would mean he'd have fewer lunatics to walk past—except one—probably the maddest of them all—the legendary Bomber McPhee.

Thrust walked past Bomber McPhee with a respectful nod. McPhee was probably psychotic and could attack anyone for no reason whatsoever—a greeting of 'All right?' could be met with 'fuck off you ponce'—and that would be on a good day. He wasn't particularly hard, and he would more often come off worse in a fight, but he never, never knew he was beaten. After one 20 minute bout with Phil 'The Mutilator' Thomas, a premier league hard man, McPhee, with a broken nose, two black eyes and missing several teeth is reported to have shouted as he was being strapped into the ambulance, 'Let that be a fucking lesson to you Thomas and pick up my teeth, or you'll be in trouble, you twat'.

As you would probably guess, McPhee's worse feature was undoubtedly his face. His visage resembled the devil having his piles bitten out by half starved weasels. Good looking he was not. He'd often make children cry just by looking at them, and in school was often made to walk around with a bag over his head by the older boys. Innumerable beatings, industrial accidents and chronic self abuse had left him looking like some demonic cross between Lee Van Cleef and the Lincolnshire Imp.

To cap it all his alleged links to the IRA (hence the nickname 'Bomber') which he did nothing to discourage (though the nearest he'd got to Ireland was Aberavan Beach!) made him a man to avoid.

Thrust respectfully squeezed past Bomber, whose eyes bizarrely appeared to be looking both at the door and the bar and then nodded to Bombers companion, Will Dong, who was also a man to avoid, but for different reasons.

Will 'Ding' Dong (so called because his penis was reputed to resemble a bell on the end of a thick rope), looked like a refugee from a German heavy metal band—skinny, pinched faced, with long bouffant hair, tight jeans and an armadillo like pouch where his crotch was.

Will was related to Gloria, but otherwise he would have been of no consequence to anyone, but for his great generally unseen asset—the aforementioned huge penis, which made him literally a firm favourite with the women of Port Talbot, who invariably ignored his ridiculous look and lack of communication skills for the obvious asset of his massive genitalia.

When not being employed in sexual activity Will also achieved notoriety for his member by using it in a variety of pub games / exhibitions all videoed by Glyn for his legendary archive.

Picking up pennies with his foreskin, nailing it to the floor and playing it like a double bass, or folding it to resemble the ancient cockney actor Arthur Mullard were key parts of his repertoire. His most famous moment, which Thrust had witnessed was his display in an Edinburgh pub, after a Wales v Scotland Rugby International, when Will had managed to stick 3 steaming haggises on the end of his nob. A passing Japanese tourist had to be sedated and helped out of the pub following this exposure to the cultural interaction between the Welsh and the Scots.

Thrust took up a seat in the corner and supped his beer. A few minutes later he was joined by Vic and another two friends, Stan Marbles and Archie Stanton. They were already quite pissed as Archie and Vic regularly went to the pub at lunchtime, and Stan was not often slow in joining them, when his girlfriend let him. They had nipped out to another pub 'for a change of scenery' but now joined Turpin in the corner.

Stan was quite tall with curly brown hair, and worked as a sales rep for a local brewery. Initially he had taken advantage of this post to indulge his alcoholic leanings to the full. However a drink driving ban, and settling down with a steady girlfriend, had calmed him down. However he was always allowed out on a Friday night, 'It's in the marriage contract boys', he would regularly declaim and he certainly attempted to make up for lost time.

Whilst in a steady relationship, Stan was a bit of a 'ladies man', he was always open to a 'dalliance' with another woman, and he often got into difficult situations, relying on his wits and sharp tongue to get him into, and out of them.

Many a gullible woman had written tear stained letters to Brett Stimpson, c/o All Blacks Training Camp, Wattawoppa, South Island, New Zealand, or Piet Van Niekirk, Department of Gynaecology, Stellenbosch University, South Africa. One even sent him a cheque for £100 to help pay for his (fictitious) triplets in Sydney that he had to support due to his faithless wife leaving him for a ball bearing manufacturer.

Stan spoke Welsh and often got on Glyn's nerves by insisting on ordering rounds in Welsh. Glyn's retaliating conversations in Klingon equally upset Stan, though Stan was secretly trying to learn Klingon in order to understand what Glyn was saying to him. It was a sad rivalry, but it kept them amused. Such was the fabric of rivalries and tensions that always added to the entertainment at the Penderyn.

Stan also had a habit of beginning or ending his sentences with bizarre sayings or observations such as 'nail my knob to a swingbridge' or 'I'd rather neck the Pope in a snowstorm'. His sayings seldom made any sense, but were always entertaining.

Archie worked for the council with Thrust, but in the Community Development Department. His job, such as it was, was to visit groups in the community to assess whether they were entitled to council grants. This took him all over the council area, and enabled him to augment his salary by outrageous expense claims.

"The finest writer of creative fiction since H. G. Wells," said Owen-Jones as part of an official investigation into Archie's expense claims. Luckily, due to Owen-Jones' ineptitude Archie got off the charge, and still ranged over the town visiting such unlikely organisations as the Neath / Aberafan Beach Levelling Society, the Cymru-Hibernian disabled philatelists (which only had 2 members) and a Welsh Buddhist who had dedicated his life to translating the sayings of Confucius into Welsh.

Archie was short and slightly balding with a traditional Welsh beer belly.

His other great interests included a fanatical support for Aberavon RFC (which never stretched to supporting the current team who he consistently and strangely berated), and also being the proud owner of the finest porn collection this side of Soho.

"Allright boys?" said Turpin.

'Aye, big one tonight. Been drinking steady nipped over the Welcome, then back here. Bit quiet here at the moment though—no women!' said Archie.

"What do you expect—wall to wall Penthouse Pets. You're in the fucking Penderyn remember, not Stringfellows" said Thrust.

"All right, all right. Who's rattled your cage?" said Archie slightly taken aback.

"Keep an eye on my pint. I'm going for a slash" said Thrust.

It was once rumoured that Richard Burton had stopped off in a Rolls Royce at this pub and brought Liz Taylor in with him. He'd ordered a bottle of Brandy and set about demolishing it with Liz. However, he'd popped out to the bog and before you could say 'Bobby Shafto' he'd allegedly given the barmaid one out the back.

As a result of this story Glyn had had a special blue plaque made for the toilet stating 'Richard Burton shagged here 1972', which he kept polished to remind him of the proud bawdy traditions of the pub that he valiantly tried to encourage, though sadly with less involvement by himself as the years went by.

Thrust got a vicarious thrill thinking that he was having a piss in the same toilet as his hero. He felt it was a link, albeit a damp, smelly one, with the glamour and majesty of Hollywood.

He returned to his mates and sipped on his beer.

Suddenly the pub was enlivened by a group of local girls who came in on a hen party heading for Bryns, the local nightclub.

They were a motley crew, but fairly representative of the local talent and a sample of what Thrust would be mingling with at Bryns.

There were about 6 of them who came, tottering into the pub like new born foals, in a state of imbalance brought about by the combination of their wobbly 6 inch heels and an excess of alcopops.

Their clothes were several sizes too small and their bellies poured over the huge lonsdale style belts they wore around their midriffs, Their short leggings and mini skirts revealing freshly shaved and nicked legs leading down to a calloused, dirty and gnarled feet, enlivened by dollops of bright nail varnish on each toe glinting in the bare light bulbs behind the bar.

Their boobs vied with their stomachs for the title of 'most protruding part of their bodies', and had presumably been winched into their 'lift and separate' wonder bras by teams of oxen. The breasts were invariably crammed together like two bald men butting each other, and were generally highly freckled, and sometimes wrinkled.

The girls' hair was universally bleached and piled up on their heads like punched turbans, and was guarded sentry like, by huge pendulum ear-rings swaying either side of an imitation gold chain, generally proclaiming their name as Kylie or Sharon. Finally, their faces appeared to have been made up by blind epileptic plasterers who had presumably thrown the make up on from a considerable distance with terrifying force. The entire coagulated mess had then been attacked with lipstick and eye shadow to give a passable imitation of a corpse who'd been blinded by a red hot poker after having its teeth pulled out.

"Cowin el Glyn, I need a drink pronto, six Raspberry Breezers now," shouted the leader of the group, Lee, as she adjusted her bra strap whilst kicking the bar as hard as she could. "And no rambling on in Klingon you dick, we've been here before and ain't got time to indulge in none of your fucking nonsense."

"All right, all right—they're on their way. If you're interested girls, there's a promotion on rhubarb flavoured ones tonight, two for one, are you up for it?" said Glyn.

"Now you're talking. Course we are you tit, two for one, stonkin—and give me a bag of cockles, I'm starving," said Norma, one of the other girls.

33

"Girls, down your necks, I'm up for it tonight, and I'll need a few to cope with the blokes in Bryns," said Sandra, Lee's sister.

"Sandra, get the jukey going, the rest of 'ew get over here. I've nicked a load of tablets from my mother's cabinet, and we can crush em up in the corner. They'll go tidy with the rhubarb breezers and cockles," said Lee.

The group sat in the corner, huddled like the witches in Macbeth, screeching with laughter at jokes about the men they'd been shagging, as Lee ground a selection of tablets into powder before emptying them into the lines of bottles on the table.

The juke box burst into life with the song 'Bananas' from Man, a 70s Welsh rock back from across the bay in Swansea, and the entire pub started to bang on tables or stamp their feet to the boom boom stomping record.

It was a rule of the pub that Glyn didn't allow any modern records, and if at all possible kept the contents to Welsh or Welsh connected bands from the 60s or 70s such as Badfinder, Budgie, Dave Edmunds and naturally Tom Jones. The only exception was the Irish Bluesman Rory Gallagher, who had called into the pub on his way from a gig in Cardiff in the late 70's and who stayed for three days, and who's signed photograph was behind the bar with Richard Burton's. Glyn also had a considerable selection of Welsh hymns which he would play at full volume to intimidate any English people foolish enough to visit the pub, or sometimes early on a Sunday morning when the pub was quieter, when he'd had vague feelings of religious fervour sweep over him after a particularly hard night on the booze, which often gave him near death experiences.

"Hey Will, you going to Bryns tonight?" shouted Lee. "I'm busting for a shag, and if my little cocktail here works you might be in with a chance."

"Little cocktail"—Argghh Arghh—the woman howled in unison at the double entendre. Their laughter was like a jackhammer on granite, and threatened to drown out the music on the juke box.

"Fuck off Lee, I've got bigger fish to fry tonight. I've heard that there's a bus load of nurses from Swansea in town, and they're going to Bryns, so I won't be darkening your door," said Will.

"Nurses! The only nurses interested in you will be psychiatric ones, or some with microscopes to have a look at your dick," screeched Lee. All her friends howled in appreciation of what passed for wit in the Penderyn.

"Piss off Lee, they won't need any help to look for my dick, its got a government health warning and will probably blot out the light in Bryns," said Will as he turned laughing to his cronies.

"Yeah, it's so big, it's gone off for a few pints on its own in the Rugby Club before meeting Will in Bryns," joined in Bomber, amazed at his own invention.

"Fuck off. How do you know about his dick you wanker—you queer or what?" countered Lee. "Stinkin bloody billo. (Billo was a local term for a homosexual male.) "Ach y Fi!" ('Dirty pig' in Welsh.) Her friends continued to squawk with laughter.

Bombers face darkened, and his eyes squinted inwards—a traditional danger sign.

"I wouldn't want my dick anywhere near your fanny, Lee as it's been entered more times than the Eurovision Song Contest. I've heard of men who shagged you and then disappeared, and who are probably living inside you like castaways on a diet of cockles, pills and alcopops. I've heard a man's got to pad the sides of his dick with mattresses to get any pleasure from you, after needing to take a twelve bore shotgun to frighten off the crabs, lice and god knows what else lives in your pubes before trying to shag you. I wouldn't touch your hairy pie with a barge, let alone a barge pole," said Will, with for him, amazing eloquence, gained probably from speaking with first hand knowledge.

"Hairy pie my arse. The word is you can only shag pies anyway; Will—that trip to Scotland wasn't it? Pies or haggises or something, though I don't believe it was as many as they said—more like one flaky pasty that had been sat on by Mama Cass, for a month!" Lee turned and folded her arms with a gesture of satisfaction. Her friends bayed their approval for her reposte.

"Right—Glyn, get me some Evans pies and warm em up. I'll show her what I can fucking do," said Will, holding Bomber back.

"As luck would have it, I've got some ready warmed for my supper, only about eight, but I'm trying to cut down see," said Glyn apologetically, as he disappeared into the kitchen to bring back a plate of steaming oval pies.

"Right, watch this you slags," said Will, as he leapt up onto the bar and proceeded to take his clothes off. As his pants were yanked off with a flourish, the women gasped in awe at his enormous member, hanging down between his legs like a windsock with a cannon ball in it.

Will closed his eyes, and his face muscles began to twitch, as slowly but surely his penis began to rise, unfailing in its glory to stand out straight and erect, like a storm trooper's arm at the Nuremberg rallies.

With a scream of pain, defiance and triumph Will thrust his penis through the first of the steaming pies, and with relentless determination proceeded to impale five of the pies on the end of his knob.

He stood on the bar, eyes bulging like Peter Lorré in a brothel, sweat dripping down his face with a plume of steam rising from his mangy nether regions.

"Beat that you gopping twat," he sneered at Lee, who eyed his display with a look of lustful hunger, seemingly torn between sampling the delights of the pies, his penis or both. One of her friends had similar ideas and immediately launched herself at the pornographic feast that presented itself, handing off one of her friends in the process. In a flash all the women proceeded to tear, bite, lick and jab at poor Will's groin and his look turned from triumph to horror as he was pulled off the bar and disappeared beneath the melée of demented harridans.

Sadly the possibility of a sexual orgy was swept away as Bomber leapt in punching and kicking everything within distance.

"Another boring night in the Penderyn boys," said Thrust, without a trace of irony. "Let's make a move and get to Bryns before this lot."

"The way they're going they might just try to eat the bouncers on the way in," said Vic.

"I don't think there'll be much of Will left to frighten the nurses from Swansea, but if there is, we'd better get there first—he's got a way with the ladies you know," said Stan, "unless Bomber kills him."

"Ok, let's get a move on. Last one in buys a round," said Archie as the group moved off leaving the dismemberment of Will to proceed, unhindered, ironically accompanied by the deafening stomp of the Man band playing their anthem, 'Spunk Box' booming in the night.

CHAPTER FOUR

'Subterranean Homesick Blues'

They queued outside the dark door of Bryns in the cold and rain. The bouncers flanking the door, looked like Easter Island statues, and obviously took great delight in making the public queue, even though they all knew it wasn't full inside the club.

"Come on, let us in it's bollocking out ere," said Stan, shivering in the cold.

"You'll come in when you're allowed in, so shut it," replied the first bouncer, a local hard man called Jack the Slap, spitting noisily and menacingly past the queue outside the nightclub.

"Do you know who we are?" piped Archie with all the authority he could muster, "we're from the council—the Town Clerks Department."

"I don't care if your from the fucking FBI, you're not going in. So shut your cowin' gob," said the second bouncer, another local hard man known as Dai Girder, as his pug face looked like he'd been hit with an iron bar at birth, curling his lip and summoning up his most malevolent glare.

"Well actually—the Licensing Department—Bryns is up for renewal next month isn't it? Shame if I mislay the paperwork," said Thrust.

The concept of a refused license, leading to the grim prospect of no bouncer moonlighting plopped into the bouncer's consciousness like seagull shite on a bald man's head. Jack the Slap did a relatively quick mental calculation. No power, no swaggering banter, no quick blow job from the local bike, no money ... all in all bad news.

"Mmmm—I'll be back. Dai, don't let 'em in until I say so," said Jack, with a slight hint of conciliation in his rasping voice. The bouncer slouched off to take instructions. Why they wanted to get into Bryns was a mystery to Thrust. The crumbling slum was dirty, noisy, smelt like a tramps codpiece and played music so old that they lyrics had to be translated from Latin. Furthermore it was full of desperate heterosexual men, competing for some of the most hideous, vulgar, foul mouthed examples of womanhood this side of the Smolensk female penitentiary.

Why they wanted to queue to get in there, in cold and rain, suffering verbal abuse from the bouncers and risking physical abuse at the hands of the desperados that invariably made up the queue, no-one really knew.

Or rather each and every one of them did know, in their heart of hearts—it was the chance, the one in a bloody million wam bam thank you mam, yes, yes, yes, ay, ay, ay Coramba, chance that one of them might get off with a half decent woman and have a yahoo, chocks away, toe stretching 'do you want to know what happened last night boys' shag. Plain and simple. Or even a, licking the nicotine out of an ashtray fingers kneading doughy arse smooch. Anything; just to be near or in the proximity to a woman, rather than more chat, pints, music and rugby. In all honesty—even though the likelihood was of more chat, pints, music and rugby—there was still the chance of something happening. That was why they stood in the pissing rain, waiting to get into the Welsh version of Hitler's bunker known as Bryns.

"Right, Bryn said you can go in, special favour like, if you know what I mean"! said Jack the Slap, awkwardly adjusting his collar at this spectacular concession.

"Splendid, I will certainly do all I can to ensure Mr Lewis' application is processed smoothly by the good burghers of the Licensing Committee," said Thrust.

"Cut the crap, just make sure we get the license—capice!" said Dai Girder.

"No problem. Nice doing business with you," said Archie.

Thrust and his friends handed over the exorbitant entrance fee to the gangsters moll at the paying booth, and then having paid an equally outlandish fee to put their coats in the booth, made their way down the steep stairs to the disco.

It was like descending into hell. The place was full of smoke, mostly from cigarettes or spliffs, but also from an ancient dry ice machine behind the DJ that spluttered into life every record or so in a doomed attempt to add 'atmosphere'. The few lights in the club that worked were a smoggy red, like dying suns in a black universe, the metaphor made more vivid by dim clusters of light, like constellations made up of burning fags signifying groups of dancers or tables of drinkers.

The music was so loud that it punched your chest like an aggressive drunk, and was generally 60s or 70s rock standards punctuated by blasts from the distant past like Elvis or Lonnie Donnegan to entertain the hard core 'ancient Britons' in the corner, the ageing Teds and Rockers who provided the early evening staple at Bryns.

The floor was furry and sticky like the pelt of a slaughtered buffalo, a surface produced by years of cigarette butts, alcohol, blood, spit and vomit being deposited on the floor in layers like geological strata. The boys headed towards an oasis of dim light ahead in the gloom which experience, and an innate homing instinct told them was the bar.

As they passed through the gloom, hands on each other's shoulders like mustard gas victims, they were occasionally confronted by dismembered faces suddenly appearing out of the gloom like props in a ghost train, demanding a light, a drink or worse. The relatively safe, and better lit haven of the bar was reached without any major mishap; Archie, in time honoured fashion, ordered a round of beer. They turned to peer back into the murky depths through which they'd passed, feeling like sentries in an isolated fort in the depths of the jungle.

As his eyes began to cope with the chemical concoction swirling around them, Thrust began to pick out familiar faces in isolated groups that surrounded the bar, and began to seriously question why he'd bothered, yet again, to come to this place.

The bar contained some of the most deluded, dysfunctional and desperate of Port Talbot's inhabitants. Mere presence here was equivalent to a gold card entry to a lunatic asylum—he knew that he himself was guilty of all the charges that he himself levelled at anyone who regularly went to Bryns, but he excused himself on the grounds of some glorified diplomatic immunity—he had convinced himself he was an objective observer, and to be fair, some of the types he knew in the club were viciously funny. In any event, it was the only place open after hours, and unless you were prepared to travel to Swansea, it was the only chance of getting a shag (leaving aside the dubious delights of the few, exceedingly ropey, prostitutes in the area).

As he looked around the room, he began to pick out some of the regulars and local celebrities that were already in the club. In one corner were a group of early middle aged wannabees known as the BPs—an acronym for Beautiful People. As always in Port Talbot this statement was heavily leaden with irony. The BPs were anything but beautiful, and indeed it was debatable whether some of them were people. Nevertheless, they were undoubtedly a close knit group of ageing posers—still convinced in their minds that they were young, attractive and upwardly mobile. Probably once the nearest thing Port Talbot had to yuppies.

They stood or sat in a seemingly haphazard tableaux affecting sophistication—a concept which was totally lost on 99% of the people in the club. They were a distinct throwback to the 1980s with their permed hair, shoulder pads and cigarette holders—and that was just the men! The group imagined themselves to be Don Johnson from *Miami Vice* or Victoria Principal from *Dallas*, and many of them still dreamed of getting a part in *Howard's Way*. no-one had told them the 80s were long gone, or if they had the Beautiful People weren't listening.

Their leader was Brian Insect, a cross between Roger Daltry and Charlie Drake, who wore Hawaiian T shirts in the depths of winter, with white trousers and no socks. He had a perpetually curled lip which he thought made him look like James Dean but which bore more than a passing resemblance to an Aztec death mask. His idea of sophistication was a glass of Pimms with a cherry on a cocktail stick, which he would nibble on whilst trying to chat someone up. Once he missed his mouth and stabbed the stick up his nose which not only ruined his

Hawaiian T shirt but let to his nickname of 'Rudolf the red nosed wanker'.

Thrust had also heard him trying to chat up a girl by asking, in his best Californo-Welsh accent, 'Do you fancy being balled' which resulted in a vigorous kick in the gonads followed by the immortal reposte 'fuck off'—if I wanted to be bald, I'd shave my hair off—and then I'd have to get a fucking wig'. What's more, you twat, you talk so much shit you make me feel like a bog roll'. Turpin recalled with a warm glow of satisfaction that, not for the first time, a girl had forcefully disabused Brian of his sex god pretentions.

Nevertheless, compared to others he probably was a Beautiful Person. One of the gang, Gavin, still thought he was a new romantic, and wore ruff shirts and a tartan wrap, with a Phil Oakey lop-sided fringe that hung way over his cheek. Sadly, this made him look like a cross between Rob Roy and Hitler, whilst his sidekick Dai looked like a 15 stone Harpo Marx.

The women were equally ridiculous, with hair dos that resembled half eaten candifloss, eyelashes like barbed wire and fingernails like chisels. One of them 'Juicy' Lucy pretended she was from New York, even though she was born and bred in Baglan, a suburb of Port Talbot, and who for some mysterious reason always tried to pay for all her drinks in dollars. Another BP called Jean, bore a frightening resemblance to one of the skeletons that had leapt from the teeth of the Hydra in the film Jason and the Argonauts, and indeed in a local pool hall she had been and forced to act as a rest for a particularly awkward shot by a group of visiting Cockney Hell's Angels.

The Beautiful People lived in a bizarre world of fashion and image competition, and would construct an imaginary league table of South Walian poseurs in which they operated. They would then take themselves off to various nightclubs and pubs (once memorably in a bus, that broke down in Caerau a notoriously dangerous and wild place, which resulted in them being collectively hospitalised after a savage attack from the natives) to indulge in contests with their posing rivals elsewhere. They would return elated from easy away fixtures at Maesteg or Ebbw Vale where they would have, at least in their minds, out-posed the locals, gloating over their superiority over the opposition, who were often sporting winged collars or platform soles, before being brought crashing down to the depths of depression after difficult and demanding visits to premier league posing hotspots such as the Mumbles in Swansea, or the horror, the horror of impossibly tough encounters with the impeccably turned out youths of Cardiff or Cowbridge. What damage a visit to Bristol or Manchester, let alone London would have done to the BPs, God only knew but they had wisely kept to areas that they were familiar with, and tonight were animatedly sitting discussing the imagined victories and rebuffs of the recent local derby against Neath.

Fed up with the faded 80s charms of the BPs, Thrust turned his eyes to the local card school, who in a particularly thick pall of smoke, played poker oblivious to everything around them. These were hardened gamblers and drinkers who used Bryns as a vehicle for after hours drinking, nightly enlivened by the chance of observing a fight, or even, if the planets were in alignment, a glimpse of an attractive woman, or at least a decent pair of legs or tits, preferably belonging to the same body.

One of them was known as Jim Shakes, on account of his uncontrollable nerves, engendered by a life time avoiding snoopers from the DHSS. Boasting of not having worked since he left school Jim's inherent nervousness, made much worse by his regular bouts of cat and mouse with government officials, had been exacerbated by excessive alcohol consumption, which had resulted in him shaking like an epileptic woodpecker. Sadly, not only his hands shook. His feet continually pounded the floor in a bizarre impression of Buddy Rich, the famous Jazz drummer, at his most energetic, whilst his mouth corners slid back towards his ears showing his rotten tombstone teeth approximately every 60 seconds. However he was an excellent poker player, as his eyes, which were tobacco yellow, never betrayed any emotion, and his perpetual nervous ticks continued irrespective of good, bad or indifferent hands of cards.

Next to Jim sat Vernon Piss, who looked about as untrustworthy a poker player as could be imagined. The slyest, shiftiest, meanest face imaginable, like a weasel sucking vinegar off a stinging nettle, was perched on a tiny hunched body wrapped in an ex-army great coat many sizes too big for him. The wrap-around great coat was rumoured to carry everything Vernon needed in life, including porn mags, meat pies, flagons of strongbow, rigged packets of cards and improbably, a copy of Milton's *Paradise Lost*. For some strange reason buried deep in his past, Vernon felt he could empathise with the character of Lucifer.

Opposite him sat Duggie Smith, whose eyes peered out from beneath his fringe like a sniper in a foxhole. He was a verbal equivalent of Jim, as instead of physical explosions, he would let forth torrents of swear words totally disconnected from the circumstances he found himself in. It was almost a classic textbook case of Tourette's Syndrome, except that it had nothing medical about it. Duggie just swore because he knew no different. Thrust had many times heard Duggie just swear for minutes on end without any ostensible point, and often a torrent of fucking, bastardading, cowing, wanking, shit, piss, bollock, etc., petered out without any sentence being constructed. It was nice counterpoint, however to Jim's shaking.

The other player was Big Fat Ian, who as his name implied was big and fat, and called Ian. He would sweat incessantly and move his eyes from player to player, like an extra in a spaghetti western only stopping to lean to one side and let out huge rasping farts, which he had no trouble brewing up on his diet of Madras Curry and Bass real ale. Such was the ferocity of the farts that people in the vicinity would brace themselves against the gust which could raise skirts and dislodge wigs. Once, after a particularly heavy eating and drinking session the night before involving a vindaloo, pickled eggs, baked beans, sprouts and prunes, washed down by draught Bass, Stongbow and Stella, Ian had farted so hard that his chair had been blown from beneath him which resulted in him kicking the table into the air, and leaving Jim and Duggie and Vince swearing and twitching beneath a mound of money, wood and the pages of *Paradise Lost*.

Finally Thrust spotted a few women in the other corner, including the legendary Rose 'The Last Chance' McGrath.

Rose was known as 'The Last Chance' as she was literally the last chance you could have for a shag. If all else failed, and before the last record was played, you knew that Rose would be available for a smooch, and that if you had the last dance with her, she'd take you home for a shag.

The trouble was that Rose was not only the last chance, she'd be most men's last choice; and that included many of Port Talbot's most desperate men, who would shag the proverbial 'crack of dawn' or the legendary 'frog if it stopped hopping' or even knot holes in a wooden floor (if the splinters went the right way). Fate had dealt Rose a bad hand, which included size 9 feet, knees like Knobby Stiles and an arse like a North bound Moose. Her belly was rumoured to be hairy and was bound up by a large leather belt, like a Mexican bandit. Her tits, which resembled bin liners filled with custard, hung over the belt like sick passengers on a cross channel ferry.

Her make up was so thick that her age could only be determined by a skilled dendro-chronologist and which kept her visage expressionless apart from firstly her mouth, which remained free to consume vast quantities of alcohol, and secondly her eyes which darted about like bagatelles ringed by a picket fence of black eye-lashes. Yes—if all else failed she was certainly the last chance. However, to shag her, you would also have to defeat the laws of science as set out in Thrust's law of diminishing Thrust.

This theory had been devised by Thrust during innumerable boring council meetings, and was basically represented by a graph with two lines, one showing sexual prowess or ability to perform, the other by the amount of alcohol needed to shag a woman.

A beautiful woman, e.g. Elle Macpherson or Helen Mirren in her prime, would need little alcohol consumption to induce peak performance and therefore would have a low diminishing Thrust reading. The less beautiful the woman, the more alcohol was needed to induce sexual relations—the well known 'beer goggle' effect. However, the more ugly the woman, the greater the need to consume more alcohol, and as this increased, the ability to perform diminished. At a certain point termed 'terminal thrust', the woman would be so ugly that the amount of alcohol needed would effectively neuter the man and therefore sex would be impossible. Thrust was certain that Rose would be on or beyond this point. Nevertheless he was proud of his theory and hoped one day to publish it as a doctoral thesis, if not to patent it and retire in comfort.

"Stop dreaming, get a round in," said Stan. A glass being waved in front of him brought Thrust back to earth. "Rose has been eyeing you—you might be in tonight. You'll need a drink!" said Vic.

As Thrust dipped in his pocked for the next round of beer, he heard a rolling commotion, made up of screaming women, shouting men, exploding light bulbs, and ripping clothes.

It could only mean one thing—Royston Uproar.

CHAPTER FIVE

'Team Selection'

The shouting, yelling, screaming and general mayhem arising from the far part of the club bubbled and boiled across the dance floor full club. Raucous laughter punctuated by female screams, became louder, as the smoke seemed to part, like the Red Sea before Moses, to reveal a group of men plainly having a good time causing as much of a disturbance as they possibly could in a confined space containing a surprising number of scantily clad, inebriated women.

A voice rang out through the smoke. "Oy—Turpo—3 Stella pronto—I'm gaspin', its been a long walk across that bloody dance floor, and I've snogged a few human ashtrays. In fact, this one's a bolter, so you'd better double up to 6."

Thrust knew who it was by the voice and the general commotion, but he turned and acknowledged possibly Port Talbot's biggest character (and that was saying something) Royston Uproar—a man who could out-drink, out shag, outfight and out laugh anyone within a 10 mile radius.

"All right Roy—will 6 be enough?" said Thrust with a smile.

"Ok, make it 9. Knobby and Smeg are a bit slow tonight but the pace should liven a bit, and the barman's like a fucking statue—so yeah, get us 9 stella—I can feel a good night coming on."

Royston Uproar was, as his name implied, a perambulating party. Whenever he entered a room he caused a commotion either involving a woman, a fight or often both.

Royston was about 6ft tall and looked as though he'd stepped out of an episode of the Sweeney. As far as he was concerned, it was still 1976. Long dark hair swept down either side of a Zapata moustache fronted by a nose that had stopped more than its fair share of punches—Roy was like a cross between Kevin Keegan, Tom Jones and Henry Cooper.

Roy was a legend of epic proportions. He would regularly down three pints of Stella as an opening gambit, then move on to 'Star Treks' i.e., Strongbow mixed with Stella livened with whisky chasers. He had played a lot of Rugby in his day and was a typical 'valleys' flanker—lean, mean and always first to the breakdown, where he would try to hit whoever was there with him, friend or foe, before playing the ball. He counted any game without a fight (and there were few) as a non event, and relished, bizarrely both giving and taking a good 'shoeing', a rugby phrase meaning a severe kicking.

He'd played a few games for Aberavon, and had trained once for Newport, but as the night wore on this became miraculously transformed into a glittering 'first class' rugby career spanning decades involving appearances for Llanelli, the Barbarians and on a good night Wales A. He'd convinced himself that he was the only flanker Gareth Edwards couldn't outwit, and that he caused Barry John's early retirement. On one memorable night he tried to persuade the regulars in his local pub that he'd actually played for Wales by shaving his head and pretending to be Terry Cobner, a famous bald Welsh flanker, when the latter had to pull out of a game with a late bout of food poisoning.

However, if Roy dipped his toe into fantasy when describing his rugby career, he positively swam 20 lengths when describing his sex life. Admittedly he was, to use the local term, 'a big shagger', but even allowing for the fact that he wasn't careful where he put it, you had to divide by 4 and then halve any story Roy told you about his sex life.

He once tried to convince the pub that he'd shagged his girlfriend in the morning (three times) before going to work as a PE teacher in the local comprehensive school, where he shagged the pretty female gym teacher over the vaulting horse, before playing a policewoman in tennis and shagging her in the shower, then, on his way home, picking up a Swedish hitchhiker and shafting her in some local woods before nipping in to have a 'full makeover' in the local massage parlour then moving on to have a quick one with his girlfriend followed by a good night in Bryns and climaxing with a two in a bed romp with two nurses from Swansea. As one of the boys pointed out—he'd need a diamond tipped cock, dipped in surgical spirit, strapped to a theodolite to come anywhere near his alleged tally.

Nevertheless, exaggerations or no, Roy was a character and certainly livened the evening up—not only with his drinking or stories, but also with his antics such as wearing a strap on dildo that glowed and fired peanuts, or a stuffed joke parrot that sung Bread of Heaven when it's claw was touched. Roy would also regularly slide on his back a across the dance floor 'looking for kit' (i.e., suspenders and stockings) or even better 'Geoff Capes laughing' if the lady in question had no knickers.

"Tidy, I needed that," said Roy wiping the remnants of the third pint from his mouth.

"Smeg. Get a round in, those boys need a bit of livening up—we'll have a chaser as well!"

Smeg, Roy's oldest friend, who bore a striking resemblance to Mutley, Dick Dastardy's dog, and who could probably match Roy for drinking, turned and bellowed the round to the barman and chortled happily to himself.

"What's the crack then boys," said Roy. "I heard there's a busload of nurses here tonight."

"Yeah should be a good night Roy, they've been saving themselves sexually for months, as all the Doctors have turned gay and caught syphilis," said Thrust.

"And as luck would have it, they've had a backdated payrise paid today," said Vic, sensing a wind up.

"That's right, and they stopped in Madame Swish's in the way over to take advantage of her half price lingerie sale," said Archie, rounding the wind-up off with a flourish that he knew would appeal to Roy.

"Fucking ell—we're in boys, we're in," said Royston, eyes rolling. "Smeg—better double up—it really is going to be a good night."

"Roy, don't listen to 'em, how many times have you seen a nurse in here?" Interjected Knobby, a rare voice of sanity in the uproarious triumvirate. Knobby did possess startling quantities of common sense, and generally drank in relative moderation until 'the silicone chip inside his head switched to overload' and he became a one man brewery buster—feared by both Roy and Smeg.

"Roy, I tell you, they are just winding you up. There'll be no busload of nurses, only the same old dogs. If you're lucky you might get off with someone from the cigar factory. If not, it's Last Chance or a curry followed by a J. Arthur Rank, so leave it out and concentrate on the next round," said Knobby.

"No Knobby you're wrong, nurses do turn up," said Roy, refusing to let go of his private fantasy.

"Yeah, but only after fights" said Knobby.

"Mmmm, I've got a feeling they'll be here and when they do get here, they'll know all about it from Roy. A few smooth lines, an 'arf of lager and lime, a drag on my Woodbine and wam bam thank you mam—back to nurses hostel for a good drill in the operating table and a bit of anatomical exploration. Oh yes," said Roy, still hanging on to his fantasy.

"Here you are Roy," said Smeg. "Are they here yet?"

"Not yet, but it's early yet. Let's play a game before we wreak havoc with the women. Right, let's pick an all time bald rugby XV to play an all time hairy rugby XV. You lot pick the baldies, we'll do the hairies" said Roy, supping the next pint.

"Ok, baldies first. No shaved heads. Only genuine baldies—and no patches—must be the full works. Full back—mmm—mostly poseurs—not many bald ones are there?," said Archie.

"Dusty Hare," said Vic.

"OK," said Roy.

"Yeah. Wings—Brendan McAloon," said Thrust.

"Not a wing," said Knobby.

"Yes he was, well he was a back," interjected Stan.

"OK, I'll let you have that" said Roy.

" P.L.Jones" said Vic.

"Fair enough" said Smeg.

"Right Centres—Jim Renwick," said Thrust.

"I've got one—Dai Burcher," said Archie.

"Too much hair, but I'll give you that, ok" said Roy.

"Outside half—Les Cusworth, Scrum Half—Jacko Page," said Stan.

"This is like shelling peas," said Thrust, "We're bound to pick a pack. Forwards have a propensity to go bald. All that pushing in the scrum."

"Right, Colin Smart, Jeff Lloyd and any Cross Keys prop," said Vic. "They were all splendidly bald."

"What about shaved heads—think of the Neath Team," said Stan.

"No, I told you, don't count, got to be naturally bald," said Roy, ever the stickler.

"Fair enough—Derwyn Jones and Nigel Redman in the second row," said Archie.

"Cobner, Mike Biggar and Bastia. A full back row in one. Done, over to you" said Stan taking a well deserved drink.

After some initial debate as to what constituted hairy, Turpin announced that it entailed having a beard or wild unkempt hair, (preferably both).

In a few minutes Roy, Smeg and Knobby picked a splendidly hairy XV.

"Bastards," said Thrust, "you've been swotting."

"No, just one fucking step ahead of you lot," said Roy. "Right—what teams can we pick next?"

As the night wore on, with no sign of any nurses, they went on to challenge each other to pick a variety of teams, and went on to pick short XV to play a skinny XV, followed by an effeminate or soft XV to play a dirty or hard XV.

The contest started to become silly as it descended into a cheerful XV to play a sullen or miserable XV, an untrustworthy XV to 'the men you'd like to have next to you in a Somme trench XV and even a smelly farts XV versus a big shagger XV. No-one inquired as to how any of the participants in the contest were able to verify the latter categories. Bored with these categories, and rapidly sinking into alcoholic stupor, they broadened the ambit of the game into a British Actors versus an American Actors XV.

"Right—British Actors first," said Roy.

"We'll go first," said Thrust, confident that his knowledge of the cinema would pay dividends.

"Right," answered Stan, Vic and Archie in unison.

"Full back—Michael Caine," said Vic.

"Wings—Peter O'Toole and Ewan McGregor" said Archie.

"Centres—Richard Harries and Stanley Baker" added Turpin.

"Outside half—Charlie Chaplin" said Vic.

"Scrum half—Syd James" said Turpin.

The boys then conferred for a few minutes, and Turpin said "Right, I'll name the rest boys:

Props—Oliver Reed and Nigel Green; Hooker—Bob Hoskins; Second Row—John Cleese and Bernard Bresslaw; Back Row—Sean Connery (blind side), No 8 Liam Neeson and open side and Captain Richard Burton. Thank you and good night."

"Good back row," sad Roy, "but isn't Burton a bit small'.

"Small! Wash your fucking mouth out, they've got plenty of height in that pack—but what he'd bring is not only guts and hardness, he was an Aberavon boy after all, but also..." He couldn't think of the words. The 10 pints of beer didn't help, but still he struggled to articulate his thoughts.

His mind spun. What was the word he was looking for? Charisma? In a team of actors? Well yes and no, it was more than that, it was that something that not only made someone stand out in a team of personalities, but also enabled him to lead it.

"Come on Turpin, what would he bring?" said Roy.

"What would he bring?" said Thrust. The words suddenly came to him. "He'd bring himself—Richard bloody Burton—he'd lead and inspire the whole team to outplay, out run, out fight, out act, out everything the other side, then off the pitch out drink them, tell better stories than them, do better impression of them than themselves, then drink everything left in their glasses as they slid to the floor comatosed, before nipping off and shagging their wives or girlfriends or both (at the same time) before returning to recite a poem in a voice they'd all die for, about the whole event." Turpin was on a roll.

"Look" Thrust slurred, "Burton was the best example of the traditional Welshman. Tough, bright, got on with people, liked to drink, to socialise, knew what women liked, the best."

'He was the leader we've been missing for so long, in a line stretching back to Lloyd George, Dic Penderyn, Owen Glyndwr, King fucking Arthur, the lot!" Turpin had rehearsed these words in a thousand Committee meetings.

"He stood for Wales and stood up for Wales on the world stage. When he was around we were somebody. Since he left we've been going downhill at a rate of knots. If only there was someone like him today—we'd beat the English and everyone else at Rugby, we'd have proper jobs in proper industries, and nobody would dare write anti-Welsh comments in the Sunday fucking Times," Thrust declaimed with a flourish, and wiped the beer from his lips.

"Well—there's no heros around any more that's for certain and Burton's not going to come back is he?," said Vic. "He's buried in Switzerland isn't he?"

"Aye, it wasn't up to him. I reckon it was a cover up; they didn't want him buried in Wales" said Turpin. (Who 'they' were was a nebulous concept in Thrust's mind, probably English public schoolboys who had manipulated Burton's next of kin in all sorts of nefarious ways).

"Why would they want to do that," asked Royston. "He lived in Switzerland for ages, so it's right he should be buried there."

"No. It's not right. No way. He should have been— should be—buried in Wales. Then things will be like the old days," said Thrust staring into the distance, lost in deep thought.

"And we'll beat England at rugby!" said Stan, laughing.

"How much have you had to drink?" said Vic.

"Not enough" said Royston as he downed yet another Strongbow.

"Anyway, we'd better get a move on—it's nearly last orders and they'll be playing the last dance before long. Still no sign of those bloody nurses though—but I did see full kit Gloria coming in with a few friends so there's a chance of something happening."

Gloria! Thrust's mind suddenly stopped daydreaming and went into overdrive as he conjured up images of Gloria in her ever present full kit, leaning back on her king sized bed and beckoning him to sample her wondrous wares.

Thrust immediately regretted having drunk so much as he realised he would be unable to say all the things he really felt about Gloria and that in any event his best chat up lines would also be submerged beneath the lake of alcohol he'd consumed.

But—he reasoned—he'd have to try. Gloria didn't often come to Bryns and Thrust had certainly felt a high level of interest coming his way from Gloria of late—perhaps she'd heard from one of the many councillors who called in to chat to her that Thrust was in line for promotion, or perhaps even that she might even like him. He just knew he had to do something, there and then, or else he'd bitterly regret it.

Staggering through the dimly lit night club like an extra from the 'Night of the Living Dead', he searched desperately for Gloria. Suddenly he glimpsed her, behind a man with his back to Thrust, standing protectively next to Gloria, like a coral reef surrounding a tropical lagoon one arm lightly touching her shoulder, the other laconically holding a gin and tonic.

That should have alerted Thrust. There were few men in Port Talbot who would drink a gin and tonic, let alone do it in Bryns.

Thrust stumbled on regardless. He knew he had to tell Gloria everything, and that he could then whisk her away from this life to a life of happiness, contentment … and hopefully rampant sex. Sadly it was not to be.

"Oh hello Turpin, nice to see you outside the council, even if it is in Bryns," laughed Gloria nervously. "Have you met Finley?"

Finley fucking Quench. The words sucked all hope from Thrust's heart. He had no chance with Gloria if Finley Quench had got hold of her.

Quench was possibly the richest man in Port Talbot, certainly for his age, which was mid 30's. He was the local doctor, and looked like a slightly nastier Jeremy Irons, crossed with Terry Thomas. The only trouble was that he had the personality of Heinrich Himmler. He was the proverbial flash git. Lots of money, with enough sense and time to make the most of it. He held all the right cards in the game of life and to be fair, knew how to play them. A Porsche car, a flat in Marbella, and posh house in the countryside with a swimming pool. He was the average Port Talbot woman's concept of a perambulating pools win.

Thrust couldn't stand him. They'd been at school together and where Thrust's career had faltered and spluttered up the road to nowhere that led to his current job, Quench had, with considerable investment from his parents, gone on to achieve professional respectability, which coupled with extremes of cash, courtesy of a brace of rich relatives who died leaving everything to him, left him as the biggest catch your local girl next door could conceive of. Trouble was, he rubbed everyone's faces in his wealth and flaunted it at every opportunity—preferably to land his conquest of the week and to revel in his alleged sexual prowess.

"Thrustie Boy. Good to see you. I'm glad the council pay you enough to get into Bryns," sneered Quench through a curled lip that resembled an unmade bed.

"Embezzled the councillors expenses did you," he chortled and turned to Gloria. "We'll have to get you out of there my girl. Too many no hopers in dead-end jobs. A pretty woman like you deserves sooo.. much better." Quench slapped her bottom. Gloria winced.

"I'm singed by the warmth of your sincerity," said Thrust. "What brings you to Bryns—a research project into sexually transmitted diseases?" (Thrust regretted saying that as Gloria flashed him a distinctly frosty glance!)

"There are some nice girls here you know," said Gloria, scowling.

"Yes. Shame on you" said Quench. "There's a bit of class here tonight, who have raised the tone, although you're too drunk to notice. Gloria and I however, I'm afraid, will have to let it slip back to it's normal depths as we're going for a few late drinks at the golf club and some cocktails by the pool.

"If you had a female friend I'd invite you along, but you seem a bit lacking there, and I don't think Gloria would appreciate a gooseberry turning up," said Finlay, flashing his designer dentistry.

"Oh, I like Turpin. He's a tidy boy but I don't think he'd really be happy at the golf club. Too many old men and it's a bit nippy for a dip," said Gloria, laughing nervously, anxious to placate Thrust, who was looking on the verge of explosion.

Quench slid off with a sneer to get their coats.

"Don't worry. I'm happy enough here. At least there are real people, who don't have to be bribed into doing things. Anyway Gloria, what are you doing with him?"

He paused and decided to change the topic. "Anyway, what's happened to your cousin Will? He was going mad in the Penderyn," said Turpin, glad to have Gloria to himself.

"Yeah, he caused ructions in the Penderyn tonight. The police came and arrested Will for gross indecency with a foodstuff or so they said, though everyone who was there, said the attempts the police made to get a statement out of Glyn, who would only speak Klingon, was the funniest thing they'd seen for ages. One of Lee's friends laughed so much she peed on the floor and short-circuted the juke-box, and started a fire. The place was in uproar," said Gloria.

"I was walking past, intending to go in, but only to see some friends. Anyway, Finlay was driving past in his Porsche, and offered to take me for a few drinks, and to be honest I'm having a great time. Nice to see how the other half live and all that. The Penderyn's not my cup of tea really," Gloria smiled weakly.

Quench came back holding their coats.

"Come on Gloria. We'd better move on, it's getting a bit … tacky in here, and I'm not just talking about the carpet," said Finlay, swivelling his eyes.

"See you Turpin," whispered Gloria in Thrust's ear. "He's not that bad really, but it's nice to have a good time and see a better side to life. I'll tell you about it on Monday."

"Ok. Don't worry about me. I'm having a great time anyway" (playing name the greatest bald rugby XV? he thought). "See you on Monday. I'll pop down and wind Owen-Jones up. A few sexy snippets and he'll be salivating all over his pink carpet. I may even do some Burton poems for you."

"Yes, that'll be brilliant. See you Turpin," called Gloria as she was led up the stairs, away from the smoke, smell and din of

Bryns like an angel ascending to heaven. If only, thought Thrust, if only I had more money, a better job, more confidence, a better voice—if only I was Richard Burton. I'd take Gloria from Quench, Roy, the lot of them. Nevermind, let's have another drink. How many Welsh dreams had floundered on the rocks of that sentiment. Get one in with the boys and stay at the bar. Downing the remainder of his glass, Turpin walked a lonely path, deep in thought across the dance floor as the DJ announced the last dance, and the bell for last orders was rung. Turpin felt a light tap on his back, followed by the words "Why's a good looking boy like you leaving when there's one last dance to go."

He turned and was overcome by a mixture of shock, panic, excitement, curiosity and comfort to see smiling in front of him—the Last Chance!! Rose McGrath in all her dubious splendour.

CHAPTER SIX

'Last Chance Saloon'

The dim light seemed to grow darker as Thrust stared into the heavily made up face that hovered in front of him, like a dangling pumpkin at a Halloween party.

It was the legendary 'Last Chance', Rose McGrath, the butt of a thousand shagging jokes, such as 'she'd held more knobs that the doorman of the Hilton', 'had more rubs than Aladdin's lamp', 'had more shafts sunk into her than the Kimberley diamond mine'—the list just went on and on, and seemed part of the folklore of the town. She was however, a formidable woman, and certainly was not a woman to mess with. She also was, or had been, depending upon how much you'd had to drink, quite attractive, though this was usually well hidden by liberally applied makeup. Being singled out by Rose was a bit of a complement, though if the rumours of her sexual appetite were to be believed, it also had an edge of danger attached to it. Certainly, many an unsuspecting man, who had thought they were using Rose (for whatever reason— though generally sexual) ended up literally, and metaphorically the worse for wear. A socio-sexual psychologist could probably produce a lifetimes worth of research papers analysing whether Rose was a victim, a predator of men, or a victim of society or her upbringing. Rose would probably put it down to too much drink, too many men, and too much time on her hands, too early in life. Whatever it was, Rose had a mission in mind, and that mission, for good or for bad, was Turpin Thrust.

Thrust swayed unsteadily, the helpless victim of a volatile cocktail of conflicting emotions, vast amounts of alcohol, rejection by Gloria, and a libido fuelled by quantities of, ok rather ropey, but still bonkable, female flesh in the club. He stared incomprehensibly at Rose—what should he do? His brain said go, his loins said stay. What did he have to lose? He weighed up the options. Just one dance. Close your eyes, pretend it was Gloria, thanks for the dance, then off with the boys for a curry. 'A curry before your willy, Thrustie boy', that's what Roy would say, somewhat hypocritically as he would probably shag a coagulated curry, poppadoms and all, if he couldn't get a bonk.

"Oh hello Rose, how's it going. Been here long?," Thrust said lamely.

"Ages. Seems like anyway. Crap here init. Fancy a dance?" replied Rose, as she put both her arms around him.

"Yeah—tidy," he said with a gulp.

Thrust loosely held Rose as they began to swirl slowly to the 70s classic ' I'm not in love' by 10cc.

The smell of perfume and smoke added to his already high level of intoxication. He was dimly aware that she had a bottle of something in each hand which were draped over his shoulder, which enabled her to swig from each alternately as they slowly spun around.

"Fancy a drink Turpin?" Breathed Rose, inches from his face. 'Ave a drop of this, it's my own concoction, Whisky, Malibu, Southern Comfort and Absinthe—it'll make your balls bang like castanets. Get it down your neck!" she said with a drawl that told him she'd already sampled a considerable amount of the bizarre cocktail.

He nervously poured the strange brew down his throat, and whilst it didn't make his balls bang, it certainly stirred something down there, and after the initial shock, made him feel more relaxed, carefree and strangely happy. Certainly Rose's face, which moments ago resembled an old yellowing artexed ceiling framed in straw, now began to become smooth, mellow and well vaguely fanciable. Indeed her breasts, which he had held at a discreet distance now developed a strange allure for him, and he pulled her closer, feeling her nipples, like inquisitive voles, burrowing into his chest.

As the record played on, the music began to hammer away at his rapidly diminishing resistance to Rose's charms, and inevitably their faces drew together. The former artex ceiling of her skin now began to change and began to take on the appearance of a satin sheet, her hair billowing behind her like soft drapes. Her eyes, which earlier had resembled half sucked gobstoppers now became wide pools of honey, reflecting harvest moons. Soon their noses began to nudge one another like tentatively sparring boxers.

The next minute Thrust found himself clamped in a passionate kiss, his tongue fencing wildly with hers and probing deep into areas of her mouth that whilst sober he would not have gone near with a deep space probe.

As the final record, 'Angels' by Robbie Williams, was played, he felt her hand on his crotch, and despite his alcoholic stupor, he felt himself becoming turned on.

"Turpin, will you walk me home? It's wet and dark and I'm a bit nervous. You can come in for a coffee if you like," said Rose, blandly oblivious to the directness of her sexual advance.

Ho ho, come in for a coffee! That was woman speak for 'let's go to bed' if ever he'd heard it he thought. Normally he had to beg, bribe, promise undying love to get a cup of coffee. Here was Rose chucking it in as an opening gambit. What should he do?

He looked around. Some old faces, some old jokes, what if he went with the boys for a curry? Another Sunday with a stinking hangover, a stinking room, a J. Arthur Rank followed by a long walk through dirty wet streets to watch the stripper at the Rugby Club. The brutal fact was that he hadn't had a shag for months, end of story. What the hell, he thought, just go with the flow, I can always back out, and you can't look a gift horse in the mouth so to speak. He made his mind up to 'go for it' and walk her home.

"Yeah, ok. I'll walk you home and I'll come in for a coffee too. Might sober me up after all this drink you've given me," he lamely joked.

Rose smiled and ran her tongue around her mouth provocatively.

"Oh, Turpin, I'm so glad I'm going to have a nice man like you to walk me home."

This led to another passionate snog and he then suddenly found himself being led away by Rose.

"One minute I'll tell the boys," said Thrust.

"OK, I'll see you by the door," said Rose, wandering off to find her coat.

There was no easy way out of this thought Thrust, in the absence of being beamed out of Bryns a la Star Trek. Just tell it like it is, then get out as soon as possible—he'd get masses of verbal abuse whichever way he played it, so he might just as well tell it like it was.

He wandered over to the boys, who were still at the bar, no doubt still inventing bizarre rugby teams. He knew he had to say it. He gulped hard, then spoke.

"I'm going back to Rose's for a coffee. Probably see you in the Indian, if not, tomorrow at the Rugby Club (he knew they'd be there at midday, for the stripper)." He smiled lamely.

The boys conversation froze, and they looked at one another for what seemed like eternity.

The abuse ripped into him like a burst of machine gun fire.

"The Last Fucking Chance!"—booked yer place in the clap clinic Turpie boy? I've got the number here," said Royston, roaring with laughter.

"Wrap your knob in a lead lined condom, garnish it with garlic, tell it to make it's will and get it blessed by a priest. It's going on a one way mission to hell," said Vic.

"Ay, and say hello to all the good men who never came back from where you're going. They're all probably playing cards in there, and watching that guards regiment she 'ad', doing manoeuvres, waiting for some kind hearted soul to come and get them back out. Trouble is Turp, you'll probably join in their game" said Stan.

"She's a shunko Turp (a particular brand of Port Talbot lowlife), leave her there" said Vic.

For God's sake don't do it. It's a senseless waste of life, or at least a healthy knob. Go have a J.Arthur, or drink a pint of bromide, but what ever you do, don't go back to Rose's. While your shagging her, the kids will have nicked all your money and sold your clothes to the rag and bone man. You'll come back naked, skint and riddled with pox—no way is it worth it. Have an Indian and think about the strippers on Sunday. You know it makes sense," said Stan nodding sagely.

Thrust had had enough of sense. He wanted sex, Rose was up for it, so was he and as far as he was concerned, it was game on. He'd face the consequences when he was sober. Tonight he would forego the pleasures of Chicken Tikka Masala for something a bit spicier. As for the pox—well he had a couple of condoms left over from his trip to Edinburgh and if things looked really bad, he'd double them up. Desperate times required desperate actions.

"Goodbye moral majority, I'll see you later or in the morning," said Thrust with a defiant grin.

"There's nothing moral about it—it's public health we're concerned with. They say there's only two certs in life; Death and Rose; and you'll probably end up with both. Leave her go, and have an Indian," said Archie.

Turpin turned his back and strode purposefully towards Rose.

"Leave him go, it'll be a laugh listening to his stories in the morning—if he comes back alive," said Stan.

"Or if he can still talk!," said Vic.

"Or if he's able to describe what went on—yeah, that would probably be an ordeal in itself" said Stan. "What's the phrase, 'post-traumatic stress'"?

"Balls to him! Let's finish these and go for an Indian. These fucking nurses never turned up again. Something not right there!," said Archie, negative as ever.

"The only thing not right around here is you, for believing that crap," said Smegs as they finished their pints.

"No problem boys—they are probably waiting for us in the Indian, come on, the last one in's got to eat the relish tray in one," said Roy. The boys meandered across the dancefloor and out into the street.

Turpin waited for Rose to get her coat, and they walked through the drizzle through the drab washed out streets, avoiding the late night refugees from the take-aways and kebab shops who either loped along the pavements like tumbleweeds, or who lay propped against the shopfronts trying to dock the burgers like miniature space probes in their oscillating mouths.

She pulled him into a darkened doorway, and they launched into yet another passionate kiss.

Suddenly she pulled away.

"Turpin—just one thing before we get back to the house. I've heard people speak about you—about your talent!" Turpin grinned and nodded confidently. He assumed, wrongly, that she was referring to his sexual prowess. "I've just got to ask you. Say some poetry for me. I'm told you're really good at it—clever with words like you. Know loads of famous poets like Byron and Shirley and all their poems, I've heard."

Thrust was taken aback. He was surprised that Rose had heard of poetry, let alone Byron and er Shirley. Perhaps there were hidden depths to her. He was also flattered.

"Well thanks Rose. I'll give it a go. Any particular poet or poetry?"

"Yeah, that local poet. What's his name? Dylan Davies? You know, the one from Swansea."

Thrust was puzzled. He once knew a bloke called Dylan Davies who played prop-forward for Aberavon, but he was sure he wasn't a poet.

"Dylan Davies?" he asked.

"Yeah, the one Bob Dylan took his name from" said Rose.

"Oh, Dylan Thomas—is that the one?" said Thrust.

"Yeah, that's him. Under Milk Tray or something—isn't that his famous poem?"

"Well, not quite—Milk Wood actually. Nice play," said Thrust.

"Nice play, stupid name. Who ever heard of Milk Wood— he was a fucking mad alcoholic though, so God knows where he got it from" laughed Rose. "Probably from Swansea— they're all mad over there."

"He did drink a bit" said Thrust, going with the flow.

"Don't we all" said Rose. "Anyway, say some poetry for me, lover boy."

"Ok, ok, I'll just gather my thoughts" said Thrust. His head was spinning with drink.

"And one thing more" she said with a knowing smile. "If you want me to be very nice to you when we get back to my house..." She stroked his inside of the legs of his jeans.

"What's that" he said with a gulp.

"You've got to do it in your famous voice."

"What's that?" he said.

"You know—the Richard Burton voice. It's famous. It drives all the girls wild, specially that girl who works with 'ew' Gloria Whatshername. Anyway I'm a really naughty girl—as you'll see later on!" she bit him sensually on the side of his neck. Turpin gulped.

He tried to think of a Dylan Thomas poem. Normally, it wouldn't be a problem—he could reel off dozens. However, in his severely pissed state he was having trouble remembering his name.

Bugger it, he'd just start something off, and see where it led. She'd be unlikely to know at the best of times, and in this state she'd have no clue. He slipped into his deepest Burton Voice.

"It was spring, moonlit night on the heaven scented down. The ding dong dangling drooping dogs dug downwards into the vole nestling, flower trestling worried earth. Oh, we were young and strident in our love, on the cusp of eternity, in the high lofted mansions of desire, vibrant and warm, as we sang like doves under silken moon, glorious in our ...."

He was interrupted by her mouth clamping over his. She was trembling like an inquisitive weasel's snout. She eventually pulled away.

"Christ Turpin, that was fan, bloody tastic—that poetry—it was brilliant. Words like that, in a voice like that. Shit—I never hear any man say anything like it in the places I go. It's always fucking this, fucking that—you are brilliant— and in that voice. The most romantic thing I've ever had said to me was 'do you want curry sauce on your chips?' Having someone recite poetry to me is cowin' stonkin'. It's made me go all .... Wow! Quick Turpin, let's get back to my house now. I'm all a-quiver and we've just got to go to bed, and I know you won't disappoint me. Lover boyo. Come on. Let's get going."

A slight twinge of unease entered Thrust's mind as she grabbed him and led him vigorously from the doorway. Had he done the right thing? The look in her eyes disturbed him.

Thrust knew that he had to go with Rose back to her house as quickly as he could, before the drink wore off, as otherwise he'd realise what he was doing and back out. Accordingly, he went along with her at a pace rivalling a pair of committed entrant in the Oklahoma land grab.

Rose, as was her want, was also keen to replenish herself with alcohol, and to slake her considerable sexual thirst which had been fuelled by his impromptu poetry recitation. She therefore swiftly increased the pace, so that they resembled a couple of dancers refining their entry for hoedown as they sped along the by now empty streets.

They soon arrived at Rose's, a not insubstantial terraced house in one of the tougher neighbourhoods and stopped for the obligatory mating ritual of a swift snog, followed by an obligatory 'do you want to come in for a coffee' followed by a 'yes' and another even swifter snog.

"Watch out for the kids Turpin—they're really lovely, but can take, well, a bit of getting used to if you know what I mean," said Rose as she opened the door.

"They are often up this late watching something or other on TV. It doesn't do 'em any harm, but 'ew just can't get any baby sitters around here. Don't be frightened of them, they're really nice" she added unconvincingly. He decided not to go through the door alone. You just go in there, and I'll get us a drink. What 'ew avin?" said Rose.

"What have you got?" he ventured, a gnawing fear starting to intrude into his drunken stupor.

"Stella, whisky or vodka. No mixers, the kids have drunk everything; though if your really desperate I've some tinned rhubarb, and you can have the juice to take the edge off things," Rose smiled apologetically.

"Whisky's fine, just a bit of ice" he added, in trying to be helpful.

"Fuck off Turpin—Ice?, Who do 'ew think 'ew are? Prince Phillip—you'll 'av' it straight, just like I'll have my vodka," said Rose.

"There we are" she said putting a large glass in his hand. "Come and meet the kids!"

They went into the living room. The scene that confronted him resembled a joint St Trinians / Bash Street Kids outing to the battle of Stalingrad.

The room had presumably been visited by a particularly irate poltergeist, who had hurled furniture, clothing and particularly food in a broad circle surrounding the TV which had, by some miracle of divine intervention remained untouched by the raw, atavistic forces that had erupted around it. The TV screen itself was framed in a halo of what initially he thought was blood, brains and offal, but as his eyes grew accustomed to the darkness, it thankfully revealed itself as a curry.

There were, he guessed, four children sitting on the, just about intact, sofa engaged in a Welsh version of the Eton wall game, as they appeared to punch, kick and bite each other in a loose rolling maul along the sofa from end to end and back again. The language would have shamed a docker, and only the bellowing shriek of 'shut up 'ew bloody sods' by Rose, managed to dim the cacophony to below that of the TV which was incongruously tuned into edited highlights of the all Wales sheepdog trials.

A mound of foul smelling fur twitching on a chair in the corner (which Thrust guessed was a dog) suddenly opened one eye before loudly farting and going back to sleep, which in turn caused a parrot, perched upside down in the other corner of the room to squawk 'Up the Wizards. Fuck Neath, Fuck Neath'! Before falling off into a mini sand dune of sawdust at the bottom of its cage.

The rolling maul on the furniture came to a stop and four pairs of eyeballs peered at him over the top of the sofa.

"Kids—I want you to meet my new friend, Turpin who's come in for a nice cup of coffee," said Rose.

"Turpin, meet Julio, Che, Panache and Gudrun, my lovely children, and oh of course Roger, the dog (you've probably smelt him by now) and Muriel the Parrot—big Aberavon fan as you've guessed" said Rose, uncharacteristically blushing.

Thrust could not believe what he saw. The eldest boy of about nine (whom he took to be Julio and who looked like a

Latin American version of Pugsley from the Adams Family) held a clump of ginger hair—probably from Che, in one hand and a large buzzing dildo in the other. Thrust hoped that the dildo had been used merely to beat Che with. It was however a debatable point. A chill went up and down his spine.

Che, the smaller of the two boys had a face like a vole sniffing chlorine, and Turpin deduced from the boys by now clumpy ginger hair and freckled face, that Che was probably of different stock to Julio. Che grinned at Turpin, and then poked his finger up his nose, right up to the second knuckle, and proceeded to rotate it like a vigorous plumber as his already malevolent face screwed up further in a grimace of resentment, pain and suspicion.

The eldest girl, aged about seven, probably the one called Panache, was the living antithesis of her name, as she had a flat plain face that resembled an uneaten nan bread, surrounded by a candy floss of unkempt, possibly nit ridden ginger hair in which dwelt some red, white and blue ribbon presumably left over from some bizzare political rally. She held in one hand the video remote, and in the other a curling tong, no doubt to defend herself and / or the TV remote control from any unwanted interference.

Finally his gaze alighted upon Gudrun, who again had a weasely face, with pulled back blonde hair which gave her the appearance of someone advancing up a very strong wind tunnel. She was chewing gum and at metronomic intervals, and would suddenly blow (God only knew how) a double exploding bubble which echoed like a ricochet around the room.

"Hello children," said Turpin nervously affecting his best 'social worker earnestly wanting to be accepted' voice that he had heard a thousand times at the council. "You seem to be up a bit late, anything good on telly?"

"Where you get him from Mam?" said Julio, with undisguised malevolent contempt.

"Not another one from Bryns. Why do they always come in for coffee—can't ew go to a café?," said Che, flicking the mucous on the end of his finger at the dog.

"Why don't we ever see them again Mam?" said Panache, squinting like a suspicious sniper.

67

"There are loads of 'em" said Gudrun. "Never the same ones."

"Why do they always shout in the night?" said Panache, still inquisitive.

"When are 'ew going to the doctors in Beulah Road again Mam?," said Julio with a malicious flourish.

Thrust winced as he knew this was the address of the local VD Clinic.

"Be quiet now you lot. I'll have none of your cheek. You're only doing it to wind me up. I never bring men home — well only now and again. So don't tell such wopping fibs to Uncle Turpin," said Rose, smiling apologetically.

"Not another uncle. We've had dozens. Why can't we have real uncles like everyone else in school," said Che.

"Cos 'ew fathers are from exotic far away places like Brazil, Norway and, er, 'Cwmavon'," she laughed nervously and turned to Thrust.

"Don't listen to them. They're lovely kids, but a bit, well, unruly, but only 'cos I can't get a baby sitter. Don't worry. They'll go to bed now. I'll pop into the kitchen and get them some ice cream. They'll go to bed quiet then and we can get some … peace" said Rose in a husky, come hither voice.

"Right. Four choc ices for you lot, then off to bed. It's ten past two and you should be tucked up safe in bed, not watching TV," said Rose, her voice hardening appreciably.

Rose went off to get the ice cream and Thrust reverted to concerned social worker mode.

"Like sheep dogs then do you?" he said.

"Fuck off mister—we've been watching 'Hell death murder zombies 6' til you came in, we just switch over to make her think we're good see," said Che, before resuming burrowing for more mucous.

Before Thrust could respond by asking how watching sheep dog trials with a dildo in your hand at 2 in the morning could be evidence of being good, Julio beckoned him over.

"Three quid each and we'll go to bed quiet like—you and her can have some time to yourselves. If not, we won't move and you'll have to go home early. All the other men do it—so make up your mind" said the child with a particularly malevolent leer.

Che, who's finger was now in his nose up to his knuckle said "Fuckin' right" and slyly swivelled his eyes towards the kitchen.

Thrust balanced the conflicting demands of his libido, his hatred of blackmail (and the children) and the wish for a quiet life. His hatred of blackmail gave way, in particular to his still vivid need to have a shag.

He rummaged impatiently in his pockets, and fished out 8 pound coins.

"Here, that's all I've got. Take it or leave it. And if you don't go quietly I'll stick the dildo, the dog and the parrot up your arse and seal 'em in with superglue. A deal?" said Thrust in his best council rent collector voice.

"OK. Done" said Julio, curling his lip.

Thrust put the money into Julio's hands and turned just in time to see Rose coming in with the choc ice.

"Here we are kids, so say goodnight to nice uncle Turpin and make sure you eat them before you go to sleep. They make such a mess when they melt.."

The children sloped off to bed slurping on their choc ices. The dog let out another fart, and the parrot squawked in retaliation.

"Right Turpin, come and sit by ere' and we can finish our drink" said Rose, patting the rancid sofa.

No sooner had he sat down next to her, their mouths slammed together like limpets, and their hands frisked one another as if they were over zealous customs officials.

"Oooh Turpin. I've been dying to get a real hold of you all night, but let's not mess around. I've had a shower and there's a fresh pack of johnnies in the drawer. Let's go to bed—NOW!" said Rose with startling firmness.

He thought it would be quick, but not this quick. Fighting back any considerations of morality, squeamishness or even fear, he concentrated on doing the dirty deed with an almost fanatical determination.

"Yes, ok let's go to bed, but can I have one more drink" (he needed it to give him Dutch courage).

"Aw, fuck off Turpin, I'm better than any drink you've ever ''ad," Rose replied as she dragged him from the sofa, spilling his whisky everywhere.

The dog and the parrot burst into a cacophony of noise as Rose almost manhandled Thrust up the stairs, kicking and pushing him like a particularly vicious bailiff.

"I didn't realise you like S and M," he feebly joked as her fingers dug into his arm, and he gingerly danced to avoid her piston like legs.

"What you want sweets?" said Rose, "you've had a drink haven't you?"

"No, I didn't mean M&Ms" he weakly replied, realising with dawning unease that he was rapidly entering a situation in which he was not in control.

They got to the top of the stairs, and she pushed a door open.

"Here we are luvver boy — sexy Rose's naughty room. We'll have the lights on to get a good look at each other while we 'get friendly' shall we," in what she took to be her sexiest voice.

Thrust immediately realised that he was seconds away from seeing a sight which few men had survived, compos mentis, to tell the tale. Rose naked! The thought of fold after fold of her dimpled, pimple punctuated, sand paper skin wobbling over, under and around him sent a shock to his penis which threatened to turn it from a Sierra's exhaust into a gnat's tongue.

"No, no don't put the light on — it's more, um, sensual, yes sensual, if we do it in the dark. It increases the pleasure of touch, taste, smell, the lot. It must be true, I read it in 'Ask Deirdre' column, in the 'Sun'," he said.

"Oh well, if you read it in a paper, it must be true, anyway, I think the lightbulbs bust anyway — come here big boy, show me what for!" said Rose with a gleeful chuckle.

They fell onto the bed kneading, grappling and wrestling like two person rugby ruck. Thrust was vaguely aware that her bra, which was like two pith helmets joined by cabling, flew off nearly decapitating him after his first clumsy touch.

She dragged his clothes off him as if she were trying to get to the bottom of a bargain basement bin in a sale, and soon they were both naked save for her knickers.

"Take my knickers of Turpin and see what I've got in store for you tonight," she whispered.

Shit. This is it, he thought. I've come too far to stop. He could feel his penis oscillating between a hard on and a slow retreat. He winced at the holes he could feel in the voluminous cloth of her large muslin like knickers, and strained his fingers to get behind the strengthened elastic embedded in folds of flaccid fat.

"Like my knickers? Sexy eh? Got em in the market— Madame DeSade's—very posh. She tried to sell me one of them thongs. I told her, if I put one of them on, I'd never find it again, ha ha ha," Rose threw her head back in a screech of laughter.

With a determined heave and swivel of his body, he succeeded in yanking the knickers off, loudly ripping them in the process.

Her pubic hairs stuck into him like razor wire. Could he really go through with this he thought?

"Like rough stuff eh—ripping my best knickers 'ew tinker. How do you like this!" she said as she slapped him with the force of a Neil Jenkins penalty on his protruding buttocks.

"Fucking 'ell—that hurt! You stupid …!"

He was unable to say anymore as her mouth clamped around his like a gintrap. The moment had come—he had to maintain some sort of erection or the whole dreadful process would have been in vain, and what was worse was she would probably kill or maim him for failing to satisfy her.

He immediately fell back on his vivid imagination and with every fibre of his being conjured up images of Catherine Deneuve (an adolescent favourite of his) in black underwear, with stockings, suspenders and stiletto heels cavorting lasciviously before him.

This started to have the desired effect, and his penis soon hardened to a satisfactory rock like consistency. In the dark, alcohol filled vortex in which he was threshing about, Rose's fat, pimply body became transformed into a Hollywood starlet and throwing caution to the wind he entered Rose's voluminous, wet yet disconcertingly cold vagina.

"Yes Turpin. More, more. I luvs you I do" gasped Rose as Thrust began to pound away at her love nest.

In his mind Catherine Deneuve had started to perform all sorts of lewd deeds upon him, and he began to sense that he would soon climax. With any luck he'd be out of there in 10 minutes and catch the boys for a curry.

"More Turpin, more—I want a good performance from you—no 5 minute wonders here," said Rose, and with that she crushed him firmly between her huge pill box shaped knees and dug her nails into his arse cheeks.

Shit! he thought, I'd better calm down. Right—goodbye Catherine—I need to think of something less sexual.

In his mind Turpin rattled through the stock images he used to delay climaxing—he had embraced the concept of 'new man' before, and unlike most of his contemporaries prided himself putting pleasuring the woman before his needs.

The usual images of favourite cars, or scenes from the film *Zulu* flashed through his mind, before he settled on the Pontypool front row of the 1970s. In his mind he imagined packing down against the hard, uncompromising, grizzled faces of Graham Price, Bobby Windsor and Charlie Faulkner and soon any chance of ejaculation fled from his mind and loins. Only a seriously depraved rugby loving masochistic homosexual would have any sexual feelings when confronted by the 'Viet Gwent' and Turpins coital momentum began to fade.

Suddenly he realised that his penis was going soft inside Rose—in particular Charlie Faulkner's determined grimace was causing it to shrink quicker than a lollipop in the Sahara.

"Turpin. Is something wrong? You're not letting me down are you?" Rose's voice rasped menacingly in the darkness.

Fucking 'ell he thought, back to Catherine!

Concentrating as never before he banished the Pontypool front row from his mind and concentrated on Catherine Deneuve. Slowly but surely his penis grew, and concentrated grunts emanating from Rose told him that he was back on track.

This process was repeated for about 20 minutes, with Catherine, in various states of undress and / or costume alternating with the Pontypool front row or in the interest of variety, the Soviet Politburo and Motorhead until Rose shouted "Now Turpin, now give me your best shot—let it go."

Bloody hell! thought Thrust as he jettisoned Lemmy from Motorhead into the darkness. Catherine was summoned back, together with Helen Mirren (in her prime circa *The Long Good*

Friday) and Pamela Anderson at her best in *Baywatch*. In his fevered mind, the three were then involved in an all out sexual assault on Turpin.

With his buttocks pumping like Louis Armstrong's cheeks, and sweat pouring down his nose, Turpin screwed his face up like a scowling Japanese sniper and heaved himself against all odds into a starburst ejaculation.

He immediately sank into Rose, in his mind mouthing a satisfied 'thank you' to the grateful actresses he had metaphysically satisfied. His warm glow of post coital satisfaction was rudely interrupted by Rose.

"Thank fuck for that Turpin—I'm knackered. Be a sweetie and get me a drink—there's a nice cold can of Bow in the back of the fridge that I hide away for little moments like this."

"Yeah, ok" mumbled Thrust as he slowly began to comprehend the dreadful act he had perpetrated.

"Come on, chop-chop—be a good boy, and mummy might give you another treat when you come back" said Rose with an edge of impatience.

The horror, the horror—Thrust had not given any thought to repeating his exploit, his plan had been to get away pronto. He hadn't reckoned on her... assertiveness.

"Cold isn't it? I'll put some clothes on to get the drink" he said.

"No need lover boy—I want you as you are for round two. Now get a move on will you, I'm gaspin'," she said with a disturbing edge of violence tingeing her voice.

Shit he thought. I'll have to come back. I need time to think of how to get out of here and she won't give me any. The bitch!

He stumbled down the stairs in the dark and succeeded in sneaking past the parrot and the dog to retrieve the can from the fridge. He could hear the rain hammering outside. What had he done? No way was it worth it, and what was worse, he had to probably do it again. He was now nearly sober, and the thought filled him with panic, fear and loathing.

He tried the back door—locked! He then tiptoed to the front door—he'd make a run for it—he'd resolved to take a chance of being arrested, soaked or even being buggered by nit ridden tramps—anything rather than going back upstairs.

The front door was locked as well. Shit, bollocks, piss ....
He was trapped.

"Turpin, come back to bed now – where's my drinkie poo?" Her voice floated down the stairs.

He trudged back up the stairs like a condemned man ascending the scaffold. He opened the door, and instinctively reached to switch on the light.

The light came on to reveal four pairs of eyes looking straight at him over bedclothes – the bloody kids! He'd gone into the wrong room.

He was standing there – bollock naked with a can of strongbow in his hand and her four children staring intently at him.

"Urgh... don't he look ugly with his clothes off" said Julio.

"Yeah, and a funny shaped willie – like a white chunky chewed twiglet" said Panache.

"Well at least it looks clean. Not like most of the ones we've seen coming in and out of mam's bedroom" said Che.

"Yeah – remember the one with the wooden leg, who's willie got caught in the joint of his leg? He really yelled and yelled" said Panache.

"Shut up you monsters. Breathe a word of this to anyone and I'll saw your heads off and piss down your necks. Failing that I'll send the public health in to demolish this pox ridden house. Understand? Sso shut it now or else" hissed Thrust with all the venom he could muster.

The children sensed he meant business. A sullen silence descended on the room.

Thrust switched the light off and turned into Rose's room.

"Come 'ere my sweetness – more nippity nip for ever lovely Rose eh? Come on Turpin boy, lets be having you!"

He pulled back the bedclothes and slid beside her. Her fleshy arm gripped him close. I can't do this again he thought. It's beyond suffering. I never thought it would lead to this. He felt like crying.

His cock had shrunk to a threadbare frazzle, hanging limply like a guilty criminal in an identity parade of pubic hairs – it was drained, battered, pounded and washed out. It's get up and go had got up and gone, and then probably emigrated from wherever it had gone to.

"ZZzzzzz" – it dawned on him that she was snoring.

Thank you God, thank you – she's gone to sleep. I haven't got to do it again he thought.

He lay there in the dark thanking as many deities as he could recall for this blessing. However, by the time he'd arrived at Quetzacoatl, the Aztec plumed serpent god, a dreadful realisation hit him like a sonic boom from out of the darkness. He couldn't risk moving her arm, in case she awoke, as if she awoke she would demand more dreadful shagging – which he was incapable of. A failure to perform, or heaven forbid, a refusal to perform, would result in ridicule, abuse, physical violation and probable castration no doubt aided and abetted by the dreadful host of delinquents lurking in the next room.

He lay there in a cold sweat. The effects of the alcohol were wearing off and the gnawing dread of the situation started to box him in claustrophobically, as her snores rasped on in a symphony from hell in his ears. Tiredness started to pull him into the blissful, yet temporary reprieve of sleep, but he resisted with all his strength, as he feared waking up to find her leering face over him demanding all sorts of deprivations that would never end.

As time passed the steaming stew of dilemmas that bubbled in his head were brought to boiling point by the slow realisation that the room was getting lighter, and that soon dawn would break – bringing nearer not only the living hell of her waking, but also, in a deliciously malevolent twist, the illumination of the scene by broad daylight.

His only hope was to get out before that point was reached, and in the growing light on the room he spied her house keys lying on the dressing table with her stained and torn underwear. He decided that he'd grab the keys, run down the stairs and be out before she awoke from her dreams of group sex with G watch in Swansea fire station.

Inch by tortuous inch he slowly moved his body from under her arm, beads of sweat running down his forehead, as his breathing got slower and slower. With an explosion of joy, he realised he was free. He turned over, as slow as stubble growth, to plop noiselessly out of bed.

One leg on the cold floor. He slowly moved the other, scarcely believing his ingenuity, suppleness and luck.

"Ooos a naughty boy then – sneaking out for a pee eh! Not without some ding dong first." Rose's voice slid out of her mouth like a snake.

An iron grip seized around his ankle, and jerked him back into the bed. Fuck, shit, bollocks, tits – his plan had been lumbered he thought. What could he do now?

The only weapon he had to use was his wits and Thrust suddenly determined upon a way out.

"Rose – you sexy, sexy woman" he said in his most amorous Burton voice. "I was only going out to get some soap and your lady shaver to do a 'Yul Brynner' – you know – a totally bald shag – it's all the rage in Cowbridge – and just to heighten the pleasure I'll do it doggy fashion – it's supposed to be out of this world," he added with a hint of desperation.

"Oooh – Cowbridge. There's posh. You're a bit of a dark horse Turpin aren't you. I quite fancy that – it's a bit, well, kinky. Can I shave yours?" said Rose.

"No, no, you might cut it off," he added with a shiver of realisation. "No, I'll shave us both. You need to get in the right position first, then I'll get the razor, a bit of foam, and – wooaahhh! Orgasm city here we come" (ha ha – what a pun he thought).

She simpered her agreement.

"Ok, Rose head down. He looked around the lightening room. Here put these pillows around you, and get your arse up. I'll be back in a minute" he said with an edge of assertiveness that surprised him.

He gently pushed her face into the pillows, and stacked the blankets around her head. Her arse stuck out like a sphinx as she breathed her muffled anticipation through the cotton surrounding her head.

With scarcely a second glance, he grabbed they keys and slipped out of the bedroom door, and in seconds he was fumbling at the front door.

"Turpin, what the fuck's going on?" came a shout down the stairs.

The door sprung open and he had scarcely time to grab a bright red womans plastic mac before running out into the rain full pelt out into the street.

A volley of curses followed him as he galloped down Inkerman Street heading in the direction of his house. In a further moment of inspiration he pulled the mac over his head and face, leaving the rest of his bloody and bruised body to full public view. He reasoned, probably correctly, that no one would recognise him from his penis or torso, but everyone would recognise his face above a woman's plastic mac. The headline 'Unknown, well endowed streaker runs through Port Talbot' read a lot better than 'Transvestite council Clerk Thrust's morning dash'.

The dwindling elderly band of early morning Chapel goers never could work out what flew past them that Sunday morning, and put it down as a product of ever worsening moral climate in Port Talbot.

A swift detour via the back streets brought him safely into his house and he bolted the doors in pounding fear of any pursuit by Rose. Thankfully it never came, he threw himself into his bed and he fell into a deep yet tormented sleep.

CHAPTER SEVEN

'Rugger Buggers'

He awoke feeling like animated road kill. His body ached, his feet were bloody and raw, and the red plastic mac hanging on the corner of his bedroom door brought the night's terrible events thudding back into his consciousness like mortar explosions.

He looked at the clock—it was mid-day. Another half hour and the boys would be knocking him up for their regular Sunday visit to the Rugby Club, for a general discussion of what happened on Saturday night, a few beers, a bit of food, bingo and strippers, then home for a nap and to watch highlights of Saturday's rugby on TV.

Thrust stared at the ceiling and willed himself to go back to sleep, where he would find some respite from the disjointed parade of horror that continually marched through his by now fully awakened mind.

An horrific kaleidoscope of leering grimy children, huge pendulous breasts, physical assaults, raw vodka, a lung bursting naked dash through the rain sodden streets, swam before him as finally he recalled peering between the folds of a plastic mac before the holy refuge of his back garden brought him to safety. Why oh why had he gone back to the Last Chance's house? Why hadn't he gone for an Indian with the lads. Why had he allowed his penis to rule his brain. What would he tell the boys? What would they say about him? What if it got back to work? Owen-Jones? Gloria? What if ...

A loud banging on the front door shook him from his anguish. Pausing briefly to examine the shrivelled string of bratwurst that had apparently replaced his penis, he flung on his dressing gown and hobbled downstairs.

"Who is it?," he asked in a high pitched voice, fearing that Rose McGrath and her children had followed him to demand the return of the mac, or to force him into further depraved actions or to burn his house down.

"Turpin's not in. I'm his mother and I haven't seen him for days," he added for good measure.

"Fuck off Turpin, we know it's you. Open the door, it's pissing down and the club is already open. We ain't got all fucking day," said a voice he recognised as Stan's.

Shit. It was the boys—he'd have to let them in, and probably confess all in a fit of remorse—he couldn't do that. He hesitated a while. More pounding on the door convinced him—well better get it over with, they couldn't kill him—unlike Rose.

He opened the door to see Vic and Stan standing in the rain. He let them in to his house.

"Good night eh?—Did you shag her then?" asked Vic, cutting to the chase.

"No names, no packdrill" said Thrust, hoping to stonewall any questions.

"Course he did. The Last Chance would get a shag out of a castrated eunuch. I'm just surprised he's lived to tell the tale. If she or her mad children don't kill you, then suicide caused by severe angst, or the pox normally finishes you off. She must have been really drunk to allow him to get away in one piece" said Stan, stroking his chin thoughtfully.

"Yeah yeah—leave it out, a cup of coffee and a quick drink and I was home by two. Nearly met you boys in the Indian, but I was a bit tired" replied Thrust hoping against years of experience that they would move onto another topic.

"You missed the naked streaker then. Some lunatic running through Aberavon in the nude, bollocks mangled and glowing like braziers—talk of the town. Two old ladies from Chapel fainted clean out. Said he headed down this way. No-one recognised him though—he had a red ladies mac on his head. Strange story innit," said Vic.

79

"Nice mac Turpie boy—mother bought it for you did she?" commented Stan as he looked up the stairs at the bedroom door. "Came home early eh—pull the fucking other one."

Stan then turned and pulled Thrust's dressing gown back to expose his nether regions.

"Ach y fi—like a pound of giblets—you did shag her—or more likely she shagged you" said Stan his lips curling like a worn out sheet of lino.

"Lots of times by the look of it. How could you, Lord have mercy" said Vic, rapidly ascending the moral high ground.

"There was no mercy there" said Stan. "She doesn't know the meaning of the word 'stop'."

"And you ran away with her raincoat—she'd probably hidden your clothes," said Vic.

"I've heard it's an old trick of hers—'morning glory' she calls it—likes a final grind to round things off" said Stan.

"It's legendary" said Vic. "The shag, not the coat."

"But you used the raincoat to get home—and, being a clever university educated boy—used it to cover your face rather than your flabby smashed up dick" said Stan "as no-one would recognise it, or at least admit to it."

"Elementary" said Vic.

"Thank you Watson—elementary indeed" said Stan.

"All right, all right Sherlock—leave it there. I'm guilty. I feel like shit, my knob aches like a hookers shin, and I will confess all as I can't live with the memory any longer. I'm not a Catholic so I can't see a priest, but as you've got religious studies at GCSE you'll do" said Thrust, confronted with the stark reality of his paper thin story crumbling before his eyes.

"Right, excellent. I knew you'd crack sooner or later" said Stan. "Wash your dick in TCP, Vim and Carbolic soap and get some clothes on. We're meeting Roy and the boys up the club, and the strippers won't wait. They're from Clydach, and I know one of them, so I don't want to miss a thing. Get a fucking move on. You can tell us the gory details on the way."

Thrust went up to his room, got dressed and came back down stairs within five minutes. They walked through the farm to the rugby club in the falling rain as Thrust related the previous nights experiences blow by blow.

"Mad, bad and dangerous to know. Stinks like hell and will sleep with anything" said Stan.

"Don't say that about the parrot" said Vic.

"Ok. We all make mistakes" said Turpin, rapidly tiring of the questioning.

"Book yourself into the VD clinic, that's your best bet. However, looking on the down side, If it's Aids, what hymns do you want for the funeral?" said Vic.

"Fuck off, it's better than beating the bishop like you did this morning—you know the saying 'half a shag's better than a dozen wanks" said Thrust, getting more irritable.

"How dare you—I'd rather wank my knob into a bloody thread than go with the Last Chance" said Stan.

"I prefer the wanking to anything" said Vic, "except drinking and eating. But it depends," he paused. "Generally I prefer it." Another pause. "Yes—to anything—though it is a close call."

By this time they'd got to the Rugby Club, signed in and made their way to the bar. Brynglyn rugby club was just outside the centre of Port Talbot and was the focal point of the community in that part of the town. Turpin looked up at the honour board which was a monument to over 100 years of rugby playing. Faded sepia photographs of teams going back to beyond the First World War looked down in waxed tableaux of barely caged aggression that still spoke and reached out to you across the decades. One photograph—was the most revered in the clubhouse, as it contained, in the front row Thrust's idol—Richard Burton—who had played for the Club as a young man. Still esteemed as a no nonsense flanker who tackled hard and late, and who in one clubhouse legend had not only floored some Oxbridge number 8 with a devastating tackle (plus a well timed short arm), and to emphasise that you could be Welsh, good at rugby, hard (and to round things off, well read) recited 'Do not go gentle into that good night' over him as he was carried from the field on a stretcher.

The club had produced quite a few internationals and their faces, like the Welsh equivalent of Mount Rushmore framed the bar in a pantheon of honour. If you were up there, you were someone in Brynglyn, and everyone knew it.

Thrust looked around the large bar area and noticed that the stage was draped ready for the strippers, and that Lance Bristow, the club steward, resident master of ceremonies and bingo caller all in one, was connecting up his microphone.

Roy and the boys were already seated playing cards, whilst a few regulars were sipping their pints and reading the Sunday papers. It had obviously been a good night last night as a few were being held upside down. A few of the younger men had got front row seats for the show, as the strippers often involved some of the younger men in their acts, and shagging the strippers was an acknowledged 'rite of passage' at Brynglyn RFC. At one end of the bar stood some of the living legends of the club—men either nearing the end of their playing days, or who had recently retired. These men represented an older generation of Welsh rugby, a game built on the ethos of 'an eye for an eye' where you sorted out your differences on the field, and where the referee was merely there to keep the score and blow up for time.

The concept that underlined their attitude to the game was 'do it to them before they do it to you' and whilst they were happy to give out punishment, they were equally content to take it. The idea of going off injured was alien to them, and in their minds you only left the field whilst the game was in play if you were sent off or as a last resort carried off, preferably comatose, ideally for the sake of your reputation, dead.

Turpin looked at them with a mixture of awe, respect, envy, fear and curiosity. They already seemed to belong to a different age—certainly none of the younger players seemed at all like them, and you could imagine them at El Alemain, The Somme, Rorke's Drift, Waterloo, Agincourt—the lot. They were the sort of men you'd want next to you in a fight, though indeed, playing with then was nearly as bad as playing against them. If they said to do something—you did it and in a ruck or maul they sought to injure and maim all flesh—their teams or the opposition. Thrust had played in the same team as some of them, and had thankfully escaped relatively unscathed, probably because he was on the wing.

This morning they seemed to be in a particularly ill tempered mood, and were discussing the decline of Welsh Rugby.

"Gone to the fucking dogs. Never been the same since the Ringer sending off—they're all pansies now—all they care about is their match fees, their kit, their hairdo! Their cars— anything but winning!" Meredith Jones' voice boomed around the room. He was unique amongst the group as he was a back, not a forward, but still hard enough to be welcomed into the select band. Still, his physique was a million miles away from a stereotypical full back—shaven headed, built like a weightlifter and with just one front tooth.

"Fucking right Meredith's right enough. They need a reason to punch someone these days. A fucking reason. In our day the only reason you needed was that they weren't on your side, and we often didn't bother about that. Right enough— they haven't got any dog in 'em—too obsessed with image."

"They're all fucking ponces" said 'Kamikaze' Parry, a wiry, but powerful former flank forward.

"Yeah, the game in Wales has gone down the pan big time—an it's not just the players, it's the fucking hawkeyed, artsey fartsy refs, intent on rooting an honest punch up out of the game, and it's the fucking WRU who back them up, when they've not got their cowing snouts in the hospitality and expenses trough. Wankers the lot of them!" said 'Wintergreen' Watkins, the smallest but certainly not the weakest of the group. He had a face like a particularly weathered gargoyle having his bollocks bitten off by a leopard, and had never flinched from putting it in the way of an opposing fist or boot. He made Jack Palance look like a cherub eating a marshmallow.

"Exactly" said Billy Bowen, another ex prop forward, "there's no room for any hardness in the game any longer—we weren't particularly hard, certainly not compared to the likes of Dai Gomper, but we knew what our fists were for and we knew when to use 'em."

A rumble of 'oh aye' rolled around the group in acknowledgement of the earlier group of players, particularly Dai Gomper, who had played in the 50s and 60s and who was rumoured to be hewn out of rock, fuelled by drink and afraid of nothing except closing time and who spent most of his time fighting entire shiploads of foreign seamen.

"We never played touch fucking rugby in training did we, in fact we often trained without a ball," said Parry.

"No point in it—certainly in the forwards," said Watkins.

"Yeah, an remember we used to hit each other with sticks as part of the warm up—common sense mun—the opposition always seemed much weaker after that" said Billy.

"Often tackled lamp posts on our way home after training—cost the council thousands. No problem tackling some poofy back after that was er?" said Meredith.

"No we just played for the fun of a dust up—the glory of winning and you and your team's reputation—that was the key—and a few pints and a sing song after—that was what rugby was about—sticking together—physically beating the other team—fuck the ball, fuck the score—in your heart you knew whether you'd won—and the other side knew it as well" said Pross, the legendary Dai 'one punch' Prosser, the oldest and still the hardest of the group. He had played prop for Aberavon for many seasons and held the record for being sent off most times in first class and club rugby. He had nearly got chosen for Wales B but in a row over the pronunciation of the word 'coat' attacked a Cardiff committee man in the bar before the team was announced and he never came close again.

His small eyes were hid behind thick pebble glasses, but ceaselessly darted around the room like an assassins. His nose was bent and crooked like a gnarled rock formation and his huge fists cupped his pint like a thimble. He was rumoured to have knocked numerous men out with one punch, and even to have actually killed someone in a mass brawl on a tour. Suspiciously he was never charged, and cynics, like Thrust felt this was merely part of the 'so hard they don't shit' legend cultivated by this group of ageing ex players, collectively known as 'The Wild Bunch'. Nonetheless no-one would dream of telling this to him face to face.

"Right enough—we ought to dust our kit off, turn up for training and sort some of these novices out. They'd crap bowls at the thought of a bit of 'business' said Parry, who had actually done time for GBH, robbery, theft, ABH and most other things. It was a wonder he was ever out of jail long enough to have learnt the game, but, to be fair, when he did play, he certainly made an impact. He certainly lived up to his nickname 'Kamikaze'. His nose was nearly as bent as Prossers and his sending off record came frighteningly close—indeed as a games played ratio it was almost off the chart.

"Come on—let's do it—we can take 'em, in fact, let's do it now—are any of the wankers in the bar?" Parry's eyes lit up like charcoal braziers and his fists (which he had tattooed himself using broken glass to read 'DETH' and 'PAYN') smashed together as his mouth parted in a rictus grin to reveal rows of blackened, broken, yellowing teeth.

"Yes—let's 'ave some now boys" he said as his eyes leered around the room in a desperate bid to catch someone willing to take up his challenge.

"Leave it Kamikaze. There's hardly any of the firsts here, they're all shagging their girlfriends or polishing their new cars" said Billy in tones of utmost contempt, though it was hard to work out which activity he felt the contempt for, "the only ones in aren't worth the fight, and they're decent boys anyway—few beers, watch a stripper—tidy boys. In any event smashing up our team isn't a good way of preparing for next weeks cup tie against Pontycymmer, and as most of us finished playing years ago, you'll be playing Pontycymmer on your own."

"Yeah, they're still all softies, not like in the old days. Hey, remember that game against the Quins, Pross when in the first scrum, you hit their prop so hard he shat in their second rows face!" said Meredith, grinning like a Gargoyle.

The group burst into raucous laughter as they reminisced about past matches, and the inevitable fights.

Suddenly the door of the rugby club flew open and four men blowing whistles ran into the room and brought the laughter to a sudden juddering halt.

"Out, out, we'll make him come out, we'll sing and dance and shout, shout, shout." The thin weedy chant ebbed feebly away.

Four shaven headed, skinny, moustached men in tight leather laderhosen type shorts and bondage gear stood incongruously in the middle of the rugby club shouting the above slogan, carrying placards above their heads proclaiming

'Thomas—get out of the closet now!' and 'We all say Thomas is gay—hip hip hooray!'

"You all would love a dick, so let's made it quick," shouted one of the less alert member of the group, as a simmering fragile silence descended on the club house. The whistling and chanting seemed to echo, then die as the four gay activists realised that they were in the middle of Brynglyn rugby club.

A deep voice growled from near the bar.

"Parry, bolt the door. Bill, I think these boys have made a big mistake" said Prosser.

"Oh fucking 'ell Julian, I told you to turn right at Station Road. We're not in the bloody Labour Club, it's the cowin' rugby club, and these boys don't look happy to see us" said the leader of the group as he began to turn a whiter shade of puce. The four backed into each other and some held hands. The one who had just spoken started to pray and cross himself. Thrust recognised him as Dominic John, one of Port Talbot's few gays and indeed a militant gay rights activist who had, quite understandably gone off to London many years ago to pursue his interests and to apparently engage in militant gay activities. Thrust recalled that John had been in the press recently stating that he intended to 'out' prominent Labour politicians in Wales, and that this was an obvious attempt to confront the resident Labour MP Iestyn Thomas, who, despite being married with three children, was often rumoured to be 'on the other bus'.

Sadly for John, his memory and grasp of local geography had let him down badly, and instead of being in the Labour club, they had found themselves in Brynglyn RFC. In terms of blunders likely to endanger human life, this was right up there with the Light Brigade and Custer's last stand.

"What shall we do Dom?" trilled one of the gay activists who had started to sob loudly, obviously fearing the worst.

"There's nothing else for it Quentin, run boys, run like the fucking wind, and don't stop till you get to Hampstead Heath......" Dominic John's sage advice was brought to an abrupt end by a large hand clamping around his windpipe. The clubhouse erupted into scenes of cold calculated precision targeted violence, as the Wild Bunch proceeded to make the gay rights activists bitterly regret ever venturing into Brynglyn rugby club. Tolerance of male homosexuality was not a particularly well developed trait in Brynglyn rugby club and the concept of gay rights was alien to most of the older rugby crowd. Certainly anyone proclaiming themselves of the alternative persuasion in the inner precincts of the rugby club would be foolhardy, and likely at best to be verbally threatened if not physically attacked. However a full scale 'outing' was about as great a desecration of the Rugby Club as the Wild Bunch could conceive of, and their barely controlled fury came erupting forth at this, in their less than enlightened view, the most flagrant insult to their club, their values and their masculinity.

The retribution was swift and brutal, and Thrust was, in spite of his broadly left wing, enlightened views, initially reluctant to speak out to try to stop the mayhem. He also partly felt that the activists deserved it, not only for the dubious ethic of 'outing' but also for not knowing the Rugby Club from the Labour Club. He'd always said sport and politics shouldn't mix. However, as the wild bunch began to wreak havoc with the unfortunate intruders, Thrust felt that things had gone too far, and moved to try and break up the slaughter. A strong arm grabbed him, and pulled him back. "Leave it there Turp" said Stan. "You'll make no difference—the Wild Bunch are on a roll—they'll kill you as well. Just let it be—you know it makes sense."

Turpin stepped back with a reluctant sigh of relief. Stan was right—he'd make no difference, and could well end up maimed himself. He looked on with detached curiosity tinged with horror (as he sometimes did in watching lions despatching wilderbeasts on a wildlife programme), as the gay activists were dealt with in a variety of brutal, yet innovative and frankly amusing ways. These generally consisted of considerable punching and kicking, but also the violent application of pool cues, ash trays and (funniest of all) a sooty charity collection box against, and even into various parts of the activists bodies, before the traumatised crew were piled into a bizarre tableaux (loosely resembling the death of Nelson) in the corner of the dance floor.

"Six pints of best Roy," said Prosser, wiping spit from the sides of his mouth. "Hope the ambulance fucking hurries up — they're bleeding all over the dancefloor."

"Right, where were we?" continued Prosser. "Yeah, Welsh Rugby's gone to the dogs, remember that game against Cwmafon Billy — when the ref was sick during the punchup!" The Wild Bunch laughed heartily.

The conversation continued as if nothing had happened. Turpin Thrust stared in amazement and thought that perhaps his analogy with the animal kingdom was apt — they had inflicted violence in an amoral dispassionate way. It was as natural to those men as breathing; though whether that would be of any comfort to the activists would be debatable. They were right to an extent though, hard, violent men were once a key feature of Welsh rugby and this was undoubtedly missing today, though in Thrust's view, this analysis of the demise of rugby in the Principality was a gross oversimplification.

He mused to himself, as the activists were loaded into the ambulance, that Welsh teams in the past had indeed beaten all corners, and in doing so had undoubtedly stood toe to toe and refused to be intimidated and, indeed were deeply often intimidating to the opposition. However, he was firmly of the view pure violence didn't win the match, nor did it account for the deep rooted love of rugby in the collective Welsh soul — this was put there by the skill, the innovation and the quicksilver combination of mind and body to beat an opponent or to sieze an opportunity that made Welsh Rugby great, and this was the key to what was missing in today's rugby, indeed in Welsh society at large — and this point was lost on the group at the bar who continually rehearsed the 'they were real men in th old days' trip down memory lane without really getting to the key to the problem. In Thrust's view it was simple — there was a basic lack of ability show at senior level, and a failure to harness natural talent — that was the major problem, and furthermore this went across the board. Thrust thought of getting up and joining them and telling them this view — but he rationalised correctly that this would get him, at best into an argument he wouldn't win, and at worst, a broken nose. Better off waiting for the strippers he concluded.

He sat down towards the back of the club with Vic and Stan and nodded over to Roy and the gang. He looked around the club and noticed that it had settled down after the earlier excitement of the outer-bashing, and most of the men had by now contented themselves with playing cards, reading the Sunday newspapers or chatting about life in general ahead of the bingo and strippers.

The club compere, Lance Bristow, got up and said a few words.

"Morning gentlemen, and thank you for coming here on his bright Sunday morning for a little lively entertainment. We have already had a bit of light pugilism courtesy of the brave lads by the bar (giving a broad nod of acknowledgement) and I am sure we won't be invaded by any more chaps of the ... how can I say, the... alternative persuasion... after their brethren's unfortunate experience today. However, putting that behind us, so to speak (a chorus of laughter rippled around the clubhouse) we can now concentrate on a thrilling game of international pro-celebrity bingo—courtesy of Gwilym the Shout up here, followed by the climax—and that doesn't mean you're allowed to wank Hovis, (pointing at one of the lads in the front row) of today's events, a couple of lovely dancing girls from sunny Clydach! I bet you boys just can't wait. So without further ado—over to Gwylim."

Gwilym, 'The shout' Thomas, who had suffered shell shock in World War Two and indeed not only stuttered, but also twitched, was a bizarre choice for a Bingo caller, but most accepted it as a form of social work, and indeed his deliveries and malapropisms often enlivened proceedings.

"Ffffirst Nnnnnnumber, number 10, Mmmaggies (boos arose at the mention of the former Prime Ministers name) Den" shouted Gwilym (living up to his name) as the game started.

With a star prize for a full house of a crate of Strongbow, it was hardly riches beyond ones wildest dreams, but Thrust reasoned, it passed the time until the stripper came on.

"Crickity clit, two small duck" intoned Gwilym as he pulled out a twenty two. A crecendo of pens being tapped on glasses rose and fell like a breeze around the clubhouse, as the game settled into a rhythm of its own.

"What do you think of the incident earlier then?" asked Vic as Gwilym called in the background. "Bit of a gaffe those 'boys' coming in here eh. Certainly won't do it again. May take some time to get the pool cue out of the curly one."

"Really good cue that one. Used it often to make some splendid breaks. Never thought it would end up where it did" said Archie.

"Yeah—bad move—should've known where they were going—though I'm sure they wouldn't have got tea and biscuits in the Labour club—it would only have ended in grief whatever they did," said Stan, in his most compassionate voice.

"Terrible, terrible thing to do. I'm no fan of Iestyn Thomas—the man's a bloody hypocrite—remember that ladyboy we saw him with in Paris. Made Boy George look like Brian Blessed, but still this 'outing' caper—might be ok in London, but not really appreciated down here" said Thrust, judiciously weighing up the debate.

"Prosser and the boys certainly gave them a good tuning," said Stan. "Just like the old days really. Punch first, ask questions later. That's the way to do it. Could do with them in the current team."

"Well yeah, fair enough—you need hard men to win a game, to get the edge over the other side, but to me, Rugby is about more than beating your opponent up. If you want to do that, take up boxing or karate—at least it's a fair fight and they know you're going to hit them. The main reason to plan rugby should be to be good at rugby and to beat the other team by playing rugby—the reason that we, or Aberavon, or Wales aren't good any more isn't just because we're not as hard as we were, it's because we aren't as good as we were," responded Thrust.

"Ok, they may be a bit fitter now, may be able to spin pass both ways, or get a lock to sell a dummy, but the real skills—the side step, the deft pass, the change of tactics at the key point in the game—have gone, and were doing nothing about it—there's no heart, no hwyl, no dog, no nous, in the game anymore. If the going gets tough, the kids get going—to another team. There's no loyalty, no building of inner strength in adversity, no all for one, one for all—that's what was ruining the game, on the field and off it," said Thrust , his fervour for rugby and Wales bursting through.

"Thank you Winston Churchill. Been reading those war books again have you?" said Stan. "I feel like saluting."

"Well, I think he's right—we have lost that something from the game" said Vic. "I wouldn't say our age group were wonderful, but we certainly had more of those qualities than the current lot. Remember last years Veterans versus the current team Boxing Day game? We stuffed the current lot, even though they were younger and fitter. There's certainly something gone out of the game, and it think it will be very difficult to put back, if it ever can be.

"It's not just rugby—it's society—you don't see kids kicking a ball around a street, or playing touch rugby with a tin can like we did. They just hang around street corners or lock themselves in their bedrooms playing Nintendo Game Boy. They don't even join bands or take up acting. There's no talent coming out of Wales anymore," said Thrust linking his two favourite themes of rugby and acting in one sentence.

"Bollocks—what about Bonnie Tyler or Shakin Stevens?" said Stan, being provocative.

"Get a life, not exactly superstars are they. Anyway, that's ages ago, there's nothing of any great consequence coming out of Wales anymore. All the talent we had, left the bloody Country, and the well at home is dry—where are today's Lloyd George, Nye Bevan, Stanley Baker or Richard Burton? We, Wales, is a busted flush and that's the end of it" said Thrust.

"In fact, since Burton died, when was it, back in '84 something died in Wales, and it's been gone ever since. That was the same year as the miners strike—it really was the end of an era. What's the song say? 'the day the music died'—well, in my mind that was the day Wales died, we've been missing something ever since" Thrust concluded warming to his theme.

"Remember we went up to his 'funeral service', in Cwmavon" said Vic. "Packed out—the pubs were heaving, the sides of the mountains were covered in people—great singsong. They'd come from all over the world for that."

"Yeah—remember that Journalist from New York who bought us beers all night? We convinced her we'd been in school with Burton, Hopkins and Dylan Thomas. Gormless or what. I wonder if she ever printed any of our tales?" said Stan.

"Don't knock the girl. Poetic licence. Her heart was in the right place. Anyway, it was a great day—but, and I've said this many times, he should have been buried there—not just had a memorial service. What was the bloody point of burying him in Switzerland?" said Thrust, with an edge of bitterness.

"Someone said it was a tax dodge" said Archie.

"Fat lot of good it did him" said Stan.

"Not for him—his family, Sally or whatever you knob" said Archie.

"Seems a load of rubbish to me. How can you tax a corpse? Senseless" said Vic, ever the realist.

"You're right—he should've been buried in Wales—it would have been symbolic—a hero's return, and it would have given a focal point for visitors. Might even have brought some jobs—and like the statue to him they've never built, it could have inspired some young kid to chuck the computer or drugs and get control of his life and do something special—and possibly, just possibly, become a superstar. We all need heros don't we?" said Thrust.

"More than all that, burying him here would be right. Right for him, for us, for Welsh people ... for Wales" he continued.

"House"—the shout went up, and a huge row erupted. Whether it concerned the validity of the call, or whether the sell by date on the cans had passed, it was impossibly to tell.

The row rumbled on for a few minutes, then the compere—Lance Bristow then stepped in and announced that the girls were now ready and could we all give a warm welcome to the unlikely named Veronique and Chandee from Clydach.

Two attractive young women paraded to the middle of the stage and began to dance to what sounded like the Match of the Day theme.

"Get that fucking racket off—you useless bloody wew Gwilym. We want 'Boogie Nights' not Colonel Bogies bloody march" shouted Lance.

The girls were unfazed by this set back and proceeded to gyrate in rhythm as they took off their clothes. Due to their youth and good looks most of the men finished reading their papers or put down their cards and were staring intently at the strippers. Stripper mornings, or 'smokers' as they were known, were often hit or miss affairs, as on many occasions the stripper or strippers had seen better days, and were generally met, at best, with an wall of indifference, or at worst with verbal abuse and litter throwing. The club must have had a good takings at the game to afford these two. Thrust got another round in, and returned to the theme of Richard Burton's funeral.

"Seriously boys—the failure to bury Richard Burton in Wales was one of the great crimes of the 20th Century" said Thrust.

"What about the fucking Holocaust, Jack the Ripper or the Kennedy assassination?" said Stan.

"Jack the Ripper was in the 19th Century" said Vince, ever precise on such points.

"All right, all right—I mean from a Welsh perspective. The failure to bury him here has robbed us of one of our few real heroes. Someone who did something for Wales—someone who had the balls and the intellect to take on anyone in the world and give as good, if not miles better, than what he got. He should never have been left to be buried in bloody Switzerland—too clean, too neat, too bloody... Swiss—not Wales, not Welsh" spluttered Thrust.

"Cost thousands—anyway, they wouldn't allow it—it's against their laws probably. His family would be saddled with a huge tax bill and wouldn't wear it. Anyway, it wouldn't look good in the papers to have a collection to bring a dead body into the country—not with all the famine in Africa like; people would rather keep people alive, stands to reason," said Thrust.

The music reached a crescendo, and the stripper's knickers flew into the air like a parody of a scaled down grouse shoot. In that explosive instant, Turpin knew he had to tell them his secret plan.

He put down his pint and turned to his friends before uttering the most significant words of his life.

"I reckon we ought to bring him back, boys!"

CHAPTER EIGHT

'The Strippers'

"Bring him bloody back—you cannot be serious. Like how are we going to do this—fly over and chop him up and secrete him in our suitcases? Strap him to the top of a camper van and pretend he's a souvenir? Put him through a blender and pour him into some wine bottles. You've really lost it this time Turpin. I know working for the council can have a strange effect on someone, but this is off the Richter scale" said Stan.

"Yeah, what did Rose do to you last night—make you smoke a mound of dope, or give you a partial lobotomy with her curling tongs. You've really pushed this one into the realms of fantasy. Come on, the bin's being passed around for the strippers—if we get enough money raised they should do something interesting!" said Vic.

Sure enough, Lance the compere had got back on stage and started to address the room.

"Thank you ladies for that beautiful display of dancing—it certainly livened up my morning, and I can see from the tilting tables that it has put a bit of lead in some of the boys pencils! Now, at Brynglyn Rugby Club, we like to enjoy and savour the full range of talent possessed by our artistes, and I can assure you, these ladies have a lot, lot more to offer. So, in time honoured fashion, we're going to pass the bucket around for some financial contribution from you lads, to encourage the ladies to come back and entertain you, and themselves with a bit more—how can I say—liberated dancing. Who knows, one of you lucky boys might be invited to join in their little dance routine—bit of fun, something to tell the kids—if and when

94

you get any," said Lance mischievously knowing full well that last weeks man of the match for the Youth Team, Nippon, the scrum half had been chosen for this 'honour'.

The bucket went around and a selection of £1 coins and 50p pieces were thrown in together with the usual assortment of washers, smartie caps and eastern European coinage.

Lance and Gwilym huddled in the back counting the contents of the bucket, before Lance came back to re-address the gathering.

"Come on you wankers, £7.50 isn't going to get four bars of the birdie song and a peck on the cheek. These girls are class—good looking, clean limbed and ready and willing to do all sorts of interesting things—but we need a bit more than £7 fucking 50. And no bloody washers or fucking Zloties or what ever they are called," said Lance. "Get some real money out, or else piss off home."

Muffled grumbles rumbled around the club, as the bucket went around again, and succeeded in tripling the amount already raised. After another huddled conflab, this time with the girls and their agent (a one eyed milkman from Morriston) in which Lance agreed to top it up to £30 out of club funds, the girls agreed to do a further 'dance' for the eager punters.

"Look" said Thrust, "I've got it all worked out, all we need to do is hire a camper van or truck from Tonto's Van Hire. We'll tell them it's for a booze cruise. Drive down to Portsmouth—three or four hours, late on Thursday, night crossing to St Malo or Cherbourg—drive all Friday, stop somewhere Friday night. Saturday we'll get to Switzerland move over the border—keep a low profile, find out exact location of the grave—it's all in his biography by Melvyn Bragg—anyway, if it isn't, I'll look it up. Then, go to the nearest supermarket, buy a load of booze—especially cans etc., Saturday night we go to the graveyard, dig out the coffin, put it in the van, cover it with booze cans and some blankets then back across France for the early morning ferry, back from St Malo on Monday, back to Port Talbot. Leave it all in my garage all week, then bury him on top of the mountain, with full honours the next Saturday. Photograph the coffin, lie low for a while, then announce to a packed press conference in the council chamber what we've discovered. Deny any knowledge of how he got back to Wales. We'll be able to face off any legal threats—possession is 9/10 of the law (I've learned that from Owen-Jones) and before we know it we'll have a great tourist attraction on our doorstep. It'll re-invigorate the town—we'll open a bar called 'Burtons' and we'll soon be raking it in from gullible Americans who'll pay £5 a pint for 'Burton Ale' and we'll be able to retire. And what's more important—Wales will start to rise up again. Aberavon and the Welsh Rugby Team will start winning, we'll find 10 new Tom Jones' and discover gold in the Afan Valley and oil in Swansea Bay, everything will be smelling of roses—I'll bet on it!" said Thrust with a flourish.

"Apart from us—we'll be smelling of a decomposing corpse! Mad as a bucket of slugs. Though I've got a feeling you are partly serious about this aren't you? Shall I phone the psychiatric ward now or do you want to savour a last few hours of freedom?" said Stan.

"How will we get the body out of the grave without anyone knowing?" asked Vic, seemingly interested in the plan.

"Well, I think the cemetery is quite remote, and I'm sure the Swiss are in the World Cup finals this time around. We wait for a weekend when they've got a big game, and bingo—the place will be deserted—they'll all be in the pub, pissed. We can dig him out then" said Thrust.

"Won't the coffin be rotted away? Will there be anything to bring back? What about the smell?" asked Stan.

"Well, I'm fairly certain it was an expensive, all singing all dancing coffin, as you'd expect from a multi-millionaire, and I've heard he was laid out by the finest undertaker in Switzerland dressed all in red, with a Welsh Rugby Jersey, and a daffodil and leek crossed on his chest. Anyway, with all the drink he stuck away he will be perfectly preserved by the alcohol. After all this time he won't smell, and in any event the coffin will seal it all in. If push comes to shove we buy a gallon of 'Paco Rabanne' on the ferry and we can douse everything in that, and pretend, if anyone asks, that we accidentally smashed a bottle. I've given it some thought, during a council meeting and I bet it really can be done," said Thrust.

96

"Turpin—it's so mad—it might just be feasible. I'm a big fan of Burton—who isn't in this town, but I'm not bothered about bringing him back and I think what you say about a Welsh revival is the biggest load of bollocks since Bobby Gould's last team talk, but I may just come along for the ride with this. It'll only take a weekend and it surely promises to be a laugh if nothing else" said Stan.

"I'll think about it" said Vic, "Money's a bit tight, but I've been meaning to do a booze cruise for ages and as Stan said, it would undoubtedly be a laugh. So do you think we need anyone else to come along?"

"I'll give it a go" said Archie. "Quite fancy a trip to France."

"We don't need anyone else—we can do it. In any event I'm going to do it whether you lot come with me or not—I could do with getting out of this bloody rut and I'm fed up with our annual 'is it Spain or is it Greece' debate, which only ends up with us getting ratted every night in bars where the music is loud enough to loosen your fillings and where there's ten blokes for every woman. Anyway, I'm convinced if we bring him back I'll become a national hero—and rich, so if you like I'll only be fulfilling my destiny" said Thrust with surprising confidence.

"Oooh—fulfilling your destiny—well if you shut up and turn round, you might fulfil something else. The strippers are back on, and it looks as if the legendary bucket has persuaded them to do something interesting" said Stan.

They turned to see the two girls appear on stage in sexy Nazi style uniforms, stockings and suspenders, high heeled Jackboots brandishing two bayonet tipped rifles.

These outfits obviously tapped into the deep vein of fascist dominatrix weapon wielding fetishism that ran not only through Brynglyn Rugby Club but probably Welsh rugby culture generally.

The booming sound of 'Caberet' filled the Club as even the Wild Bunch stopped talking about the decline of Welsh rugby, and turned to observe the two girls as they not only danced in a provocative manner but began to make obscene and suggestive gestures with their guns.

Gwilym, who had till now been busily counting up the raffle tickets for the annual Edinburgh trip rapidly became fixated at the spectacle in front of him and even though a virgin at the age of 85 began to experience a kaleidoscope of emotions ranging from the stirrings of long dormant sexual longing (he'd normally be gone by the time any strippers came on) to dreadful flashbacks to his experiences at Pegasus Bridge in World War Two.

His mouth hung open as the two girls dancing became more and more provocative and as his lower lip began to quiver, his cigarette fell into the sack of raffle tickets on to his lap where it began to smoulder.

The two girls had by now begun to kiss and smooch each other, and, in the tradition of the club, invited one of the young boys sitting in the front seats to join them.

Nippon, the youth team scrum half had already taken off most of his clothes in anticipation, and as the nod came from Lance to join the girls went out, he sprang onto the stage bollock naked with an erection like a storm troopers salute to join in the climax of the dance which was namely Nippon, shagging one or both of the girls as the traditional reward for outstanding performances in the youth team.

The sight of Nippon joining the girls on stage was too much for Gwilym who was by now conscious of a fierce burning sensation in his groin — caused not as he thought by a reawakening of youthful desires, but by a small fire now raging in the cloth sack of raffle tickets. This caused Gwilym to leap from his chair in the wings of the stage and run into the middle of the stage where, battling with a psychological maelstrom raging in his mind, Gwilym sought to do battle with evil Nazis, relieve long dormant sexual frustrations, and to save innocent Welsh maidens from the evil ministrations of the youth team scrum half who unfortunately in Gwilym's disturbed mind had morphed into Himmler.

Before leaping onto the stage, Gwilym had thrown the bag of raffle tickets over his head where it landed by the streamers and tinsel that had been left backstage since the Max Boyce Christmas special at the club, and in no time the burning bag set them alight as well.

Meanwhile Gwilym, his trousers also by now smouldering, launched himself at the human sandwich of Nippon and the two girls cavorting on stage.

"Fuck off you stinking old pervert—you're setting my knickers on fire," shouted one of the girls, who immediately grabbed one of the guns and stuck the bayonet into Gwilym's arse.

"Aaaaggh Aaaggh, the NNNazii Bbbastards are trying to kill me…" shouted Gwilym, convinced now that he was indeed back at Pegasus Bridge. The acrid smoke that wafted from the back of the stage only added to his illusion of time travel, as he thrashed out with his walking stick, only to connect with Nippons steaming erection. Nippon howled in pain as he stood up and started to kick out at Gwilym.

The rest of the club watched the bizarre scene in open mouthed astonishment.

At this moment the police arrived to investigate the reports of a disturbance earlier in the day at the rugby club, accompanied by cameramen from BBC Wales who had arrived there to follow up the breaking story of the gay activists who had been forcefully ejected from the club in the course of outing the Local MP.

Instead of mundane shots of the Brynglyn Club, and an anticipated low key voiceover to the story, they were able to film a scene resembling a mélange out of *The Night Porter, The Texas Chainsaw Massacre* and *Carry on Camping*, as a smouldering geriatric war veteran battled with a naked youth and two semi naked women in Nazi uniforms on a stage circled by flames. The scene became even more bizarre as many of the clubmen watching leapt up on the stage to join in—some in the hope of sexual congress with one or both of the women, others to join in or break up the fight and others more philanthropic than the rest to try and save the participants from the inferno that threatened to engulf them. The footage was not only the lead story on the national news that night, but also eventually spawned at least two pornographic film tributes and a Harold Pinter play.

"Come on boys, let's get out of here—you couldn't make this up if you wanted to," said Thrust as he pushed open the fire door and left the clubhouse. "This bloody place—this Club, this Town, this Country… is truly descending into farce—and I'm going to do something about it!"

CHAPTER NINE

'Whizard Wheeze'

A few days passed after the spectacular events at Brynglyn Rugby Club, and the boys next met up at Aberavon Rugby Ground for a midweek match. The ground was a crumbling reminder of post war prosperity. The main stand (in fact the only stand) was a ramshackle pile of rotting wood, its faded red and black paint cracked and peeling. The rest of the ground was made up of open terracing which provided no shelter from the elements—it was about as far removed from the San Siro Stadium as the Sex Pistols were from Beethoven.

The boys took up their usual spot on the terrace and joined in the usual banter that flew both on and off the pitch. They would never, as a matter of principle, ever sit in the stand —that was the preserve of the 'cracach' the relatively wealthy upper echelons of Welsh Rugby supporters, who were invariably comfortably pleased with themselves and, who generally looked down, literally and metaphorically on the hoi polloi on the terrace. For their part the people on the terrace— gnarled, rougher, generally poorer than the 'toffs' in the stand, wouldn't have had it any other way—it made them feel more in touch with the game, and somehow more part of the game they were watching.

They collectively stared up at the scoreboard which read: Aberavon 0; Visitors 76. The score board continued to rack up the score with wounding indifference. Local rivals Neath were playing Aberavon in a League match and were running riot. Time and time again, the black shirted runners tore through the Aberavon defence to score yet another try. Time and time again the red and black hooped jerseys trooped back like extras from *Schindler's List* to mope sullenly behind the rugby post as the conversion sailed over their heads.

Even the stoic home crowd, numbed by years of decline in their teams fortune, contemplated this record score with sullen, aching silence.

"They are pathetic—I've seen more commitment at a whist drive. Neath are bound to score a ton" moaned Archie.

Archie, although a lifelong Aberavon supporter swore this was the last time he'd watch Aberavon if they lost again. He'd made the same oath at least three times this season, and in innumerable other occasions in the past 10 years, but stubbornness and loyalty, born of a childhood supporting a talented, virtually unbeatable Aberavon side had combined to compel him to keep watching a team, and a club that seemed destined for oblivion.

"They are utterly, totally, definitively crap," shouted Archie, with uncharacteristic venom. I don't know why I waste my time and money going to watch them. The front row are like Tolkien dwarves, the back row have about as much collective pace as sedated limpets, whilst the scrum half is a malnutritioned child. If he was any younger he'd be in a sperm bank. How can someone like him take on 17 stone forwards? No wonder we're seventy six points down. Get home to your Gameboy Nintendo and think of another way to collect autographs!"

Archie never had much sympathy for Aberavon teams, and Thrust wondered why he bothered coming to watch them. He knew that it was really an excuse to vent his frustrations on something, anything, for Archie loved to moan—about his job in Port Talbot, the pubs in Port Talbot, the houses in Port Talbot and the women in Port Talbot. He even moaned about the name 'Port Talbot'. In short, he loved moaning about Port Talbot and anything to do with it, and as Aberavon were the rugby team of Port Talbot, it was only natural and logical that he should moan about them. He'd probably even moan about them if they ever won, though to be fair there hadn't been much opportunity to test that theory in recent years.

"No, we're only lulling them into a false sense of security" chirped Vic, "they're tired out now, and we'll blitz them with fifteen magical tries to take the game and get bonus points." Vic was (in Vic's view) a perceptive and staunch Aberavon supporter, his never say die attitude a rock in difficult times. To the rest of the boys he was trapped in the past, and probably clinically insane, or at least inhabiting a twilight word divorced from reality. In any argument or discussion, he generally adopted positions far removed from any likelihood of success, and clung to it tenaciously. He'd have predicted a win for the Germans at Stalingrad and a loss for Tyson against Bruno.

"Vic, you are pissing into the hurricane of reality. There are only 20 minutes to go, and we've been in the opponents' half once and that was when they were warming up. It's physically impossible to score enough tries to win the game," countered Thrust.

"Defeatist rubbish—they'll crack any minute—look we've won the ball. The tide has turned" said Vic, punching the air in defiance.

Indeed, Aberavon had won a ball, and threw it along the backs in a valiant surge up field. However the passing was laboured and slow, and not surprisingly the Neath centre intercepted and raced in behind the posts.

"Hah—see they are utterly totally useless—they ought to commit mass hari kiri and put us and them out of their misery. Come on, let's go for a pint, though as we all know, all the beer's like piss here anyway." Archie pulled up his collar and started to jump up and down.

"I'm not going yet—Neath are going to get over 100 and I want to see it" chirped Stan, the only Neath supporter amongst them.

"I had to put up with you lot winning in the 70s, so this is well worth waiting for—though to be fair we were never this bad, and anyway, I'm enjoying every minute."

"No look. Aberavon have broken through—they're going to score" shouted Thrust. True enough, the Aberavon centre had got through on his own and had scored. It was a minor miracle, though everyone knew he was a former Neath player and in any event was by far and away the best player in the Aberavon side. It was however a comforting throwback to the old days. A feeble cheer rippled around the ground.

"Only 78 points to go then boys," cracked Stan. "The fight is back on—trouble is, you've now got only 12 minutes left."

The only hope was for Vic single-handedly to invade the pitch, and for him to fart in the Neath scrum. This would kill the entire pack, and would probably be the first murder to be committed on a rugby pitch and the game would have to be abandoned."

There was more than a grain of truth in the last statement as it was well known that Vic's wind was a lethal weapon which should've been outlawed along with other forms of mustard gas.

Thrust could personally testify its power and clearly remembered one night in a night club in Bridgend when Vic had single-handedly cleared the club with one fart with scenes at the exit which must have been very similar to those on the last lifeboat to leave the *Titanic*. The knowledge that Vic had consumed 7 pints of Bass and a Chicken Vindaloo the night before also summoned up a vision of a public health disaster in the stand as he imagined Vic's rectal emissions floating across the pitch and causing a human stampede that would destroy the rickety stand leaving the unlucky survivors mentally and physically scarred by Vic's gaseous outpourings.

Thrust was brought back to reality by yet another Neath try.

The Aberavon revival had certainly been rapidly stopped in it's tracks. The players trooped back yet again, this time with the expression of veal calves on their way to export— panting, uncomprehending victims of fate. Thrust thought there must be better ways of spending a night than this. A hideous flashback of his night at Rose's disabused him of that notion.

"Yeah, but this is all a fool's paradise for Neath, there's no great credit in beating Aberavon by 100 points. It'd be a different story against Queensland or the Transvaal or one of the top English sides. It's like saying you're the most talented actor in *Neighbours*—it means sod all," said Stan.

Turpin saw Aberavon give the ball away at the kick off, and the Neath outside half lofted a huge up-and-under. The Aberavon full back peered up into the gloom vainly searching for the ball, hands stretching up like a revivalist preacher. His face displayed fear, anguish, and a fleeting knowledge of the afterlife as the ball came down from the gloom. He seemed to make the sign of the cross, as he possibly contemplated the hereafter. He could certainly hear the Neath team bearing down on him, intent on mayhem, mutilation and possibly murder. He seemed briefly to turn white, then green, then purple before bending double and retching violently. The ball crashed into his bowed head, knocking him flat into a pool of his own vomit, as the Neath forwards ran over him, grabbed the ball and once again crashed over for a try.

The Aberavon fullback was carried off hidden by a vomit and blood stained blanket. Turpin was sure he heard him mumbling the Lords Prayer.

The game ended in a few half-hearted cheers, and players and fans trooped away. The boys gathered in the bar and chatted generally about the game, and the events in Brynglyn Rugby Club the week before.

"Big piece on *Wales Today*, with a few features in the National News—the footage of Gwilym and those strippers will be worth millions in years to come," said Vic.

"Poor man's mind must have been in turmoil. One minute peacefully bingo calling, the next in the middle of strippers with your first hard on in half a century, the next in a ward full of rampant homosexuals. It'd been better if he'd been shot at Pegasus bridge—it would have saved him so much in pain and torment" observed Thrust.

"Anyway, the club is closed for repair—most of them have had to drink down here now. To be fair, it was a cracking strip show, nice looking girls and to be honest, what a funny sight— the look on Gwilym's face when that bayonet went up his arse—a picture," said Stan, starting to laugh.

"Let's get back to reality. Aberavon are crap, the town's a dump, the women are horrible and the Brynglyn Rugby Club's closed" said Archie, "What a life, what a place."

"Eh remember Turpin reckons it's all Richard Burton's fault. If he had been buried in Wales everything would be all right. The sun would shine every day, we'd be fighting women off with big sticks, and Aberavon would win every game for a decade. He's so convinced that he's going to Switzerland to bring him back aren't you Thrustie?" said Vic.

"Ssshhh—you don't want any of these Neath types getting there first do you," said Stan, continuing to laugh. "What's more, he was from Neath anyway."

"Fuck off—he was born in Pontryhdyfen—which is in Port Talbot. Anyway he was brought up in Taibach—you can't be more Port Talbot than that" asserted Thrust. "Are you coming on this trip then Archie?"

"Yeah, thinking of. I fancy a booze cruise, and it's only a bit more effort. The other boys said they were up for it" said Archie. "Do you think we can do it?"

"I think it can be done and it will work. This'll be the last time Neath beat Aberavon—when we repatriate him the good times will come back to Aberavon, Port Talbot, Wales, everywhere....." said Thrust.

"Except Neath" said Vic, trying to wind Thrust up.

"Mmmm—the jury's still out on that one" said Thrust.

"Just like King Arther eh? We bring back The Holy Grail, and spring will return to the land" said Archie, who always had a vivid imagination and, despite his mundane job in the council, was surprisingly well read.

"Yeah, it sounds interesting to me—go through your plan again Turpin" said Vic.

Thrust outlined the plan he'd already divulged to the boys. He'd refined it in a few ways—he'd discovered that there was a National holiday on the weekend they had in mind, and that the locals would probably all be out celebrating. It was only a few weeks off everything would fall into place. In any event, Thrust said he'd go on his own if he had to—he felt things were as bad as they could be, and certainly Wales' whitewash in the Rugby Internationals had seen them plumb new depths.

A particularly scathing article in one of the Sunday broadsheets about Wales and the Welsh by a toffee nosed English style guru lampooning everything about the county and its inhabitants, had driven him over the edge, and he was determined to do something once and for all to put things right.

"So, yet again, are you coming along Archie?," said Thrust.

Archie was silent for a while then said "I'll come along. I need a break and it seems to be an interesting plan. Whether it'll work is another story, but let's give it a go. If it fails we can get a few laughs in the pub—if it works we can sell our story and live happily ever after."

Thrust was pleased, but slightly disturbed to discover that Archie was coming along. Whilst he would appreciate any help he could get, Archie was seriously weird and was known for quirky behaviour. He certainly dabbled in drugs, and his sex life was rumoured to be bizarre. Never mind, he thought, Archie was certainly entertaining.

"What about you Vic?" said Turpin.

"Yeah, I'll come with you as well" said Vic. "I haven't got anything planned in the next few weeks. I've recently had a bit of a win on the premium bonds, and a 'booze cruise' is right up my street—count me in."

"Over to you Stan" said Thrust turning to the last member of the group.

"Well, if you lot are going, and I think it is the most stupid plan I've ever heard, then I suppose I'll have to come as well. I couldn't stand listening to you lot talk about it when you get back, and anyway, the sight of you three trying to dig up a body in a Swiss graveyard is something I just won't forgive myself for missing. I'll take a camcorder and sell it to *Beadle's About*" said Stan. "Just have to square it with the other half, but that shouldn't be a problem."

"Right. That's it. We're all in for this trip. I'll need a few bob up front for the van and the ferry tickets. Let me sort out the details and we'll be on our way in 2 weeks time. Trust me boys, it'll be a 'great trip', you'll have the time of your lives and what's more, you'll be putting history right. What more can you ask?" said Thrust.

"That you shut up and get the next round in" said Stan as he downed his pint.

"We need to get some practice in for the big trip" he added.

"I'll drink to that" said Vic.

"A toast—let's bring him home" said Archie. The boys clinked their glasses solemnly.

"Aye. Let's bring him home" said Thrust outwardly pleased but inside beginning to worry that he'd started something that should've really been kept as a flight of fantasy.

It could only end in humiliation—or worse he thought as he pushed his way slowly to the bar. There wouldn't be a normal bloke in that mini van—and what they were thinking of doing was certainly not normal—and probably criminal. He stood, thought a while, strangely calm in the middle of the bustling rugby club, and then inwardly resolved that whatever it was he had to do, he would do it.

CHAPTER TEN

'The Busload of Nurses'

Thrust pulled outside Vic's house in the camper van that he'd hired from Tonto's the local van hire firm. The van had more than enough room for the four of them, their luggage, and importantly the additional item that they hoped to bring back with them. There was also a roof rack if they found anything else interesting along the way.

Stan was already in the van, and Thrust blew the horn to get Vic and Archie to get a move on.

As soon as Vic and Archie came out of the house Thrust recognised that they'd been drinking.

"Ten in the morning and they're already on the pop," said Thrust. "Senseless, they'll be a liability not a help on this trip—we'll have more comfort breaks than an incontinent wine taster's outing and we'll probably miss the ferry."

Vic and Archie staggered to the van and hauled their luggage after them. There was in fact very little of it—they were obviously travelling light. Vic had brought his usual bizarre selection of CDs including a 'Best of Gregorian Chants' and 'Mongolian Throat Singing Unplugged', in order to enliven the trip, whilst Archie's case just seemed to be packed with pornographic magazines.

"You two drunk again" said Thrust. "Can't you wait until France?"

"Not drunk—just happy—we need something to enliven the trip. Anyway, it's a sort of glorified wake isn't it? Therefore we are merely entering into the spirit of things. No pun intended" said Vic, suppressing a snigger.

"Spirit—yes—we're in the spirit—and that's the main reason for this trip—to get some booze, and if it is to pick up Richard Burton's body, then he'd be the last person to object to someone having a drink. So, get your foot down and let's get moving. We don't want to miss the fucking ferry do we" said Archie.

The van pulled away from Vic's house and drove out along the grimy washed out streets of the town, past single mother's pushing prams and the gangs of gangly youths lounging around the street corners.

There seemed to be an air of hopelessness and resignation shrouding the town—an air of a place that had had it's day and that was now very much a down at heel backwater.

What did the future hold for those kids? thought Thrust, as they drove towards the motorway. Drink, drugs, sex, unwanted children (a terrible flashback of Rose McGrath's unholy brood flashed through his mind) who would grow up not knowing their fathers, not knowing who they really were, not knowing anything about where they were from, the history, the sense of belonging that he felt so strongly— today saw a generation, or now probably generations that, perhaps for the first time in history had no sense of real identity or shared tradition, other than a can of Strongbow, or a tracksuit or a Macdonalds or a flavoured condom.

If you don't know where you've come from, you can't know where you are going he thought, and these people certainly had no idea of their history. If you asked them about Burton, the sharper ones might identify him with a clothes shop. As for Dic Penderyn or Owain Glyndwr you might as well ask a spaniel to recite Shakespeare. The sad fact dawned on him that they didn't care, and they didn't care because no-one else cared. The 'me' generation had turned it's back on even itself and left a once proud culture fragmented and directionless, eventually doomed to turn itself into a pale watered down version of a New York or Chicago suburb. These kids had more regard for rap than male voice choirs, and no-one was doing a thing about it. Perhaps that was the way it always was—cultural Darwinsim would root out the weaker culture and the stronger culture would prevail. Perhaps we should all support the Pittsburgh Steelers, he thought.

Well, not if he had anything to do with it. He'd bring back Burton, and the change would take place. The tide would turn, and this place, this county, indeed all of Wales would rediscover itself and reclaim it's cultural identity. He'd be on TV, and making speeches in Parliament and ...

"Oi, Turpin. Wakey wakey. You've missed the turning for the motorway. You're rewriting history again, or telling Owen-Jones what you think of him, or confessing your night of passion with the 'Last Chance' to a tame priest. You're anywhere but here. Make sure we get on the motorway at the next turning" said Stan.

"Fair enough" said Thrust sheepishly.

"Just thinking about a few things were you. Well—enough thinking and more driving. Want a can of 'bow?" said Vic, draining the can in his hand.

"No. I'll try and keep a clear head" said Thrust, realising that he'd let his mind wander. He had a feeling this was going to be a lively trip—Vic was knocking them back with a vengeance.

The van snaked through a few miles of more deadbeat street and then rose up the feeder road onto the motorway, and was soon speeding out of Port Talbot, with the massive steelworks belching steam on one side and the barren gnarled mountain on the other. Only three and a bit hours to go before we get to the ferry thought Thrust. Never mind, at least the scenery got better. There was certainly no way it would get any worse.

They drove on for a while before Vic suddenly came to life.

"Bite the bum off a buggered bison. Oh my god boys, look at this. Our bloody dreams have come true, our prayers have been answered. Thank you God, thank you, thank you, thank you" Vic was grinning and punching the air, in between sips of Strongbow.

"What the fuck are you on about. I know you've had a few, but Strongbow doesn't normally bring on hallucinations until much much later" said Stan.

"Look, look behind us—it's going to overtake any minute. It's like living in a dream" said Vic. "If I wasn't in a mini van, I'd be having a wank!"

Thrust looked in the mirror and saw a large bus behind them signalling to overtake. It had some words painted on the front windscreen, but he couldn't make them out as the van was shaking too much.

Vic and Archie started to laugh out loud, and then began to cheer and jump about like Barbary apes on a rollercoaster.

As the bus began to pull past, Thrust turned and saw that it was filled with young women, heavily made up and provocatively dressed.

Most of them seemed to be up against the nearside windows, and were mouthing what seemed to him to be indecent suggestions. One opened her top and pressed her not insubstantial cleavage against the window.

One of the other women was drawing a huge red penis in red lipstick on the windows whilst licking her lips, whilst another two sat face to face with their tongues fencing like battling samurai in a Kurasawa film.

Thrust was beginning to lose control of the mini van and had to fight hard to prevent it overturning when one of the girls pulled up her skirt and bent down against a window revealing a 'g' string thong thinner than a cats whisker splitting two of the most gorgeous arse cheeks he had ever set eyes on. By now the van was careering wildly as all on board became overcome with excitement and delight. The rest of the boys were downing cans of Strongbow at will and smashing the empty cans into their own heads.

A final shriek of frenzied triumph burst forth all around the mini van as the bus finally pulled in front of them to reveal a legend emblazoned on the back window.

Turpin could not believe his eyes, and had to re-read the words three times before it sunk in.

"Singleton Hospital Nurses' Netball Team—Annual Tour—Switzerland." Underneath written in lipstick were the words, "There's nothing worse than a naughty nurse!"

"Oh my giddy aunt. I can't believe it" said Thrust. "If I had a fiver for every stinking pub I've gone to after being told there was a busload of nurses there, only to find they were full of overweight, asthmatic blokes, darts players, rugby teams, male voice choirs, eunuchs' conventions, rent-a-man auditions, the lot—every bloody living thing except nurses, I'd be a cowin millionaire."

"Oh happy days are here again—we've actually seen a bus load of nurses, and joy oh joy, they're not male nurses, not geriatric nurses, not faces like bulldogs, licking piss off stinking stingy nettles nurses, but rampant, gorgeous, game for anything, nympho bed bath administering bollock biting sex crazed nurses, and what's more, thank you God, they're heading to the same part of the world as us. It's a bloody miracle" said Thrust. "You see boys—it's the Burton effect— it's already happening."

"Please God let them be going to same part of Switzerland as us—and please, please make it the same ferry" said Vic.

If they are, I'll bite my own balls off and spit them into a mincing blender" said Archie. "I'm so fucking happy."

"Well. Bugger a Byzantine barber! We spend most of our adult lives looking for a bus load of beautiful horny, loose moral women, and we find them on this glorified tomb robbing trip. Fucking irony or what" said Stan, "but if it's got anything to do with Richard Burton, I'll carry him back myself."

"Quick Turpin, foot down. They're pulling away. We can't let them get away" said Vic, his face pressed against the window.

"I'm trying my best, but if my foot goes any further it'll go through the floor" said Thrust.

"Bastard van" shouted Vic who attempted to pelt the dashboard with 'bow cans, whilst holding his kit bag up with his teeth. His face had by now turned crimson.

"Look, we can't go any faster. What will be will be, but if they're going to Switzerland, the quickest route is the one we're taking. Anyway, if they're like this now, and we haven't left Glamorgan, imagine what they'll be like by the time we get to Portsmouth. Loads of drink, and not a man near them for three or four hours. We will be the cocks of the walk. Take our pick and eyes down for a bumpy ride across the channel. We'll have to fight them off with a shitty stick" said Thrust.

"I'll never stand the wait" said Stan as the bus full of nurses began to pull away further. Thrust could see cars swerving and skidding either side of the bus as male drivers lost concentration, co-ordination and/or their entire mental faculties at the sight of the nurses. He also noticed that a significant number of cars all containing female passengers also suddenly seemed to spin out of control as the women either hit the distracted drivers or fought to gain control of the careering vehicles.

Thrust imagined that in any event pretty soon the motorway would be clogged by a phalanx of articulated lorries who would form a guard around the bus, as other desperate truckers fought to smash their way into the protection zone, that would develop around the bus. It would be like a travelling war zone on wheels, a Welsh wacky races, but with added spice.

The bus soon disappeared over the horizon, and Thrust saw that Archie and Vic had collapsed in an alcohol soaked heap in the back of the van (with Vic lying with his kit bag still in his teeth, splayed over his head) whilst Stan stared straight ahead like a man possessed.

"We've got to get after those nurses—we deserve it—if we can track 'em down I'll help you exhume Burton with my bare hands. It'll show his magic is working. I've dreamt of a busload of nurses for years, nothing's going to stop me now" said Stan. "When we catch up with them they'll be back in intensive care—for sexual exhaustion."

Thrust was disturbed by the words and the look on Stan's face, but he too felt a need to close in on the nurses as soon as possible. It would be the perfect start to a journey that would transform everyone's lives. It had to be a sign he thought. A sign that the trip would be worthwhile.

A more obvious sign of the bus passing however, was the alarming number of crashed cars littering the hard shoulder either side of the road. Most seemed to be accompanied by dazed men weeping or shaking uncontrollably some oblivious to the blows being rained on them by their female companions.

Most poignant was a van half way up the grass verge with 'Porthcawl Octogenarian Bowls Club' written on with white suited bodies lying around it—arms and legs twitching upwards like bleached dead ants, presumably yet another, hopefully not fatal victim of the bus load of nurses.

If Turpin was a man on a mission before the sighting of the bus, he certainly was now and what's more, so were his friends. The van shuddered and heaved as they willed it to follow the nurses, their minds and bodies eagerly contemplating what they hoped would be an eventful voyage.

Stan was in a seemingly catatonic state and continued to stare ahead like a demented gargoyle. The veins on the side of his head throbbing, as his nostrils flared, and his mouth moved around like oscillating hula hoop.

Thrust knew better than to disturb him, as even though Stan had a steady girlfriend, it was not the happiest of relationships and Stan would often 'play away' if the opportunity presented itself. It was probably due to his desire to get away from his girlfriend that Stan had agreed to come on the trip. Whatever his reason, he certainly seemed to have been shaken up by the sight of the nurses.

Not long after they went past Newport, Vic and Archie started to come around.

"What happened to you two then?" said Thrust.

"Passed out with the excitement. I assume that all my blood went from my head to my dick, and It all just went black. I can't believe what I saw. All our prayers have been answered" said Archie.

"Well, yes, if they are going to the same ferry port as us" said Vic.

"Bound to. We've got to be positive" said Stan.

"Ok. Even if they are. Are we guaranteed to do anything with them?" said Thrust.

"They might not want to get off with four clapped out sad gits from Port Talbot who are intent on grave robbing. What's your chat up line going to be? Why don't you come back to my camper van to look at my recently acquired cadaver?" said Stan.

"Don't they see enough of them anyway?" said Vic, revealing that he knew more about nurses than seemed obvious.

"They won't want to bother with the likes of us anyway — they get enough Welsh blokes in Swansea" said Vic.

"What are they going on tour for? What are they, Nurses! Right! — You can bet they'll be after blokes, any ones will do, even us!" said Archie.

114

"Maybe, but there's bound to be other men on the ferry, not unless the world goes mad, and I bet those nurses will prefer anyone, even Englishmen, to our little gang. Just you watch" said Stan.

"Never. They'd much prefer a Welshman—finest men in the world. It would be like having prime fillet in the fridge and going out for a kebab. They'll know which way their bread is buttered when we get amongst them. A few beers, a few jokes, a sing song and then Bobby Shafto—oh yes, they'll appreciate a real man, not some lah di dah public schoolboy with a dick like a peeled prawn in a snowstorm who'd been buggered senseless as part of his so called education at some poofs paradise like Eton or somewhere, or alternatively some shaven headed loud mouthed lard arsed cockney football hooligan with terminal syphilis and breath like a hottentots enema. They'll want real men—and that's what we are. Real Welsh men" said Stan.

"Yeah, he's right. Some of the finest men in the world have been Welsh—not only that, but big shaggers all of them—Lloyd George, Tom Jones, Richard Burton—we're in good company, and got a lot to live up to as a nation" said Thrust, with a patriotic flourish.

"Yeah, and that includes David Bowie, Prince, Bruce Springsteen" said Vic, nodding vigorously.

"'Hold on! Bowie, Prince, Springsteen—they're not Welsh. What are you on about" said Thrust, with a puzzled look.

"It's gospel. They are all Welsh. In fact, they're all from Maesteg, though if you want to be picky, Prince is actually from Nantyfyllon, but in effect they're all from Maesteg. A bloke told me that in the Old House pub in Llangynwyd. I thought everyone knew."

"Not that I am aware of. I must have led a sheltered life" said Vic, taking a fresh swig of 'bow.

"Leave it out will you. Have you ever heard any one of them speak?" said Thrust.

Vic just stared out of the window.

"Well I have, and not one of them has got a Welsh accent, and they certainly don't sing about Wales, let alone bloody Maesteg."

"Yeah. Springsteen sings Born in the USA, not Born in Bangor you dick" said Stan.

"Well, I'm sure Meatloaf mentions Maesteg in 'Bat out of Hell'" said Archie, "he may have a point."

Vic and Archie then chorused, "Nothing's gonna stop me now, I'm gonna make 'Maesteg'," from the song in question.

"I don't bloody think so, but even if he does, how does that prove that Bowie, Springsteen and Prince are Welsh?"

Fair point, but Kylie Minogue's mother is definitely from Maesteg" said Archie.

"And Bowie's gran!" said Vic

"Just shut up—this is the most stupid converstaion I've ever had. None of those stars come from Wales, not even Maesteg. In fact no-one famous comes from Maesteg," said Turpin.

"What about Gwyn Evans" said Stan, referring to the former Welsh Rugby fullback.

"Get a life" said Thrust, "he was famous in Wales for 3 minutes in 1979, hardly a superstar!"

"Well, this man, the one in the pub in Llangywyd, he told me that they all left Maesteg at an early age, and that's why they don't have Welsh accents" said Vic.

"Leave it out. He must have seen you coming a mile off. He did if for a laugh, to tell his mates—bloody Prince is from Nantyfyllon my arse. If he was, he'd have been strangled by the time he was 5. Can you imagine him walking into the Collier's Arms and asking for a Chateaux Lafite' 54 and a line of Coke? He'd be dead before you could say 'Kiss'" said Thrust. He really worried about Vic.

"Well. It sounded plausible to me, and, it helped me get a shag" said Vic.

"How the fuck did that happen?" said Stan with a puzzled expression.

"Well. I met a girl in Bryns, who told me she was a big Prince fan. I said that I had a big secret to tell her, and after a few drinks, I told her the secret which was that Prince was born in Maesteg, and that I know where. She went crazy over me, and asked that I'd drive her to see Prince's house in Nantyfyllon. We got in my car, even though I was pissed and drove to Maesteg. Amazing really, 'cos when we got there, there really was a Princes Street in Nanyfyllon, and someone had painted their house bright purple. She was really gobsmacked. I told her we couldn't go in as the National Trust closed it after 5. She was so impressed, as a lifelong Prince fan, that she repaid me in the appropriate manner in the lay-by near Maesteg Golf Club—great shag" said Vic taking another sip of bow. I won't tell you what she did when I said I'd sung on 'Sign o' the Times'."

"What a load of rubbish. Taking advantage of a poor deluded girl. You should be ashamed of yourself," said Turpin.

"So, if he wasn't Welsh, who cares? At least I had a good shag out of it," said Vic.

"Did you see Elvis when you were there?" asked Stan.

"Fuck off, he's living in Brecon isn't he?" said Archie laughing.

"She must be brain dead to believe that story" said Stan.

"You don't shag a brain do you. Anyway, we both enjoyed it, and at least she was better than the Last Chance" said Vic laughing into his can of 'bow.

"That man from the Old House—very clever, a mine of information" said Vic. "He told me, that in effect, the Second World War started in Pontypool. Gospel. He saw it with his own eyes."

"This I've got to hear. How did World War Two start in Pontypool Vic?" said Stan.

"Well, the story went like this. A young German was working in the mines in the 1900s—name of Schiklegruber—playing for Pooler in rugby on the weekend. Not very skilful, but very aggressive, a bit of a born leader. Very confrontational. He was their hooker like, and in the local derby against Newport—who should be playing but a squat Russian from the docks, played prop like, named Djugashivilli or something like that. Big punch up, the two fought like dogs. Later on, club officials discovered that Schiklegruber's real name was Hitler, and that the Russian later changed his name to Stalin. The rest, as you know is history. If it wasn't for that fixture, no Dunkirk, no Stalingrad, no H bomb—nothing."

"They've got a lot to answer for in Pontypool!" said Stan.

117

"And Newport" said Archie.

"What a load of bollocks. It's frightening to think what you lot would be like if you took drugs. I've never heard such a cock'n'bull story in my life. Stop talking, and think about those nurses" said Thrust, as the van ploughed doggedly down the motorway.

"Yeah well there's more—proof if you need it—apparently the German had a huge Zapata like moustache, very similar to the one the Russian had, and before the kick-off, he'd been preening and prancing around, twirling the end of the 'tache' and laughing at the Newport players, and this really upset the Russian" said Vic.

"Well, a while into the game, like I said, there was this huge punch up, both front rows going at it like windmills, and the Russian bloke grabs the German by the moustache and lifts him up off his feet."

"Get away" said Stan, feigning disbelief.

"Held him up there for a couple of minutes then, Snap! Pulls both ends of the moustache clean off! The German, Hitler, went mad, the German then got sent off by a Dr Isaacs! After the game, the German runs into the other changing rooms—threatens the Russian with everything. Ranting and raving. The Russian just grinned and smoked his pipe, and another huge fight erupted. The German was eventually carried off swearing that he'd get even with the Russian one day.

"The old bloke in the pub said the German looked really stupid with both ends of his moustache pulled out, just like Charlie fucking Chaplin. And—later on as I said, the club officials checked the team sheets, so there," said Vic.

"Amazing, but true" said Archie.

"Exactly. Hitler and Stalin. The start of it all. Hitler's moustache, his hatred of the Jews, the Russians, Stalin, the whole shebang!"

"All over a poxy game of rugby," said Stan.

"Yeah, in Pontypool" said Vic "of all places."

"Where else?" said Archie.

"Yeah, leave it now, we're nearly at the bridge," said Turpin.

As the bus pulled up the bridge over the river Severn

crossing, a spontanious burst of 'Mae hen wlad fy nhadau' broke out, as the by now happy band left Wales behind following their much fantasised about quarry over the border into England.

The journey was now really underway.

CHAPTER ELEVEN

'A Load of Claptrap'

They piled into the four berth cabin, exhausted after the journey, and by the seemingly endless queue to get onto the cross channel Ferry. Their spirits had soared when they saw that the nurses bus was ahead of them in the line of vehicles boarding the ferry, but their ardour had then been dampened when they saw considerable number of other buses bearing various markings of male rugby or football tours also in the queue. It suddenly dawned on them that if they were going to realise their dream of getting into bunks with the nurses they would have to fight for it.

"I'm in the top bunk" shouted Stan as he threw his bag onto one of the higher level bunk beds. "I wouldn't want to be down there with your stinking farts all night."

"You've got that one wrong Stan—hot air rises, it'll smell more up there" said Vic laughing.

"I don't know why you're arguing" said Thrust, "there's hardly any room in here, and in any event it's not as if either of you are perambulating deodorant sticks anyway. I'd just as well be down here as when we get back pissed tonight, when I can just fall into bed."

"If we get back pissed? If you get back pissed. I'm aiming to be staying with one of those nurses, so you lot can do what you like. Won't bother me" said Archie with a self satisfied grin.

"I'll believe that when I see it. You've got about as much pulling power as an asthmatic butterfly," said Stan wriggling into the bunk bed.

"Anyway—as I was saying before you interrupted. I'll be happy down here. First choice for the bunks isn't really the choice you want to fight over. It's first crap in the bogs!" said Thrust.

With that Thrust leapt into the cubicle and locked the door. Possession is nine-tenths of the law, he thought, as he settled down for what Stan referred to as an Eartha Kitt. He could hear the others arguing outside as to who would be next in the toilet. It sounded as though they were arguing over a place on the last lifeboat of the Titanic. They eventually settled the order in which they would go into the toilet by listing as many rugby players as they could think of named after animals. He listened intently as frenzied debate ensued with a wide variety of names being put forward and discussed.

Finally the argument was settled, Stan came first, Archie second and Vic last.

Thrust could hear Vic banging his head against the bunk in despair.

"If I go in there last, I'll probably die of asphyxiation or airborne ebola virus. It's not fucking fair. Bloody rugby players named after animals—what crap. Jamie bloody Salmon!! Mike fucking Catt. Why couldn't we have decided on something normal like, I don't know … like famous Belgians or 70s porn stars. I never had a chance," said Vic ruefully.

Turpin had finished his business in the toilet, and decided to vacate the throne.

"Hard luck Vic" said Thrust as he stepped out of the toilet gingerly. Stan immediately bustled in. An eruption of muffled screams bubbled up from within the toilet as Stan settled down.

"It smells like Baboons afterbirth in here, you must have been saving that from the early 80s. My eyes are watering so much I think I'm going blind" yelled Stan between gulps from within the toilet.

"Ah shut up and get on with it" said Thrust. "With all your sobs and gasps, you sound like you are making an Oscar winning acceptance speech, not having a dump."

"Right, where are we going first" said Archie as Thrust began to change.

"Head for the bar, but do a swift recce for the nurses. If

they're on a different deck, we move on asap. Liven up with a swift burst of claptrap to get us in the mood, then a bit of smooth talking followed by a bit of bump 'n' grind on the dance floor, then pick your spot girls—a bunk, the van, a lifeboat, the prow, anywhere. I'm bustin for a shag and tonight's the night" said Thrust, rubbing his hands.

The hissing of deodorant and the sound of stamping on the floor of the toilet cubicle indicted that Stan was setting in for a long haul.

"If it was bad in there, it's getting worse by the minute" said Archie.

Poor Archie, thought Thrust, poor poor Vic. Pathetic really. They hadn't the sense to go to the outside toilet, though to be fair they also needed to shave and all that. Still, not his problem now. As Confuscious may have said 'He who dumps first laughs the longest' or something like that, he recalled, in an impromptu ad lib to himself.

After a while, Stan came out coughing and spluttering, eyes squinted and red like a firefighter. His experiences had robbed him of the power of speech. Archie pushed past with a determined grimace on his face.

"Aiyeeeee" there came a blood curdling yell as if Archie had been bayoneted by a Japanese infantryman. A series of screams, yelps and moans indicated that the atmosphere in the toilet was moving from foul to putrid.

"Uh, Ah ooch, bluh, bluh—I'm going to be sick" shouted Archie from within the toilet.

"You're in the right place then, get on with it" said Thrust with another helping of smug self satisfaction.

The sound of a vigorous chunder indicated that the smell in the toilet had indeed caused Archie to be sick.

"Ach, you animals. You'll pay for this. The paint's coming off the walls in here, and the toilet paper is levitating. I can't stick it any longer" yelled Archie between retches.

"Well if you come out now, you'll eventually have to go after Vic" said Stan recovering his vocal powers, "and that is really a fate worse than death. Think about it. Hang on until you've finished. You know it makes sense."

A pregnant silence ensued, and they briefly thought that

Archie had taken Stan's advice literally, and had committed suicide. Thankfully, the tell tale noise of grunting and plopping revealed to them that Archie had weighed up the alternatives and decided to choose (probably) the lesser of two evils.

A sound like cement and chippings being thrown into a large plastic bin caused them all to wince. It would be bad in there—very bad. It would be hard on Vic, thought Thrust, but that would teach him for not knowing enough about rugby. Anyway, it would be a form of character building he concluded.

Vic had started to pour aftershave onto his shirt and some spare pairs of socks, and proceeded to wrap them around his head like a Taureg warrior. He then sprayed deodorant onto his pillow and doused it in some more aftershave.

"It's the only hope I've got" he said in a muffled voice. "I'm going inside now, and I may be some time" he said in a bizarre pastiche of Captain Scott's companion Titus Oates, to whom he now bore a striking similarity.

Archie staggered out, hands held in front of him like a mustard gas victim. His eyes were clenched tight and were streaming tears.

"Arghh, that was terrible. I'll crap out of the porthole rather than do that again. It was a living hell" said Archie, between gulps of air.

Vic, with cloth trailing behind his head, burst into the toilet yelling a muffled 'Geronimo'. He had a passing similarity to Red Adair leaping into a burning building. Three pairs of hands reached after him and closed the door, a propped a bunk ladder against it.

"Thank God we were in time" said Stan. "If any of that got out it'd be curtains for the lot of us."

"And the rest of the ship" added Thrust.

The sound of muffled yelps and whines, followed by desperate clawing at the door signified that Vic's protective garmets were of little use. They held the door tight to stop any chance of escape.

"Poor sod. He didn't deserve this" said Stan in a rare display of compassion.

"Could have been any one of us boys, he knew the rules"

said Thrust, banishing pity from his heart.

"Dog eat dog—survival of the fittest, someone has to be last. Knowing how he smells, it's probably fitting that he went last. He's probably best equipped to deal with it" said Archie.

A sound as if Vic were trying to run around the walls and / or the ceiling was followed by more muffled sobs and gasps. This was followed by dreadful noises resembling a symposium of water jets, explosions and gurgles all of which seemed to indicate that Vic had accepted the inevitable and was using the toilet for its designated purpose.

"When he gets out, we'll give him some time to change, then we hit the bar. Any aliases for tonight boys?" said Stan.

They often made a point of inventing bizarre occupations, generally coupled with outlandish names to try to bamboozle any women they met on a night out.

"Yes, I'm going to be a flint knapper called Rex Ormskirk. I'll say I've just won the lottery and I'm trying to keep it low key by travelling like a student" said Archie with a smirk.

"I think I'll be Brinley Craphammer, and I'll be a feng shui expert who advises local authorities on the layout of their offices to ensure good decision making" said Thrust.

"Some good lines boys, but you'll never fool the nurses. They've heard it all before. Be worth a try though" said Stan.

"Well I'm going to be Conrad Humpage, a former personal injury lawyer and a fine art dealer from Penlan," said Stan with a defiant jut of his chin.

That's one of the toughest areas in Swansea" said Vic. "You know you won't see any fine art dealers living there in a month of Sundays, what a crap alias."

"I know, and they'll know. And they'll know I know they'll know. That'll give them a fright. Let's see if that gets them thinking" said Stan, jutting his chin out further.

The other two looked at each other. Sometimes Stan was just too mad. They decided to humour him.

"Yeah ok, anything's better than telling them what you really do—anyway it will be entertaining to see how long it takes them to guess that your lying—and it also enables you to gauge how bright they are," said Archie.

"I once had a girl believe that I was an official curry taster for the council" said Thrust. "I said I could tell a Vindaloo from a Madras from twenty paces. Good story—inventive like."

"Yeah, I remember when she discovered the truth. Poured a bloody curry over your head, didn't she?" said Stan.

"Yeah, didn't take it well. No sense of humour really. Good idea though" said Thrust. "Nice way to earn a living—eating curry all day—tidy!"

An urgent banging from the door brought them suddenly back to Vic's predicament. They had forgotten he was still in there.

"We'd better let him out. We don't want a death on our hands" said Archie.

"Yeah, trying to smuggle two corpses back into the country would be a bit of a tall order" said Stan.

"Right. I'll open the door, pull him out. Then we need to slam it shut. A seconds delay could be fatal," said Thrust.

"I'll light some paper and throw it in. It'll burn up the methane and neutralise the smell" said Archie fully utilizing his GCSE in Chemistry.

"No way. It could cause an explosion or set the ship on fire. Look, just leave it and God willing the smell should be gone by the time we return" said Stan.

"Ok enough debate. I'm ready to let him out" said Thrust. "Let's just do it."

They pulled the bunk ladder away and leapt back.

The door opened and Vic came stumbling out like a marathon winner. He collapsed onto the bunk, with the shreds of socks and shirt still around his head. His body heaved as he buried his head deeply into the aftershave soaked pillow.

Stan hesitated slightly before shutting the door. This allowed a waft of the contents of the toilet to escape into the room.

Thrust caught the smell in his nose and it then travelled to his throat. The stench was almost beyond description. Even though he'd lived in Port Talbot, and played rugby for many years (once packing down behind a prop who hadn't washed his shorts for 8 years) and was therefore used to some terrible smells, this was undoubtedly one of the most dreadful stenches he'd ever experienced. The urge to throw up was almost irresistible. He succeeded in holding back the urge to be sick, and reaching into his case, managed to spray aftershave on his hands and press them to his face. Never, never, never share a cabin with three other men he thought. This has probably knocked years off my life.

They all lay still, trying to gather their senses.

After some time a voice rang out.

"Right, come on boys, up guards and at 'em the ship is well out of harbour and the night is young. If we don't get a move on the nurses will have been shagged senseless by the hooray Henrys on that other bus and we will have blown the biggest opportunity since Pete Best left the Beatles" said Vic, showing both a remarkable power of recovery and a knowledge of pop music history.

They left the foul smelling cabin and set off to find the nearest bar.

On reaching the nearest bar—imaginatively named 'Le Pub', they grabbed a spare table and Stan got the first round in. There was no sign of the nurses anywhere, though the bar was quite full, mostly with young English men going to France on some kind of sporting activity.

"Wonder where those nurse are then?" said Archie. "They're either holding themselves back for a spectacular entry, or else they've gone straight to the disco bar. It's down the other end of the ferry.

"Why don't we finish these and get down to the disco then?" asked Vic, impatient to meet the nurses.

"Don't want to go there too early. Need to get a few down you first and anyway you won't be able to hear yourself think down there. It'll be a waste of time. We'll be like exhibits from Madame Tussauds. Just silent mute statues just looking on. What a waste of time. No, we'll have a few beers here, have a chat about life etc., and then go to the disco when its nice and lively then get straight into the nurses. You know it makes sense" said Thrust, drawing upon knowledge gained over years of nightclub attendance.

"Yeah. Let's not go down the disco straight away. We'll only sit there unable to say a word, and that only makes me feel depressed. Let's stay here and have a chat—at least you can hear yourself think in this bar," said Stan.

They continued with their drinking and talked about the route they would take to Switzerland and Celigny, before moving on to the well honed topic of the state of Welsh Rugby.

A voice interrupted them.

"I say. You chaps Welsh, are you?" inquired a young-ish looking man with a upper class accent on the next table.

"No. We're Americans pretending to be Welsh just to impress people" said Thrust with an added dash of sarcasm.

"Oh. Strange thing for you to do. What part of America are you from?" said the man, displaying breathtaking naivity.

"Don't listen to him. Yes, we are Welsh—from the best bit, Port Talbot. Just popping over to France to stock up some booze and to have a bit of a laugh. Where are you boys from?" said Stan.

"I'm from Guildford, but I'm a student at Exeter University. We're on our annual rugby trip—good fun every year, but this year might be even better. We've seen a bus full of nurses down on deck D, from down your way actually. Well, we won't go wrong there. Nurses, Welsh nurses, on a girly trip to France, it's the nearest thing to a legalised travelling brothel your ever likely to come across. We're going to have a few beers here before going to the disco. They're bound to be in there. It'll be like shooting fish in a barrel, can't go wrong eh!," said the student with a guffaw.

Fuck shit bollocks piss thought Thrust. Bloody English Public School gits. Why don't they stay at home buggering each other in the dorm, or if they have to travel, just lock themselves in their cabins to play whist. The last thing we need is competition for the nurses!

"Oh—we hadn't realised. Down in the disco eh! Where are they from did you say?" said Turpin.

"Swansea I think. Is it Singleton or something like that?" said the student.

"Oh, not the Singleton nurses? Some terrible things have happened there—the entire medical staff were infected with syphilis by a sex crazed bisexual male surgeon. I'd heard they'd sent the ones still surviving off on a therapeutic trip to the Continent—it must be them," said Thrust.

"Yeah, they are probably the ones being treated for

paranoid schizophrenia" said Stan. "Since they became infected they've not only developed an incurable strain of syphilis, but also a pathological hatred of men, particularly well educated English Public School types. Reminds them of the infected surgeon, you see. He was an Exeter Graduate I think. If I remember correctly, some have even indulged in genital mutilation of any English men they meet. Not a pretty experience for anyone to get involved with them. You'd better watch out, boys."

"Yeah, they are rumoured to lure men back to their dormitories then hand them condoms laced with grated glass—shreds a blokes dick like marmalade—shocking. You wouldn't want to bother with those types boys. Better of staying here and having a few beers" said Vic, deciding to embellish Stan and Turpin's attempt to put the students off the nurses trail.

"Oh, thanks. Didn't think they could be like that—you'd think customs wouldn't let them out of the country. Perhaps we will stay here. Hear that chaps—better leave those Welsh tarts alone, rotten to the core" said the student, turning to his friends.

"Wouldn't touch them if they're Welsh anyway. Thick, dirty and inbred. The men shag sheep and the women everything else. I wouldn't put my dick anywhere near them" said one of the rugger types with broad shoulders and cropped hair, who looked like a prop forward.

"Nice to hear an English person speaking so fairly and objectively about the Welsh" said Thrust. "No doubt your observations are based upon well researched facts and made from a position of total objectivity."

"Gosh, an articulate Taffy! Never heard one before, not even in University. Most of them were beer swilling idiots who had filthy habits, and who only got in because they could play rugby, or had managed to get some decent A level grades in their own, how shall I put it, less stringent examination board. You must feel quite unique across the border, being able to string together long words, and deal in abstract concepts" said the prop forward with a condescending sneer.

"Fuck off, you English twat" said Stan. "Haven't you got a good word to say about anyone who's not English? You ignorant stupid bastard." The student had ignited Stan's barely suppressed hatred of anyone from the wrong side of Offa's dyke.

"Stupid? I'll have you know I went to Oxford!," said the student, shocked by Stan's outburst.

"I don't care if you went up your own arse with a six string banjo serenaded by a troupe of singing nuns—you're still an ignorant stupid bastard," countered Stan, obviously upset.

"Oooh, no need to get personal dear chap. Calm down. You see, to me, well, some people are known for particular skills or talents, I mean the French do a good line in wine, food and lingerie; the Germans in uniforms and composers; but sadly the poor old Taffys don't feature anywhere. Used to be quite good at rugby but that was a long time ago and we try to keep them on the fixture list as a gesture of goodwill. To be honest, nowadays the Welsh team simply hasn't got a hope anymore. Apart from a small contribution to rugby I can't think of anything that Wales is good for, or has given to civilisation. Don't want to upset you, but surely you agree I have a valid point" said the prop, with a malevolent grin, deciding that attack was the best form of defence.

"The current state of our rugby is just a temporary blip" countered Thrust deciding to enter the row that he had started.

"Your chances of winning anything in rugby are non-existent. They are defunct. Washed up, washed out. In fact they have in reality gone for a Burton. Not a fucking hope" said the prop with a defiant jut of his jaw.

'Gone for a Burton', thought Thrust. What a cheek! Gone for a Burton—gone up in smoke, gone West, fallen apart. It was ironic that his phrase should mean an abandonment of hope, when in fact their trip, going for a Burton was intending to do the exact opposite—to give hope, rather than take it away. How ironic he used the words 'Gone for a Burton'. The cheeky twat. The cheek of using a great Welshman's name to rubbish Wales' chances in rugby. We can't stand for this. I'll show him. Thrusts mind was reeling. The prop had unwittingly touched a raw nerve. He knew he had to speak up to right this verbal slur on his hero, his country, and their secret mission.

"Welsh Rugby is the very soul of rugby" said Thrust, his

voice rising in anger. "It's what breathes life into the game. When the Welsh play rugby to the best of their ability it takes the game to a different level. It's the bubble in the champagne, the spice in the curry, the glint in an eye. I'll admit we haven't been too good lately, but that's a momentary aberration—we'll be back and rugby will be a better sport for it. He paused for breath. At least we try to be creative and do something with the ball, not like the brute force and sterility of English rugby teams. You don't know what you're on about."

"Well apart from rugby what have the Welsh done or given to anyone?" said the prop with an aggressive flourish, jutting his jaw out even further. "As far as I'm concerned Wales is a glorified county of England that could realistically be split between Lancashire and Gloucestershire and no-one would really miss it or them. I'm surprised we didn't stamp out all this bloody nationalism in the first place. I suppose it gave us someone else to play apart from the Jocks and the Paddies, but other than that I don't see any real point in allowing 'a Wales' to exist."

"What do you mean 'we stamped out'?" said Turpin, rising to the challenge. "As far as I'm concerned when you say 'we' you mean the English. In my view they didn't stamp anyone out. My reading of history was that the Normans conquered England in 1066 in a relatively short space of time and then took over 200 years to do the same to Wales. If you lot were so bloody wonderful you'd have stopped them conquering you, or at least kicked them out, rather than packing in with indecent haste, then jumping on the Norman bandwagon in attacking Wales, Scotland and Ireland and anyone else around at the time."

Thrust was on a roll, on one of his favourite topics.

"In any event," he continued with an equally firmly jutting jaw, "Wales may have been physically 'conquered' whatever you mean by that, but it was certainly never wiped out, and stands for a great deal more than Lancashire, Gloucestershire, or any other fucking county in England. It may not have dawned upon you, but most of the world didn't take very kindly to being turned into England, and in roughly historical order, the Scots, French, Americans, Boers and the

Irish all kicked you out, followed by the rest of the British Empire. So why would anyone want to be part of England?."

"Oh, touched a raw nerve have we?" said the prop, intellectually stepping backwards at this vigorous, and to the prop's way of thinking, novel interpretation of history.

"No," said Thrust on familiar ground. "But it just might be the first time you've had anyone take the trouble to tell you an alternative view of history—it's not necessarily true that the English brought the benefit of civilisation to all points West, or wherever—an alternative view could be that Wales—or whatever you wanted to call it at the time, was the only part of the Roman Empire to withstand Barbarian invasions and that it exported Christianity to Ireland—St Patrick was Welsh wasn't he Vic?."

"Yeah, from Banwen, near Neath. It's well known he was Welsh," said Vic, who didn't know anything about St. Patrick other than a loose association with Shamrocks, Guinness and Ireland.

"Yeah, like Prince, David Bowie and Bruce Springsteen" said Archie suppressing a giggle.

The prop laughed. The others joined in. Thrust felt that perhaps he wasn't such a bad type after all. The laughter deflated his growing anger.

"Shut up" said Thrust impatiently. He was glad however that Archie's words had lowered the temperature between him and the prop.

"Anyway," he continued in a slightly more conciliatory manner, "the Welsh exported Christianity—where it eventually reached the English—who then had the cheek to call the Welsh 'uncivilised'!"

"The Welsh had written poetry, codified laws, had monastic 'universities' when most of Europe was in turmoil—but you don't get taught that in your traditional history books do you?" Thrust thought he'd wrap things up on an educated, religious note as the anger within him subsided.

"Boudicea, Caractacus, King Arthur would all have probably spoken 'Welsh' and even London is a Welsh name—so I'm not saying Wales is wonderful, or even 'better' than England, but that for a small part of the world it's got a lot to be proud of, and it just isn't fucking fair or even right, to dismiss it like you, or many English people do." Thrust concluded his speech with a long pull on his beer.

"All right, all right, you've said enough—why hasn't any other Welsh person I've met said all this then?" said the prop in a gesture of conciliation. "Most of the ones I've met are only interested in beer, singing and women, and act daft all the time. Remember that Flanker from Abergavenny who could drink a pint through his nose? Mad or what?"

His mates burst out laughing in a good natured way. Thrust and the boys joined in.

"I don't know. A lot of them, or should I say, us, are mad. What's more, a lot of us don't really know anything about being Welsh" said Thrust. "I don't think they get really taught Welsh history—it's often a watered down version of English history. The only significant Welshman in English eyes was probably Henry VII—though recently history teaching has descended into empathising with peasants' experiences under the three field system, or pretending to be lesbian floor sweeps in Yorkshire Cotton mills."

"Can I do a role play on that one?" said Stan butting in. Both groups again burst into laughter. The atmosphere was now quite friendly.

Turpin decided to bring his speech to an end. "Someone once said 'conquerors write history—but in Wales' case it's now a case of the conquerors version is now diluted to a sort of pick 'n' mix sociology lesson, and that the Welsh haven't been bothered to replace it with anything meaningful. Are all of us— the Welsh, English, Scots, Irish, whatever are soon going to turn into some Disney / MTV bland one World Culture, with no-one even bothered to do something about it. Perhaps we'd better realise what we've got in common, rather than what divides us?" He looked around, and realised most of his audience just wanted to get pissed.

"Shit. He's off on one" said Archie. "He thinks all this up in those boring council meetings he attends. He's talking through his arse—most people in Wales are happy to have a few pints, watch a bit of sport and shag their wives or girlfriends, preferably both—just like you said!" patting the

132

prop forward on the back.

"You don't want to listen to him, he's fucking mad—he's even brought us over to try and get Rich."

Thrust's hand went over Archie's mouth.

"Ssshhh we don't want to let anyone know how we're going to get Rich" said Thrust laughing out loud.

"It may involve us smuggling back some rare wines" said Vic, "but we couldn't possibly say too much in case it jeopardised our plan, and we're not likely to make any money out of it, let alone get rich."

Thrust hastily pushed a bottle of beer into Archie's mouth and Archie found himself inadvertently gulping down its contents in order to prevent him divulging the top secret nature of their mission.

"Let's leave this nationalistic crap alone boys," said Stan. "How about a quick game of claptrap to break down the barriers and to get us tanked up. We can then all get stuck into those nurses—there'll be plenty to go around."

There was a murmur of agreement on the students' table.

"Ok, let's have a game of claptrap. You all know the standard rules?" asked Thrust.

"Yeah—most of us have played except Will—I'll tell him the basics, he's a bright boy and he won't be in too much trouble. Whoever is chairman will need to go easy on the boy" said the prop, who introduced himself as Gavin as he gave a knowing wink to the Welsh boys.

The two groups sat in a circle and the rules of the drinking game were explained to Will. Basically the object of the game was to get as drunk as possible in as short as possible a time period, whilst displaying a modicum of knowledge coupled with manual co-ordination. In the hands of seasoned players however, the game could really come alive with complex challenges and debates, and variation on themes which generally produced a considerable amount of amusement. The game also enabled players to push the pace of drinking or to rein back, or hammer particular individuals. Claptrap also encouraged innovation in the approach to topics and or answers which also got more bizarre, funny or insane the longer the game went on. Ideally, a game of claptrap could be an entertaining sociable start to an evening's drinking. In the wrong hands it could lead to comatose drunkenness, mass vomiting and possible death.

The game would start with the Chairman nominating a player to begin the game. This player would then shout 'going down' before slapping his hands on his knees, then clapping them and then finger clicking in rhythm. Then (and it had to be done precisely at the same time) the other players would clap and click in time with one another. The Chairman would then shout out the refrain, 'give me, names of famous…. inserting whatever then took his fancy. This could be at a simple level, animals or plants or, sometimes much more obscure and demanding matters or topics.

Potentially, the danger is naming something that there was a lot of, or that everyone knew answers to, was that if every player came up with a valid answer (and there could be a lot of debate about that) and if the players completed the circle—he would be punished—normally with a pint on the head, or even more depending upon who he was or what he said.

Cleverer or more skilful players could, and often would come up with obscure and or entertaining topics such as names of famous porn stars, American Civil War generals, or Italian suits, or whatever really they felt like.

The only restriction on the topic chosen was that a player couldn't 'talk shop' i.e. chose a topic related to his job—so a Doctor couldn't choose 'bones in the body' or 'treatments for herpes'. The only other substantial rule was that any player could challenge a person choosing a topic by demanding that they name seven examples of the topic chosen.

However, such a challenge was a high risk strategy, for both challenger and the person being challenged. If the challenge failed, then the challenger had to drink a pint, though if it succeeded then this would be the fate of the person being challenged.

Turpin recalled that claptrap had been the staple of many a rugby drinking session for decades, and had developed it's own culture and folklore. Games had been known to go on for hours and regularly resulted in mayhem, rioting and behaviour beyond the comprehension of mankind, which, for most rugby clubs, took some doing.

Thrust volunteered to be Chairman—another risky strategy because while he could effectively control the game, he was also in a high profile position, and were he to make a mistake, he would be liable to double penalties. He felt however it was a risk worth taking, and in any event, hoped to use it as a device to 'hammer' some of the English boys, so that they would be in no fit state to pose a threat to Thrust's designs on the busload of nurses.

Sitting in the hastily designated Chairman's seat, Turpin prepared to start the game.

"Right Gavin—you're familiar with the rules so you can keep your boys in line—I'll go easy on you lot anyway for the first five minutes, so ready when you are" said Thrust.

"Right. Introductions first, then we'll start" said Gavin.

"Just to lay down the rules—happy game—no miserable looks—or else minimum fine of three fingers of beer" said Turpin exuding an air of confidence as Chairman.

"Furthermore," added Turpin, "no crossing legs and / or other limbs, no pee breaks without permission. Compulsory drink with Chairman on the signal. No speaking out of turn, Gavin and Vic to be cleckers (specially appointed 'aides' to the Chairman)."

"Right, Stan kick off" said Turpin.

Stan started gently with names of famous rugby grounds. The usual ones wee trotted out on the clicks 'The Arms Park', 'Stradey', 'Twickers' etc., Luckily one of the English boys blurted out 'Old Trafford' and was duly penalised. Stan had started to worry the answers would get back to him.

The next player started with Post War American Presidents—obviously he was either no fool and / or in addition an experienced player. Archie came up with his response. 'Roosevelt'.

Immediately a row broke out—'Which Roosevelt? A fresh row then erupted. It was established that it was F.D.R. Was Franklin D post war?

Thrust was firm 'Archie—out of order; Franklin D Roosevelt died before the war ended—therefore he was not a post war president'—three fingers." It was essential to be firm as Chairman. It also helped to have a good general eduction and

135

a clear mind—which got more difficult as the game wore on.

Archie muttered something about 'University twat' and downed his drink.

The game began to hot up. Thrust's heart stopped a beat when the bloke next to him asked for famous Opera singers. It was not Thrust's strongest suit.

Luckily one of the English boys blurted out Oprah Winfrey in a panic attack and Thrust was left off the hook.

A few interesting ones surfaced such as electric guitars, Beatles number ones and Grand National winners. It was not long before one of the boys threw the sucker punch of naming days of the week. The days run out just before Stan.

"Sorry Stan, three fingers."

"Fuck off. How can I name another day of the week when there are only seven" said Stan quite reasonably.

"Well, that's your problem. You could have said 'today or yesterday', or the day after tomorrow—you need to have your wits about you" responded Turpin with a false smile. The English boys laughed as Stan drank three fingers.

The game was beginning to loosen up and get interesting.

Thrust rashly called for a pint on the head with the Chairman, as he felt a rush of adrenaline coming on due to his generally competent chairing of the game. Sadly the next call came to name stars of the 70s television series *Crossroads*. He prayed that someone would forget Shoey McPhee—it was the only one, apart from the obvious, that he knew. The names rang out, Bennie, David Hunter, Sandy then, the words he dreaded, Shoeey McPhee, shit he thought, the bloke next to him had stolen his ace name. He had no time to think of another. He immediately considered making one up—this could sometimes work—he'd once got away with Otto Von Trapp as a first World War German General. However—there seemed to be some real soap fanatics in this game, and he decided to take it on the chin.

"You've got me boys" he said with a resigned shake of the head.

"Chairman—pint on the head!" the voices rang out.

He swiftly downed the fizzy ferry beer and regretted calling for the Chairman's drink earlier on.

He then started the game, as required, and in a moment of madness decided to show off by choosing Renaissance painters. Even more rashly, instead of sticking to da Vinci or Botticelli, he said Hieronymous Bosch.

"Challenge—Bosch wasn't a renaissance painter—he was mediaeval. I should know, I've got a degree in history of Art," shouted one of the English boys.

A whoop of joy went around the group.

"Got you there Turpie boy—on the fucking head," said Stan with glee.

Thrust felt like arguing, but realised he would not win, as any dispute would be determined on a vote, and he would pay the price for trying to be too clever anyway. Sometimes you just had to roll with the punches.

Another pint on the head, and he was now in danger of getting pissed, losing control of the game and not making any meaningful attempt at meeting the nurses.

He needed to do something drastic. The only solution would be a call for a 'themed chunder'. This was an old trick from the rugby club which would enable him to get rid of the beer, hopefully sober up a bit, and, if the theme were funny enough, retrieve his standing with the English boys. He decided it was the only option.

"Right. Chairman's prerogative—themed chunder. Tonights theme—Roman Emperors!" A few of the players nodded in appreciation. Other's looked puzzled. Turpin decided to explain.

"What this means is that I'm going to spew—anyone is welcome to join me—it only requires that you shout out a name within the theme or genre whilst spewing. The spews are verified by independent 'tellers' who then announce them to the group. The funniest, most original name wins £5 from the kitty. It's the Chairman's prerogative, and I've named the theme as 'Roman Emperors'. Any of you boys up for it?" said Thrust, beginning to slur his words noticeably.

"Your all fucking mad! I've never heard anything like it," said one of the students.

"I'll give it a go," said one of the English boys obviously the worse for wear.

Will, who had been particularly badly hit, as you'd expect for a novice, also indicated a willingness to participate.

Two 'tellers' were nominated by the group, Stan and Gavin. It was their job to make sure that the theme was adhered to, and to give a score out of 10 for the effort. The game was then 'stayed' for the themed chunders..

The small side group of themed spewers loped off to the nearest toilet—vaguely concerned that any bystanders might consider them to be some sort of perambulating cottaging entourage, sneaking off to the nearest toilet for a homosexual orgy.

Thrust pushed this thought from his mind, as he was more concerned with ensuring that he could survive the game of claptrap and achieve his goal of meeting the nurses. "Right, I'll go last—Chairman's prerogative" said Thrust narrowly avoiding a spontaneous retch.

Will muttered "I'm ready to have a go," and braced himself for a chunder over the nearest toilet. A huge vomit gushed forth, and in the aftermath a gasping, coughing gurgle of what should vaguely like 'Nero'.

"Is that it Will?" queried Stan, who was one of the tellers.

"Yes" rasped Will, as another retch overtook him.

"Never mind—good try—Give you three for effort, and to encourage you for any future tries. All in favour?" said Stan.

"Yeah," muttered Gavin.

"Thanks" muttered Will, as he swilled his mouth in clean water.

"Right, Jake is it? Your turn," said Stan.

One of the students named Jake tried to be sick but nothing came out. He then stuck his fingers in his throat. Unfortunately, his attempt to induce vomiting succeeded to a far greater extent than he'd wished as a torrent of beer, pasties and peanuts came flying out of his mouth and nostrils. His face looked as if he'd been buggered by a Rhino.

A cry of 'Aaarrrhhhh' accompanied the vomit, which culminated in a limp 'Ustus' as Jake wiped the vomit from his mouth and nose.

"I presume that was your attempt at saying 'Augustus' Jake," said Stan with genuine compassion.

138

"Yeah—got there in the end. Bit lively that one" replied Jake, eyes rolling.

"Not a lot of innovation or quality in the delivery, but lots of character shown in retrieving what could have been a lost cause. Liked the split consonants. Give you a five for that boy" said Stan.

"You all in favour Gavin?"

"Aye—five," said Gavin.

"Right Turpin, over to you." Stan put his hand on Thrust's shoulder.

Thrust felt the sick already welling up inside him, but for good measure imagined eating snot swimming in a bowl of afterbirth.

He'd already chosen the Emperor, and let fly whilst yelling 'Diocletian'. The chunder was timed to perfection, and the shock of the vomit was tempered by a rush of satisfaction that he'd timed the yell to perfection.

"Good darts Turpin. Well chundered" said Gavin in barely concealed admiration. "The word came out in total sync with the chunder. Nice choice of Emperor too—not an obvious choice, and daringly controversial with his record of persecuting Christians."

"I reckon that's an easy eight, if not a nine. I'd give it a nine," said Stan. "The winner by a mile. One of your best. Up there with the Vespasian a few years ago in Cardiff Rugby Club, and in another genre, Montezuma whilst on tour in Manchester," agreed Gavin.

"Yes" said Gavin. "A classic. Couldn't have done better myself."

"Thanks," said Thrust as he wiped his mouth, "one day I'll do Marcus Aurelius. A favourite of mine. Need some more practice though."

They all laughed and left the toilet, passing some puzzled and appalled German tourists entering to relieve themselves.

The group rejoined the others in the bar, and the game reconvened. The tellers announced the result, and to Turpin's relief his chunder was greeted not only with acclaim and laughter, but also with a vote in favour of the £5 bounty.

"Thank you lads, it was a privilege and pleasure. Now after that exertion, I'd better stand down and let someone else take up the burden of chairmanship. What about one of you boys?" said Thrust, glad to be feeling no longer in danger of alcoholic poisoning.

They all nodded, and gave him a brief round of applause as he vacated the chair.

Gavin was then unanimously elected Chairman.

Turpin got a round in and rejoined the game as a player. The game continued apace though Turpin managed to avoid any heavy penalties.

The game eventually petered out in a welter of arguments, comatose bodies and vomiting players.

Thrust grabbed Vic, Archie and Stan and tried to talk some sense into them.

"Come on boys, lets see if we can do some damage to the nurses. We've been waiting for this for years—it's now or never."

They said goodbye to the few students able to speak, and moved off to find the nurses.

CHAPTER TWELVE

'Dancing Fools'

They lurched down to the rear end of the ferry where the disco was being held.

They could hear the pounding of the disco before they got there. At that range it was impossible to make out any individual songs, but there again, to Thrust's ears there was little to differentiate songs these days—they seemed to involve a variety of chants or screams overlaying a pounding bass line which sometimes went faster or slower, but generally religiously following a 4 / 4 beat.

He used to remember enjoying discos or nightclubs now and again mainly due to fairly decent songs played at a lively level. However, his enjoyment had steadily diminished in recent years as he concluded that all music played in modern clubs was a leaden bass and synthesised drum dominated insipid broth of musical diarrhoea that he had steadily grown to hate. This feeling was no doubt mostly due to his age, but he genuinely felt that there were hardly any good, let alone classic songs being written anymore, and even if there were, they were certainly not being played in nightclubs. He admitted that you could always hear quality old songs in the clapped out bars like Glyns but he reasoned that you were then trading decent music for uglier women and potentially more violent men. It was also true that the rougher the club, the older the clientele, and the higher the risk you ran that your 'boogie night' would be interrupted by 'Agadoo' or 'Una Paloma Blanca'. He'd once had a dance interrupted by 'They call the Wind Maria' accompanied by a mass outbreak of spontaneous farting throughout the club. This was a Brynglyn Rugby Club speciality—they always tried to engineer public participation in a song—especially if it had 'sex' in the title. Thank God they never played 'love me, love my dog' he thought. He laughed inwardly and his mind began to wander. Whatever, he certainly felt that all modern music was crap. He longed for a decent club playing decent music.

Never mind he thought, once he'd repatriated Burton, become a millionaire and made Port Talbot a cultural and entertainment Mecca, he'd open his own club, with decent music, played at a decent level, full of decent women—and about five men. All of whom would be his mates. Sorted. And then...

His mini daydream was interrupted by Vic.

"Turpie, it's your round boy. I'm having a pint of 'bow. Hope you're in a position to drink some more after that chunder. One of your best that. Pity about that English bloke collapsing though," said Vic.

"Yeah, we'll if you can't stand the heat, etc., you know what I mean" said Thrust with a hint of self satisfaction.

Turpin was secretly going to ease back on the drinking, as he knew that if he drank much more, he'd be unable to speak to the bevy of nurses he confidently expected to dance with, let alone give them the vigorous shagging they undoubtedly deserved.

They stepped into the disco and were hit by the full blast of the music. It was like being run over by a prop forward—the force of the speakers nearly knocked him back out of the doors. The pitch blackness was pierced by shafts of coloured light that illuminated a floor thronging with dancers. Turpin thought he recognised a few of the girls from the bus that had passed them back in Wales, though he accepted that may have been wishful thinking.

He struggled to order the round over the pounding beat, and, drinks in hand, he fought against the lurching of the ship, battling through the crowd and the darkness over to where the rest of the gang were sitting near to the dancefloor.

"Here we are boys one 'bow, and two Stella, but go steady on the Stella boys" said Turpin—"you know it drives you both mad, especially if you turn it into a 'Star Trek'."

"Uh?" said Vic.

"What?" said Archie. "Can't hear you."

"The drinks—the round—here they are" shouted Thrust.

"What? Who's car?" said Stan.

"No. The fucking round. Here it is," said Thrust.

"Oh, right. How much do I owe you?" said Stan.

"What's he got to show you?" said Archie

"No. How much" said Turpin, beginning to get fed up with the need to say everything twice.

"Never mind. Let's grab the drinks and move to the back. At least we can talk there," said Stan.

They moved to a free table at the back of the disco and sat down.

"Thank fuck for that. The noise down there was unbearable" said Vic. "I can't stand that bloody music. Why don't they play some decent music—Tom Jones or Man or Budgie—something like that."

"Budgie. Are you serious?" said Turpin. "No-one remembers Budgie any longer—are you trapped forever in the mid 70s? I agree the music today is rubbish, but there's a world of good music to choose from without confining yourself to the same half baked, out of date marginal prog rock from the valleys."

"Breadfan—best record ever made" said Vic. "If you put that on—that'd liven them up. What a great riff! One of Budgie's best."

"Liven them up! They'd have to leap about like fleas on a hot plate in order to dance to that. You'd look like Steven fucking Hawking wired to the mains if you succeeded in dancing to Breadfan" said Stan. "Look you just can't dance to that type of music."

"Oh yes you can—you can stamp, or power dance" (this was a dance invented by Vic which resembled a rigid phalanx of soldiers, advancing over their most hated enemies heads, whilst miming trying to get out of a straight jacket). "It's this crap you can't dance to," said Vic, argumentative as ever.

"Yeah, it's the women what matter" said Stan, "but if you can't dance to a record then it's no good for pulling women. God only knows I've seen that enough in Glyn's with you asking for some heavy metal or 70s psychedelic track, only to see people more quickly off the dancefloor than if you'd shouted 'Child Support Agency' in the Rail and Transport on a Sunday morning. In any event, I can't stretch the English language to describe your movements as dancing."

"Yeah, and you are always left looking like a right dick and, what's more, I agree that whatever you do to the music, it can't be described as dancing" said Archie.

"The last time I saw anyone moving like you on a dance floor was when I rewound a Wales v All Blacks game and saw the 'Haka' being done backwards—very funny, even moving, but in no way could anyone call it dancing," added Turpin.

"Fuck off all of you. I know I can dance, and what's more, I know good music, and I'll get some tonight by one means or another—and pull one of the nurses" said Vic. "Anyway, need a bit of drink first. Archie, I've finished the Stella. Get another and some 'bow. I'm going for it tonight Archie. I'm going for it." Vic's eyes began to glow like anthracite.

"Where the hell are these nurses anyway?" said Archie. "We're too far back to see them now. Ahh—bollocks to it all, I'm going to get some Star Treks in and see what happens."

"Well, they are out there somewhere" said Stan pointing at the dancefloor, and the only way to find them is to go in there. Come on boys—on fix bayonets—we're going in. First back to the cabin gets squatters rights, and the rest of you can splice the mainbrace or whatever, because I'm going to be the first to cop off. Come on, follow me" said Stan, striding off towards the dancefloor.

Vic and Archie shrugged their shoulders, and said that they'd prefer to have another pint, especially if they were Star Treks. Thrust felt he had to accompany Stan or else he'd be letting him down. What's more, he'd been thinking about this moment since they'd worked out that the nurses were on the ferry, and he was ready with his best lines, to be delivered, as ever, in his finest Burton voice.

Thrust scrambled after Stan.

Turpin and Stan stood momentarily on the edge of the dance floor, peering into the swaying gyrating mass of bodies, partially obscured by billows of smoke. He certainly saw lots of attractive women on the dance floor, but sadly, most seemed to be dancing with men, who all appeared to be tall, good looking and well groomed—probably thought Thrust, from the fucking busload of doctors.

Why couldn't we be on the same ferry as 20 busloads of severely wounded D Day veterans, thought Thrust, preferably gay sex offenders who had been physically or chemically castrated. No such luck. Even if they were a few busloads of deaf mute librarians or stammering flint knappers he'd have a chance. But it had to be these bloody flash, fancy Dan, let me take you for a spin in the soft top whilst I tell you how a I saved a dozen children's lives, bloody like to work out as well you know—healthy mind in a healthy body fucking doctors.

His insecurity welled up inside him, as the hatred he'd stored up against Finlay Quench for continually taking Gloria from him became transferred to Doctors generally.

Just then Stan touched his arm and pointed. He mouthed 'those two over there' as the noise of music made verbal communication impossible. Thrust turned and saw two women dancing together in the far corner.

Like two hunters alerted by fresh spoor, Thrust and Stan re-enacted scenes that must have been in their gene pool since time began, as they skirted their way through the heaving mass of humanity, eyes targeting their prey, with a surge of excitement increasing with every step. Thrust's eyes became transfixed on one of the girls, whom he assumed to be a graduate nurse. He immediately assumed she would be caring, worldly, sophisticated, yet in kilter with his stereotypical image of a nurse she would also be an atomic bomb of lust waiting to explode into a panting frenzy within moments of meeting him. His mind conjured up a vigorous and passionate sexual congress on the prow of the ship as his thrusting loins moved in time with the ship as it delved through the waves.

"Oi. Fuck off. Watch where you're going, you drunken bum!" boomed a voice from behind the screen of fog.

Thrust was brought back to reality as he realised in the noise and mist his hunter like tracking of his sexual prey had gone awry, and that he had stumbled into a smooching couple. His face was almost next to the woman's and it was only this close proximity that enabled him to hear her—otherwise he would have stumbled blithely on unaware of the chaos being caused by his passage through the crowd.

"Oh sorry, didn't see you" he mouthed, and smiled inanely, before rushing to Stan who was hovering behind the two girls.

Stan turned and shouted in his ear. "Mine's the blond— we're in luck, they're both quite tidy" before striding out and standing between his chosen target and her companion and he started to dance his usual pogo hop from one foot to the next.

Right Turpin, get in there before someone else comes along, or she sits down, thought Thrust and with one bound he was dancing in front of the girl, jiggling up and down in front of her legs twitching like a St Vitus' dancer, whilst his arms moved back like a semaphore signaller without the flags.

He grinned inanely at the attractive girl in front of him. She had long straight brown hair, wide dark eyes, a cute little nose, and a figure like the proverbial hourglass. He couldn't believe his luck. Whilst he was trying to impress her, he thought what a ridiculous ritual dancing was—two people often strangers, bouncing and jogging up and down, back and forth in front of each other eyeing each other with a view to sex, marriage, romance, friendship or possibly anything which may or may not be reciprocated. In reality most dancers were more likely be met instead with laughter, scorn, naked fear or (particularly if you were in Bryns) vomiting.

Even if both parties took an immediate physical liking to each other, he thought, there were innumerable pitfalls ahead. Setting aside the fact that with modern music it was impossible to verbally communicate on a dancefloor, progress in this time hallowed mating ritual generally depended upon a bizarre concoction of smiles, jibes, eye movements and grimaces, all of which may or may not find favour with the person in front of you. Furthermore, all these actions could be accompanied by a variety of hand, body and leg movements that were often not only embarrassing but sometimes positively dangerous.

In fact, he'd seen many a gormless dancer seek to impress another with a lexicon of hand and arm movements, ranging from sign language through the traditional 'Mick Jagger hitching a lift' gesture through to snake eye motions and obscene gestures. He'd once observed a prop froward from Neath nearly poke his own eye out doing a snake eye movement, and another pop the buttons on his trousers whilst hitching his thumbs into the waistband a la Mud. That incident was particularly memorable as the guys trousers then fell to his ankles causing him to fall into the girl, butting her unconscious and starting a domino affect they resulted in the DJ's podium being pulled off its mounting.

Turpin had also seen numerous men stick sherry glasses, socks and or deodorants down their trousers in order to impress the opposite sex, and quite a few, in a desperate attempt to win favour, 'rolled out the fire hose' to expose themselves, one memorably attaching a blown up rubber penguin to his foreskin for good effect. That unsurprisingly resulted in a severely torn foreskin when the female dancer quite reasonably in Thrust's view, decided to support the 'Free Willy Brigade' (no pun intended) and yanked the penguin free.

Letting out the 'seasick snake' as it was often called never seemed a sensible option to Thrust. Leaving aside his respect for female sensibilities, he felt you certainly left yourself open to a swift stab from a comb or even a well wielded, stiletto heeled shoe. As far as he was concerned the 'dancing dick brigade' deserved everything that came their way.

He still strongly felt that dancing was a ridiculous way of making any form of progress with the opposite sex as, especially considering for the million and one pompous, epileptic convulsive dances that could be devised. Indeed, you could move like Fred Astaire on a silken floor and still be confronted, when the music died down with any sort of person ranging from a female trappist monk (presumably a trappist nun) through a wide variety of women with personalities ranging at one level of girls with a charisma level of a lego brick all the way through to a demented man—hating PMT afflicted harridan boosted by a years assertiveness training at Spare Rib HQ.

Thrust concluded, not for the first time, that the entire process of dancing was a pathetic, cringe inducing brain deadening waste of time, before going on, again not for the first time to consider that it was the only real option available, and that, if he played his cards right, that it could result in him getting off with the pretty girl in front of him, who he was certain was his dream nurse.

He continued to sway and poke his hands up and down like a traffic cop, before deciding to grin a bit more. The girl didn't seem too put off by his jiggling, and smiled back.

Thrust concluded it was now time to move up a gear, as he was convinced his perambulations so far would not bear fruit, and that, even though there was no discernible beginning, middle or end to the 'song' they were dancing to, it could all end suddenly and he'd be left drenched in sweat with a nose full of smoke and a bulging hard on. He was going to have to say something—he rehearsed the line in his head, and spoke to the girl with his best Burton voice:

"Delighted to meet you. I must ask myself, with beautiful women like you in Britain, why on earth am I going to France?"

He cocked his eyebrow and pulled back his lip in a half grin. He genuinely thought it looked sexy. In fact it made him look as if he'd caught one bollock in his fly zip.

Nothing happened. There was no reaction on the girl's face. It suddenly dawned on him—she couldn't hear him as the music was too loud.

He repeated the line in a louder voice, with a more emphasised eyebrow lift and mouth twist to follow. Still no reaction. She smiled back at him with a slightly puzzled look on her face. She obviously thought he'd developed a nervous tic.

He took a deep breath and shouted the line, followed by a thrust back with his head, in addition to the twists, in a vain attempt to justify his third attempt at speaking.

She leaned forward and yelled 'Pardon?'.

He stooped forward and yelled with all his might his original chat up line, which the first time he'd considered cool and sophisticated, but which now felt as stale and hackneyed as Sunday morning's beer slops.

"Ah, thank you, you are very kind" the girl shouted, and continued to dance.

"Are you looking forward to your holiday?" he shouted.

Her crinkled up expression told him he was having little luck with the communication over the noise of the music.

He again leant forward and shouted the words.

"Yes, it was good" she replied.

Good? She hadn't been on it yet. Was she mad? he thought. Perhaps she'd drunk too much. He wasn't going to give up this easily. He repeated the mantra 'there are only two certainties in life, death and nurses' to himself, and again leant forward.

"Lovely place France, isn't it?"

He nodded after saying the words as if to invite confirmation, or any form of dialogue that may have eventually turned into a conversation.

At this rate they'd need to go through the entire Beatles back catalogue before he'd even find out her name. Never mind. He continued to nod and thrust his head forward in time with the music. He tried his largest 'Robbie Williams' what a cheeky chappy I am' smile—blissfully ignorant of the pieces of chewed crisp that his grin revealed on his front teeth.

The girl laughed heartily.

At last he thought—I'm getting somewhere. The old Robbie Williams grin never fails.

The girl continued to laugh, as it gradually dawned on him that whatever she was laughing at, it wasn't his infectious smile.

He started to panic and imagined that his flies had come open or that she recognised him from the TV report from Brynglyn Rugby Club.

Fortunately she pointed past him, and he realised that whatever was making her laugh—it wasn't him. Feeling slightly let down, he turned to see what the source of her mirth was.

He turned and saw Archie and Vic dancing together in a passable imiitation of a scene from the *Texas Chainsaw Massacre*. Archie was punching the air like a demented evangelist whilst thrusting his groin, from which sprouted a thin flower vase, back and fore like a piston. In his mouth hung a pair of socks whilst the former contents of the vase protruded from his ears.

Vic was dancing around like a red Indian yelling through a presumably stolen traffic bollard, whilst stabbing himself in the buttocks with an ice tong. His underpants were on his head like a balaclava and his trousers were around his shoulders like a cape. Thrust admitted to himself that it was one of the funniest sights he'd seen, including Will Dong's haggis piercing trick in Edinburgh, but was appalled that it had blown his attempt to get off with the nurse. They'd obviously been getting stuck into the Star Treks. He glanced at Stan and saw that he was, despite the music, wrapped in a passionate snog with the other girl.

He turned to his dancing partner and shrugged and shook his hands back and fore, indicating that he had nothing to do with either of the lunatics behind him. He reasoned that no women would bother with anyone with friends as mad as that, and in any event, when the dry ice cleared the bouncers would soon evict them, if not throw them overboard.

His attempt at splendid isolation came to a shuddering halt when he felt a pair of sharp ice tongs thrusting into his arse cheeks. The next thing he knew was that both Vic and Archie were dancing around him prodding him alternately with flower stalks and the ice tongs.

His obvious embarrassment only served to make the girl laugh louder, This was not how he had thought his night would turn out. Suddenly the music stopped and the dry ice lifted. Both Vic and Archie realised that their cover had literally been blown, and through the clearing smog saw a group of stewards point and start to move towards the dance floor.

In a flash they turned and fled, leaving a flower embedded in Thrust's hair and the ice tong stuck into his jeans.

He could not have felt a bigger prat, and was frightened to look at the girl, who still appeared to be laughing. He felt a hand on his arm and on looking up he saw that she'd stopped laughing and was pulling him off the dance floor.

When they got far enough from the dance floor, he realised that he could actually hear the words when she said, in a thick French accent, "Come with me—you can buy me a drink, I need one!."

Things were looking up he thought.

CHAPTER THIRTEEN

'The Owl and the Pussy Cat'

The girl removed the ice tongs from Turpin's rear, but after a slight hesitation, let the flower remain in his hair and then led him by the hand off the disco floor to the bar.

"Um, what would you like to drink?" he asked, relieved to be able to talk with some normality after the battlefield intensity of the dance floor.

"Pernod and ice if you please," she said. He now knew she wasn't British.

"Ok, oh by the way, my name is Turpin—pleased to meet you. Sorry about what happened out there." He smiled apologetically.

"Oh, don't worry—it was so funny. I'm Catherine. Pleased to make your acquaintance," the girl said with a marked French accent.

"You aren't British are you," he said.

"No. Can't you tell" she laughed, "I'm Swiss."

"Swiss—good God—I've never met anyone from Switzerland. I thought they were all fat financiers in Lederhosen firing crossbows," said Thrust with genuine surprise. "You're certainly not a fat financier," he added admiringly as an afterthought.

"My father is though! Anyway, get me a drink. I need one after all that laughing. It was very funny dancing with you. We can talk then" she said.

He assumed that this was some backhanded complement, and got some drinks from the bar. They sat then at a quiet table away from the disco area. She spoke good English, and as they chatted away he discovered that she'd been at college in London, and was returning home for the summer and had met up with a few friends. She was 22 years old and was studying English, though she spoke it, and both French and German fluently.

What she didn't tell him, was that she had a boyfriend in Dijon, named Henri who she'd known since her early teens, and who'd been the only man she had made love to.

She was deeply in love with him, but had been shocked to discover from a friend that he'd been seeing other women whilst she had been in England.

She was determined to confront him with this on her return, but on the journey back, had decided to 'get even' with him by for the first time going with another man, and then throwing this at him to show that infidelity was a game that two could play. The disco had not presented her with anything remotely suitable until this reasonably attractive Welshman, with a strange voice, and bizarre friends, had started to dance with her. His outgoing, amiable manner, and a certain something she couldn't explain, told her to get to know him better. He could, she thought, be the one to get back at Henri with.

He explained where he was from and that he was on holiday with some friends, and that they were probably going to go on to visit Switzerland.

She asked him what Wales was like. She'd heard it was mountainous like Switzerland.

"Well, it's not exactly Switzerland. There's a place called Swiss Valley in Llanelli, and we do have some nice mountains — though you'd call them hills, lots of sheep. Not really much of a patch on Switzerland though," he commented ruefully.

"It sounds very nice. I've been told you've got a beautiful coastline, which we haven't got and some interesting castles. Perhaps one day I'll visit Wales" said Catherine.

"Yeah, great, love to show you around, we could go to the seaside, though not where I live, it's a bit, well, murky if you know what I mean. We could also visit a castle or two — preferably by the sea, so we wouldn't have to move around a lot. Perhaps I'll take you to Swansea, it's near to where I live, and there's some nice beaches and castles in an area called Gower which is close to Swansea. You could also try our national dish."

"I know, I've had it—Welsh rabbit! Lots of cheese but not a lot of rabbit, if I remember correctly," she smiled, pleased at her local knowledge.

"No, well, possibly and it's not rabbit it's rarebit so you wouldn't have had any meat in it anyway, but I'm thinking of laverbread," he explained.

She looked at him quizzically.

"What is that?" she asked.

"Mashed black seaweed. Delicious with bacon and cockles" said Thrust speaking with fond memories of one of his favourite foods.

"Ugh, sounds horrible. You seem to have a strange cuisine in Wales, what with cheesy rabbits and black seaweed" laughed Catherine.

He saw the funny side of what she was saying, and certainly warmed to her open good humour.

"Ok, but well I think it's great and at least it's ours. No-one else would dream of eating wet seaweed" said Thrust. "A Welsh cuisine," he continued, "that was surely a figment of the Wales Tourist Board's imagination. Cheese on toast, seaweed, lamb soup and a few current cakes. All washed down with .... Brains best or Felinfoel. Hardly Cordon Blue eh" he smiled apologetically.

She seemed to follow the point he was making and smiled in return. "Why do you run yourself down like that? It sounds fine to me. Not everyone has a national cuisine. Ok the French have one, so do the Italians, but how many other countries? You should be proud of what you've got—at least, as you say, it's yours. I like all foods from all over the world, but always be proud of what your people produce. It shows you are a country. We've only made cheese. That's nothing to shout about is it?" said Catherine demonstrating a fair knowledge of cooking coupled with a strong line of independent thought.

"Yeah, fair point. To be honest, I've never heard of a Swiss restaurant. Bit cheese orientated I would imagine. Not wishing to offend you though. The cheese you make is very good cheese" he said, worrying that he might have gone too far and upset her.

153

"That's ok" said Catherine. "There's a lot more to Switzerland than cheese though. The mountains, the lakes, our freedom. We haven't been invaded since William Tell drove the Austrians out in the Middle Ages you know. We're so proud of that."

"I'm impressed, but it helps if your so high up in the mountains, you could roll the cheese down on any invaders, and yodel through your horns to create avalanches to crash down on them — so you've got a head start in fighting invaders" he joked feebly.

She laughed — thank goodness he thought — as his humour could sometimes backfire on him. She also seemed to be interested in what he was saying, and in his mind therefore interesting. He'd met very few women who were prepared to discuss either history or food apart from 'What did you think of Coronation Street last week"?, and "what are you having in the Indian tonight?" minutes after meeting you. In fact he was quite shaken by Catherine's response.

"Yes, we Swiss like to yodel and sing, though you Welsh are famous for your singing aren't you? My favourite Welsh singer is Tom Jones. What's that song? 'It's not unusual to be loved by anyone'," she sang and pretended to wiggle her hips. Thrust laughed.

"Tom, yes, brilliant. Have you heard 'Delilah?'" he said.

"Yes, that's were he stabs her for having sex with another man. Good song. I like the bit where she laughs 'ha ha ha'," countered Catherine.

He was a bit disturbed by that comment, particularly in the light of the look on her face when she made it, but chose to ignore it.

"Brilliant. My favourite is 'The boy from nowhere' but you probably haven't heard of that one. I can relate to it" he mused, thinking of his hometown.

"No, I haven't heard of that one. Have you ever met Tom Jones"? she asked staring deeply into his eyes.

Thrust had only once seen him at an outdoor concert in Cardiff castle. He didn't let that hold him back though. He had to try to impress her.

"Yes, yes in Cardiff I met him, had a good chat. Indeed, I've met him quite a few times. In fact you could say he was a friend. Don't see so much of him now that he's living in America. But I may bump into him now and again. If I do, I'll get you his autograph" said Thrust carried away by the combination of his own imagination and the need to impress Catherine.

"Oh please, If you could" she seemed genuinely delighted. "I would be so grateful. Could you get him to write 'To my darling Catherine—love Tom'. Oh yes." Her eyes misted over.

"I'll see what I can do" he said with a wink, knowing he had no earthly chance of getting an autograph from Tom Jones.

"Are there any other great singers in Wales?," she asked.

"Oh yes, many. Every town, every village has dozens of great singers—have you heard of Geraint Evans, Bryn Terfel, umm Ivor Emmanuel, you know, the singing soldier in the film—*Zulu*? Never mind... Ivor Novello?" The look on her face told him he was not getting very far.

"Are there any modern music singers in Wales?" said Catherine.

"Well, apart from Tom?" He thought hard, "well apart from Shakin' Stevens, Bonnie Tyler and the Alarm and there's a few new bands—the Manic Street Preachers, but otherwise ... that's about it" He began to feel he was on sticky ground.

"Wonderful—what talented people! You have so many good singers in Wales. 'Lost in France' was a very big hit in Europe. For a small country you've produced so many talented people. I studied Dylan Thomas on my course in London. He was a great poet, what was it that he wrote? 'Do not go gentle into the darkness'. Yes, that's it" said Catherine.

"Not quite," said Thrust, more comfortable now that he was firmly on home ground. He cleared his throat, and launched into a rendition of 'Do not go gentle into that good night' in his best Burton accent.

"Wow, that's fantastic" said Catherine. "You know all the words, what a great poem, and, when you spoke, your voice—it sounded so much like... the famous actor from Wales ... what is his name?" she crinkled her nose.

Thrust smiled smugly, quietly surprised that his Burton

impression had registered with this pretty lively and intelligent Swiss girl.

"Anthony Hopkins—yes—my favourite British actor... apart from Sean Connery. *The Silence of the Lambs*... what a film yes" she said deflating his ego considerably.

"Well, no actually it was Richard Burton" he said, a little huffily. "Both actors come from my home town though—must be something in the water. Anthony, I know him as well—our mothers were in school together (again he was unable to resist embellishing a story). Anthony is a superb actor—one of the worlds greatest, but to me, he is still not as good as Richard Burton. He was the best, the greatest actor Britain has produced, and without doubt the greatest Welshman ever. Brilliant. I could talk about him for hours" said Thrust warming to his favourite topic.

"Yes, I remember him. He died a few years ago. Didn't he die in Switzerland? I recall friends of my fathers talking about him. We live near to the village where he lived" said Catherine. She was beginning to feel that perhaps he was the one she was looking for.

Thrust's heart leapt at this news.

"The local inhabitants thought a lot of him" she continued. "Apparently, even though he was a Hollywood star, he would often go down to the local inn, and talk with them for hours, often leading them in singing, or relating stories or poems to them. He certainly made an impact in the village—Celigny—yes, that's it. Wasn't he buried there, in fact?" she added.

"Yes, apparently so" said Turpin scarcely able to conceal his excitement. "I'd very much like to visit his grave." He stopped at this point. He didn't want to divulge the true nature of his journey to the continent to her. He's thought it might be useful to keep that to himself. You never know, her father might be connected to the police.

"What would you do when you got there?" asked Catherine.

"Oh, walk around. Perhaps put a few flowers on the grave. I certainly would say a poem or even a prayer over the grave. I'd probably say 'Do not go Gentle' or 'Fern Hill', I love the line 'Time held me Green and dying, though I sang in my chains like the sea'." Again Thrust was warming to the subject of the conversation.

"That's beautiful—what does it mean?" she added.

"I don't really know" he said "I studied him in University, and lots of people told me what they think it meant. Personally, I think it means whatever you want it to mean. For me (and he decided to be radical at this point), it doesn't mean anything anyway—I just like the sound of the words, the way they run together, the impression they create. You need not necessarily be concerned with their literal meaning, though some people spend their lives trying to find out. Not that they ever will know exactly what he meant. That's a secret forever. Only Dylan knows that, and he's not telling!"

He realised she was gazing intently into his eyes.

"Lets go for a walk on the deck—it's too noisy and smoky here. I need some fresh air" she said. She was more and more convinced that he would be the one, and anyway, if it wasn't him she would run out of time, before confronting Henri.

"Yeah great. I could do with some fresh air as well" he agreed, all thoughts of nurses now well and truly banished from his mind.

As she led him by the hand towards the exit, he saw that Stan was still smooching with Catherine's friend oblivious to, and in the teeth of, a pounding dance anthem. They seemed an oasis of calm as all around him people danced leapt and snogged like fury. Turpin thought he recognised a few of the nurses from the bus, but by this time he didn't care—they could wait for another day—he'd found a good looking, intelligent girl, who seemed genuinely interested in him, and what he had to say, and he was very happy to find out what was going to happen next.

They got up onto the top deck and saw that the sea was smooth and calm, with a nearly full moon bathing the ferry in it's light. She whispered something French in his ear, and slid her arm around his waist. If this wasn't romantic, he didn't know what was.

They slowly wandered around the deck, which was

deserted. Most of the younger passengers were still dancing the night away, or had passed out, whilst the families on board had long since gone to bed. The evening was beautiful, but the sea breeze had a cold edge to it. In the distance the lights of passing ships glinted in the moonlight.

Eventually they stopped at the front corner railings and stood looking out to sea, arms around each others waists. It was one of those 'shall I make a move now' moments. He turned to face her. She continued to look out to sea. 'No luck' he thought—what shall I do next?

"Do you want to go back downstairs to the disco?" he asked.

"No, it is better here—we can talk more freely, and the evening is so nice. Coming from Switzerland I want to enjoy the sea as much as I can. Are you happy to stay up here?" she replied.

"Oh yes, very much so. It's not often that I'm out at sea on a moonlit night with a beautiful girl. I'm a lucky man." For one of the few times in his life, he actually meant these words.

"No not so, you are a very interesting man. Most men I've met in Britain wouldn't talk poetry to me—it is beautiful. They only seem to want one thing. I am the lucky girl" said Catherine and then kissed him.

The kiss lasted and lasted. It doesn't get much better than this he thought. Well, it can, I suppose, but one step at a time Turpie boy. One step at a time. One step at a time.

The kiss eventually ended. His heart was racing. What to do now? Again, it was one of those awkward moments. He thought he'd try and move the conversation on again.

"We're probably moving on to eastern France" he said, "we may even pop into Switzerland. We may even bump into you on the way—wouldn't that be a coincidence." Secretly he hoped that they would.

"Oh yes—that's quite likely, we're travelling through Dijon, and we'll be staying there at my friends house, her name's Michelle. She's returning from college with us. I'll give you her phone number—if you're going that way, and perhaps we'll meet there. It would be nice to see you and your friend—he seems to be getting on well with Michelle anyway. Have you any other friends travelling with you?" she asked innocently.

"No—only the two of us" he lied as panic started to grip him. The less she knew of Vic and Archie the better he thought. With any luck they'd have fallen overboard or at least been arrested, and then he wouldn't have to explain them away if they met at Dijon. He could be callous when it came to women.

"What about those two strange men on the dance floor. They seemed to know you?" she asked knowingly.

"No, not really, never seen them before. Drunks from the bar—probably jealous that I was with you. Nothing to worry about," he lied.

They kissed again and their embrace got tighter. He began to consider moving from this exposed part of the deck to somewhere more conducive to what he had in mind. He didn't want to take her back to his cabin—it probably held Vic and Archie in a state of utter physical and mental degeneration pouring forth noxious emissions from every orifice. He was not really confident that they'd been arrested or fallen overboard and just couldn't take the risk that they were back in the cabin. Even if they hadn't got back, the stench from the escapades in the shower room / toilet earlier would probably still be hanging around like plague spores. In addition, even if the cabin was free he could find himself interrupted in full flow by those two idiots. Nope—he had to try to play this one away.

"Can we go back to your cabin?" he asked. "It's quicker and… whispering in her ear… warmer there."

"Oh—you Welshmen—you are so cheeky. Just like Tom Jones" she laughed.

"or Dylan Thomas?" he said.

"or what's the name... Richard Burton?" her eyes sparkled mischievously.

"Yes, ok certainly like Mr Burton—he, we, can't help ourselves—it's the effect you beautiful women have on us. It's a national trait. We can't be blamed—it's all your fault!"

They both laughed, and kissed again.

"I'm sorry—I would very much like to be… what did you say… warmer with you, but my other friend is not well, and she was in bed long ago. Much as I'd like to, we can't go back to my cabin. We will just have to stay here" she said "anyway, It's a beautiful night"

She kissed him again in a manner that left him cursing both her ill friend, and the lack of a handy bed.

He looked over and saw that one of the lifeboats had a loose canvas cover. He'd spent many a happy hour as a younger man making love on mountainsides, football fields, in unlocked garages in fact just about anywhere. Why not try a bit more alfresco romance he thought. Always a first time for a lifeboat—variety being the spice of life and all that.

"Catherine, why don't we go into that lifeboat? It's sheltered and private and we can, I'm sure, make it a lot warmer. You said you like the sea, so why don't we get into the lifeboat?" He stared into her eyes.

She laughed. "You are a crazy, crazy man. Get into a lifeboat? What if we're caught?"

"We'll pretend we don't understand a word they say, or that we're illegal immigrants fleeing a repressive British government. I don't know, I'll think of something. Anyway, what can they do? Throw us off? They won't do anything. In any event, we'll be in port soon. No-one will know and I'm sure it's something you won't regret" he pleaded.

"Ok, just a little cuddle" she said. "It's so cold out here and now we are such good friends" her words died as he kissed her again and then led her over to the lifeboat. He undid the rope, peered inside and with a bit of effort scrambled inside.

He could just about make out that there were blankets and lifejackets on the floor which he reasoned would make a splendid mattress. That clinched it. He leant back out of the boat and pulled her up and in.

As she fell in, they rolled over onto the blankets laughing and giggling.

This had to be one of the best nights of his life he concluded. He only needed one more thing to make it complete. Typical Welshman.

Catherine, for her part, had concluded (helped by a considerable amount of alcohol) that she had better do it here and now, and to hell with the inconvenience. She would also suitably embellish the story when she confronted Henri back in

France. Anyway, she quite liked his quaint accent and interest in literature—even if his aftershave smelled like toilet cleaner. She decided to let things happen,

He held her in the darkness, as their mouths met in yet another passionate kiss. The lifeboat was quite warm and welcoming and the blankets soft. He was soon starting to undress her, and as her hands moved to unzip her jeans he felt that everything was going exactly as he wanted it to.

Unlike most women he got into such situations with, he was very attracted to her and, for the first time in ages he actually wanted to stay with the woman he was with, not only for the obvious reason, but to find out more about her and her life. Waves of pleasure flooded over him as their semi naked bodies entwined. He paused savouring the aching anticipation of making love to her in the warm snug darkness. The moment seemed to hang in the air like a crashing wave, when suddenly a voice rang out. He knew the voice well, and his heart sank.

"Quick Archie—in here—the bastards will never find us. Some idiots left the tarpaulin unfastened. If they catch us we'll be thrown overboard or arrested and Turpin's precious trip will be ruined."

Thrust couldn't believe what he was hearing.

A bloated booze belching face thrust into the gap in the lifeboat cover, and with a heave and a strain struggled into the lifeboat, the body dropping in like a new born baby. Seconds later another, slightly less bloated, but equally alcohol ridden face bobbed into view, followed by it's owners body performing an equally ungainly squirming belly flop into the boat.

"Quick—shut the fucking flap—they're not far behind us. Why you had to run bollock naked on top of the captains table was beyond me—it really pissed them off, though the sight of that man's face was priceless I really wish I had a camera. I'd make millions selling it to TV stations" said Vic.

"Shut up and be quiet. Let's hope they don't look in here" said the slightly fainter voice of Archie.

In the darkness Thrust's ardour had diminished quicker than a salted slug. He lay in Catherine's arms raging at his misfortune, but too frightened to say or do anything lest he give his own... interesting predicament away. They just hugged each other, not knowing what to do next.

At that point footsteps hurried past, and it soon became apparent that the pursuers had moved onto another deck of the ship.

In the darkness no-one moved.

"There's a nice smell in here Archie, and I'm sure it's not you" said Vic, "It's a really fragrant perfume. It sounds unbelievable, but, I'm sure there's a woman in here."

"Perhaps it's one of the nurses. They'll do anything. Shag anywhere. Let's have a look" said Archie in a rare burst of decisiveness.

After a few fumbles, Archie lit his cigarette lighter and illuminated Thrust and Catherine in a naked embrace staring directly at him in a tableaux of embarrassment. Catherine's face was a frozen mask of uncomprehending amazement tinged with shock and disbelief.

Thrust's face, however, revealed a mixture of hatred, shame, loathing and discomfort, overladen with devastating, grinding dismay. What would have been his finest moment had now been consigned to the deepest pit of despair. Of all the lifeboats in all the ships, in all the world, they had to leap into mine he thought. Bastards! He'd castrate them with a rusty comb and feed their gonads to pirhanas. The drunken good for nothing sheep shagging wasters. He could not believe it—one minute—on the brink of paradise, the next he was being leered at by the biggest lunatics on the Western hemisphere. He could not credit or comprehend it. He let vent his fury in a manic outburst of pent up frustration.

"You dog buggering piss gargling rat raping fart breathed pair of shit encrusted wankers—what the fuck are you doing in this lifeboat" hissed Turpin.

"Oy—who are you calling fart breath" snapped Archie, in a rare moment of self possessed ironic wit. "Anyway, what are you doing here?"

"Fucking hell—it's you! I, we, didn't realise" said Vic in amazement.

"Look—we were on the run—those bloody stewards, things got out of hand—we were chased off the dancefloor, and forced to run up deck by deck until we burst into a room full of these posh people, some in uniforms which we presumed was the captain's dining room. We thought ... well we're in enough trouble as it is, a bit more won't do any harm" said Vic.

"Trouble" said Archie, continuing the story. "What we did, resulted in a lot more harm—the captain went ape shit. I really thought we'd be killed. We were lucky to escape with our lives! The only way out was through an emergency door, we found ourselves on the outside deck and we just ran for it. The lifeboat seemed a good idea" said Archie.

"Not for me" said Thrust ruefully.

"How the hell were we to know you were in here shaggin' some bird! We're not clairvoyant! Sorry Miss!" said Vic, looking at Catherine.

"Turpin—who are these men?" said Catherine in truly justifiable outrage.

"Oh don't ask. I don't really know them" said Thrust, still boiling with anger.

"You lying git" said Archie—"he's from the same place as us. We're all on holiday together—going to Switzerland to steal Rich ..."

"All right—shut it Archie will you. Enough said," interjected Turpin. He realised it was true confession time.

"Sorry Catherine, I do know them. They are my friends, but I was embarrassed by them on the dance floor—they were, I mean are, really drunk. I'm very very sorry" said Thrust with genuine sincerity.

Catherine was not impressed.

"Turpin, can we go now, I'm cold and I don't want to be here anymore" said Catherine ignoring Vic and Archie's penetrative stares.

Turpin realised they were both totally undressed and that his dreams of poetry and passion had come to nothing.

Suddenly he concluded that if he hadn't been so cold, humiliated and embarrassed he would have laughed out loud, as the scene in the lifeboat, was surely one of the most bizarre and funniest he could conceive of. So much for his perfect night of passion. Should have kept to the nurses, he thought, though to be fair, none of this was Catherine's fault—in fact as he began to smile inwardly, he reasoned that it was really no-one's fault, just the way things were sometimes. C'est la vie, as Catherine may have said.

However, she was right, he'd have to take her home. He looked over in the gloom. Vic and Archie were crouched in the corner still listening for footsteps on the deck. Apart from the wind and the gulls, it was silent outside. Nevertheless their eyes were still fixed firmly on Catherine.

He snapped into action. "Right, we're going—and I don't want you two following us. Stay here all night. For God's sake, don't go back to the room—you might disturb Stan" said Thrust with frightening assertiveness. Thrust and Catherine then started to dress.

"Has he copped one then?" said Archie breaking the enveloping silence.

"None of your bloody business. Remember there's a lady present. Just keep quiet and God willing I'll see you in the morning" said Thrust. "Nos Fucking Dda"!!

Vic and Archie stayed mute.

"Come on Catherine. Let's go" said Thrust.

They lowered themselves from the lifeboat and re-arranged their clothes. They then walked in silence back to the cabin.

As they walked along the deck, two crew men came up to them and asked if they'd seen two semi naked men running around. Thrust replied that it was all quiet back there, and that they'd seen nothing. Much as he was angry with Vic and Archie he couldn't let anything happen to them.

Outside Catherine's cabin they stopped and he uttered a hesitant 'Goodnight'.

"Goodnight Turpin, I'm sorry about what happened" said Catherine a tear welling in her eye.

"You're sorry! I'm really really sorry. If I had a gun I'd shoot them. I may even shoot myself. I can't explain what happened. I feel so bad." Thrust also felt like crying.

"Lets go to sleep. Perhaps we will meet in the morning. Here—take my friend Michelle's address and telephone number. We'll be staying there for a few days. Perhaps we can meet again." She looked lovingly into his eyes. You are a really nice man. Remember some more of your poetry. Next time you see me, tell it to me in an Anthony Hopkins' voice" said Catherine.

"Ok, I will, but it will have to be Richard Burton or nothing" he said. Thrust cheered up a bit.

"All right. Good night mon cherie Richard!" said Catherine.

They laughed and kissed goodnight. As he trudged back to his room he thought that perhaps it hadn't been such a bad night after all.

CHAPTER FOURTEEN

'Strangling the Bishop'

Their van trundled off the ferry and they headed into France.

"What a fucking night. One of the best I've ever had" said Stan. "Michelle, she loves me. What a girl. Given me her number in Dijon. Said we'd meet up tonight. Got to do it."

"You would say that—copped off with that French girl you jammy bastard" said Vic, with scarcely contained envy.

"Yeah you even took her back to the cabin. We spent all night on those poxy seats. What a friend. I am absolutely knackered" said Archie.

"So you should be—serves you right for ruining my night" said Thrust. "First you get bollock drunk and dance around me and Catherine like one of Dominic John's fag hags, then you get chased off by the bouncers only to climb into the only lifeboat on the ferry where I am just about to make love to a beautiful Swiss girl. Why didn't you hide in the poop deck or the bilge or where the fuck ever, anywhere on the ferry apart from my bloody lifeboat. You ruined what should have been one of the best nights of my life. I can't believe you two exist. I even had to spend the rest of the bloody night sharing those sodding seats with you and listen to you farting, belching and giggling yourselves sober. Talk about from the sublime to the ridiculous." He stared out of the window at the passing dockyard in righteous indignation.

"Sorry Turp. We didn't know you'd be in a lifeboat with a Swiss girl—it's not exactly, what's the word ... foreseeable" said Vic with a mischievous grin.

"Yeah—we didn't search every boat on the ferry to see if you were poised to shag in it. We were fleeing for our lives. Just one of those things. Very funny though. I wish I'd had a camera" said Archie.

"Yeah—with a zoom lens on it in order to photograph his dick—I tell you Stan, it shrank like a marshmallow in a microwave, when we got in. Priceless. You should have seen the look on his face. I'll dine out on this story for years" said Vic starting to laugh.

Turpin didn't share in the hilarity.

"You didn't see anything—nothing happened—Catherine's a nice girl—though if she hadn't been—I'd never have found out because of you! Though I'm sure you will spin a fine tale. Anyway, at least I got somewhere. You two didn't get a sniff of anything. Not even with a busload of nurses on board" said Thrust. "You are just a pair of fucking wankers." He continued to stare out at the dockyard.

"What's wrong with wanking?" said Vic in his usual contrary mood, still chuckling at his recollection of the night before.

"Well—that's all your fit for" said Thrust.

Vic as usual, was up for an argument. "I've had me moments with women but in all honesty I'm quite happy wanking. In fact I'm proud to be a wanker. To be honest, everybody does it—it's just that I'm more open about it" said Vic, confrontationally.

"Look, it can't be natural. We're on this earth to pro-create, and wanking doesn't help the process. In fact if everyone confined themselves to wanking, then the human race would die out. It's fucking obvious. All wankers are evolutionary dead ends" said Thrust, determined to have an argument, preferably with Vic.

"Not necessarily—you could have test tube babies" said Archie, joining in the debate.

"Who's a pedantic little tosser then" said Thrust with inadvertent irony, sensing that Vic and Archie were conspiring to wind him up.

"Anyway, it would certainly hit the birth rate. In any event you can't seriously compare wanking to shagging a woman" said Thrust, ascending to the moral high ground that he felt his dalliance with Catherine the night before had given him.

"Well, depends on the woman" said Vic. "Compared to some of the dogs I've seen you with—I'd rather wank till my knob fell off. Look at the 'Last Chance'. I wouldn't put my dick even if it was tied to the end of the Eiffel Tower, anywhere near her. Apart from the obvious danger to my health, it would rattle around like a stick of rock in the Mersey tunnel and would probably be seized as a hostage by the gangs of unfortunate men who've fallen into her twat and never got out. Compared to shagging her, wanking has got to be the only sensible choice."

"He's got a point Turp. No-one could do what you did unless they were desperate or impervious to pain, disease and shame with an iron constitution thrown in. If I had the choice, I'd side with Vic. I'd prefer to wank rather than shag the 'Last Chance'. You can't argue with that" said Archie.

"And what's more, there are worse than her ... remember that woman from Llanelli that shagged Archie? She was terrible" said Vic.

Vic sensed that he and Archie had Turpin in on the ropes.

Vic and Archie looked at each other and made the sign of the cross, before collapsing into fits of laughter.

"Some things are better not spoken about" said Archie.

"Yeah, fair point" said Stan, deciding to join the debate. "but if you've got a normal girl, certainly a cracker like Michelle last night, then you can't compare wanking to that. It's like comparing lemonade to champagne, or a Reliant Robin to a Jaguar or whatever. There's no real comparison. It's got to be a woman."

"Well, depends" said Vic in full debating mode. "You can have a wank when you want. You do it your way. You haven't got to talk after, or hug anyone, or tell them you love them or take them to dinner beforehand and listen to what they think of last weeks episode of *Coronation Street*. You don't get nagged, or have kids to eat you out of house and home, you don't end up with a mother in law, or be made to go shopping in B&Q on a Sunday bloody morning when you've got a million better things to do. As far as I'm concerned, I think wanking's got a lot to be said for it. In fact, I'm proud to be a wanker" said Vic with a flourish.

"You are a wanker for saying that" said Thrust launching a counterattack. "In fact. It's a pathetic, solitary, sad waste of time. You'll end up a wanked out, washed up lonely old man, with a loft full of porn mags and nobody to say you've spent your life with. There's more to women, even, perish the thought, the 'Last Chance', than just shagging. They're great. Catherine, the Swiss girl—last night—she was fantastic company. We talked and talked about everything—music, poetry, history—you can't discuss those with your nob. You're just screwed up, or not, as the case may be. Just give up wanking and concentrate on meeting some more girls. If you keep on the way you are going you'll be a jibbering drained husk by the time you're 40 with pebble glasses and calloused hands. You really need help big time."

"Rubbish" replied Vic, refusing to give in. "I've read that wanking is actually good for you. It increases your heart rate, blood flow, muscular co-ordination and releases positive endorphins into your system to make you feel good. There's no harm to your body as a result of wanking. In fact, its medically proven that it is positively good for you. It's a scientific fact."

"Good for you? I've heard it all now. If we listen to you, you'll tell us that they'll make wanking an Olympic sport next. Good for you my arse. You really do need some serious help" said Thrust. Surely Vic would give up the argument now he thought.

"Well now you mention it, I've given that suggestion some considerable thought in the past, and I'm seriously thinking of organising a wanking Olympics or at least a tournament. There's a lot to be said for it" said Vic, digging into his reserves of ingenuity and lateral thinking.

"Wanking Olympics?" replied Thrust incredulously. "You really are mad. What on earth did you drink last night? Whatever it was it's still affecting you. You really do need help" said Thrust, amazed at Vic's thought processes.

"It's not so daft" said Vic. "Think about it. The Olympics are about the pursuit of human physical excellence. Wanking is definitely a physical activity. I'm convinced you can get excellent at it, and indeed can compete in getting excellent at it, therefore, it could be an Olympic Sport." His logic was hard to fault.

"Look," he said, warming to the theme, "they have synchronised swimming and shooting as Olympic sports, and there's definitely more effort in wanking than shooting—take it from me. There certainly could be skill involved. I've seen all sorts of sports on TV—bog snorkelling, worm charming ... I've even seen competitive pint drinking, pip spitting, fart lighting. You name it—I've seen people compete for it," Vic was on a roll now, "so why not wanking?"

He continued with his oration. The rest of the van was silent.

"Look, TV is crying out for celebrities—they even just train cameras on people who live in houses and call it entertainment. For fuck's sake, they need celebrities. It's the oxygen of the media. So, instead of making celebrities out of people who are bad at things, or who do boring things like playing chess or just live in houses, why not make celebrities out of wankers? It's a fact that everyone does it and therefore can relate to it—I think it would catch on in a big way. Anyway—they do have sex Olympics—longest shag, best lesbian duo etc., I've seen it on Cable TV. I'm convinced we could do the same for wanking." Vic leaned back with an affirmatary nod of satisfaction.

"You mean competitive wanking? You must be mad! It would only have one event anyway—so how could you build an Olympics around it?" said Stan, interested in where Vic's argument was going to end.

"Easy. I've thought of dozens of events" said Vic who'd obviously given the topic considerable thought.

"Such as?" said Thrust.

Vic leant forward and explained his vision in more depth.

"Well, firstly, the obvious one—fastest wank from a slack start. The 100 metres of wanking world. You could have the event aided or unaided, by that I mean porn mags or whatever. Could be interesting in terms of the sheer potential variety of the event. The sprint wank could cater for all sorts of bizarre tastes. Human ingenuity knows no bounds."

"I can't believe this" said Thrust, beginning to feel genuinely appalled.

"Yeah. Fastest wank—no problem. I bet there's some

really fast wankers around. But you could easily expand on this" said Archie warming to the theme.

"Ha ha—no pun intended" said Thrust.

"Well for example, you could have the marathon—longest erection followed by an ejaculation" said Archie. "Could go on for hours."

"Days even" said Stan.

"Not if the 'Last Chance' was around" said Archie.

"You'd need adjudicators" said Vic, injecting a note of realism.

"Obviously" said Thrust, irritated by the reference to the 'Last Chance'.

"You could also compete in terms of length of ejaculation" said Vic, ignoring the scowl on Turpin's face.

"Like a shot put or javelin" said Stan.

"Exactly" said Vic. "Though it would have to be in a fairly straight line, otherwise you'd upset the crowd."

"You could go for weight of emission" said Thrust, re-engaging with the conversation.

"Another alternative would be weight held up by an erect penis. Will Dong could enter that. Remember those haggis in Edinburgh?" said Vic.

"Yeah" they all spoke as one, united in a mixture of admiration and disgust.

"Thinking about it, you could also have relay teams" said Archie.

"Wouldn't like to be in that one, too gay for my liking" said Vic.

"Fair enough. However, you could also have events measuring accuracy in shooting the height of discharge emitted, sperm count—all sorts" said Archie furrowing his brow at the scientific turn the conversation was taking.

"Another thing, you could bet on most of these events" said Stan ever mindful of commercial potential.

"Ladbrooks would probably give it a go" said Thrust.

"Who'd compile the form book" said Vic mischievously.

"You could sell the TV rights. Get sponsorship," said Turpin, equally alert to the media angle.

"Who from?" said Stan.

"Kleenex obviously, any of the big porn mags, *Men Only*, *Playboy*, but also any range of lubricant jelly, or even thinking about it, weightlifters gypsum" said Vic.

"You could also get underwater wanking," said Stan, "or even extreme wanking—on top of Everest, or sky diving, or wanking in a shark cage" he went on, with a grim glint in his eye.

"Wouldn't be my cup of tea though" said Vic ever the coward.

"The list is endless" said Thrust in genuine amazement.

"What event would you go for Vic?" said Stan.

"That's interesting" said Vic, "probably the sprint. 4 seconds flat no problem but I'd have to banish all thoughts of the 'Last Chance' from my mind to do that. I'd also choose to do it to music. In fact that could be a separate category, probably where, just like ice skating, you'd get marks for matching it to the song or music, and be given more marks for expression, artistic content etc., just like Torvill and Dean."

"What would be the music?" asked Stan.

"I've got two favourites. Ace of Spades by Motorhead or The Phantom of the Opera, the fast bit by Iron Maiden. I've got it all worked out. I reckon I'd soon be a media celebrity—opening supermarkets, be giving interviews on local radio, endorsing products. It's my destiny I know it" said Vic looking determinedly out of the window at the French countryside speeding past.

"Get a life" said Turpin, bringing the conversation back to reality. "You'd be a freak. You'd not only be laughed at, you'd be shunned and probably committed to an institution. Society just isn't ready to accept wanking, let alone make celebrities out of wankers."

"I thought that being a wanker was an essential prerequisite for being a celebrity" said Vic.

"You're right there" said Stan. He had a deep loathing of most 'celebrities'.

The van went quiet.

"What a stupid conversation" said Stan, "grown men talking about wanking."

"We should forget about talking about crap like that, and concentrate on having a good night tonight" said Archie in a rare moment of purposeful common sense.

"There'll be plenty of beautiful girls in Dijon, and as we already know a few we'll be sitting pretty for a good time. Even you two dithering wews (a wew was Port Talbot for an utterly ineffectual dithering weak willed creep) should be able to sort yourselves out" said Thrust.

"We can't speak French" said Vic.

"You can't speak English properly" said Stan.

"Don't worry, most of Catherine's friends have studied in the UK so you'll be able to have a nice conversation about all sorts of topics — though I think you'd better avoid talking about wanking. I know the French are broad minded, but I don't think your average French girl would be particularly impressed by that mound of bison crap you were going on about just then. Try to impress them — and I don't mean tell them you can have 6 wanks in a row on a Sunday morning. Tell then you've done something useful or interesting" said Thrust, sounding like a wise uncle.

"But I haven't" said Vic, with more than a hint of truth.

"Fuck that — make something up. Tell them you're a rugby star, or a musician — they'll like that" said Stan, ever the pragmatist.

"What if they ask us to play something" said Archie.

"Look, they're not likely to whip out a guitar in a nightclub and say … play me 'All along the watch tower' mon cher. Look, just talk a good game, be friendly, buy them a few drinks, don't get too pissed and before you can say 'Ally oop', you'll be cementing Anglo-French relations in a meaningful way" said Stan, drawing upon his experiences of the night before.

"Or if you don't," interjected Turpin, "you won't at least be pissing on me and Stan's chips — metaphorically speaking of course — in other words, either get into some women yourselves or leave us alone to do what's natural with some nice girls. Once you're out of the pub or whatever you can wank your knob's into a bleeding pulp or feed them to the swans in the river — I don't care but just leave us alone" said Thrust ruefully recalling the previous night's experience.

"Touchy eh! I bet she won't look at you twice after last night—you really did look stupid. I still wish I'd had a camera" said Archie grinning like a naughty school boy.

"All right. Let's wrap it up—we've got a lot of driving to do before we get to Dijon and this conversation is going nowhere" said Stan.

"Ok, name the best Welsh left footed rugby team" said Archie.

"Mmmm that's an awkward one. Definitely Ray Giles at scrum half" said Vic recognising a difficult topic when confronted by one.

"Bollocks—how can you pick a left footed team? How on earth will we ever know if a prop or number 8 is bloody left footed? You might as well ask for a Welsh best manicured toenails team, or the devoted to their pets fifteen, or most extreme religious persuasions. There's no point in the bloody category. Think of something sensible for God's sake." Thrust was getting irritated by Vic's and Archie's predictable descent into childish madness.

"What about a nastiest stare XV" said Archie.

"Got to be Paul Ringer at number seven" said Vic.

"How do you know he didn't live in a bungalow" said Turpin, exploring the pun.

"Ha bloody ha—thank you Oscar Wilde" said Archie.

The usual teams were trotted out, as town after town sped past. Then suddenly a cry went up.

"I don't believe it! Look what's coming up behind us.

They turned and looked in disbelief. "The busload of nurses" said Stan, staring into the mirror in awe and trepidation.

The three others threw themselves to the back window and saw the familiar bus with the by now legendary sign pulling to over take them.

Several pieces of torn cloth hung from the bus' aerial, which on closer inspection revealed themselves to be men's underpants. A huge rubber dildo was also projecting from a hole in the front radiator grill, and a number of badly drawn penises, in gates of 5, well into double figures, had been painted along the top of the windscreen. The driver appeared to be in a catatonic state of exhausted nervousness as he stared vacantly ahead of him.

The bus pulled past revealing yet again numerous women in states of undress, many whom were dancing in the aisle of the bus, swigging from wine or Champagne bottles. A number appeared to be in varying degrees of sexual congress with a select number of what were probably the pick of the doctors' coach that they had bumped into on the ferry.

As the bus pulled past, bottles and stray pieces of underwear and clothing were being randomly discharged from the sky vents of the bus. Stan had to swerve to avoid a basque that came spinning towards the windscreen of the minivan.

"What I'd give to be on there" said Thrust ruefully.

"It makes the 'Good Ship Venus' look like the *Mayflower*" said Vic.

"It must be heaven on earth. Why didn't we try harder to meet some of those nurses last night" said Archie.

"You had your chance" said Turpin, "you shouldn't have got so bloody drunk!"

"I don't know about heaven on earth... look at that boys" said Stan with a look of horror on his face.

The bus had by now fully overtaken them, revealing a large number of nurses congregating on the back seat, surrounding what appeared to be a naked man with his face pressed hard against the window.

By the laughing, grinning faces of the women, and the distorted agonised face of the man, it was obvious that this was some sort of group sado masochist session, where there were a large number of active sadists, namely the nurses, venting revenge for thousands of years of male misogyny upon a solitary masochist, the unfortunate man.

The man's face boiled in agony like a kaleidoscope of Picasso paintings. One eyeball appeared to be circling in the opposite direction to the other, a feat that to Thrust's mind defied the laws of physiology whilst his mouth rippled like a feeding mussell. On the other hand, he thought, laughing to himself, if anyone knew how to defy the laws of physiology, it ought to be the nurses.

In any event they seemed to have not only found, but also

pushed back, both the limits of scientific knowledge and human particularly male, endurance. The glint of metal somewhere to the rear of the man's head sent a shudder down Thrust's spine. You certainly wouldn't want to get on the wrong side, literally and metaphorically, of those nurses he thought, with some justification. He wondered what the poor man had done. Perhaps it was better that they hadn't met up with the nurses after all. Having said that, the rest of the bus seemed to be having fun, and whatever the man had done, on further consideration, Thrust felt sure that he richly deserved the ignominies being vested upon him.

"They've got to be going to the same place as us. It's fate. We're bound to meet up with them" said Vic with growing optimism.

"Yeah, it's getting quite late now, and I think the next big Town is probably Dijon. We've got a chance now" said Archie.

"I don't know about you two, but me and Stan are sorted. You two can do what you like" said Thrust with an air of righteous smugness.

The busload of nurses slowly pulled away into the distance. 'I wonder what will happen in Dijon?' thought Thrust. Whatever it was, they'd soon find out.

CHAPTER FIFTEEN

'Jive Talking'

They booked into a seedy downmarket hotel in the middle of the city. This time they had the dubious luxury of two bedrooms to share. It was agreed that Stan would room with Thrust, whilst Vic and Archie would share the other room.

Stan phoned Michelle and, as luck would have it, she was at home. They arranged to all meet up later at a local bar. Stan told Thrust that Catherine was indeed staying with Michelle and that she'd be out that night as well. They would also be meeting some of the girls' local friends, and, if all went to plan they would have a few drinks, then go on to one of the bigger disco nightclubs in Dijon.

"Not another fucking disco. The one on the boat was bad enough, especially with those two idiots around" said Thrust irritably. "The bloody noise on that ferry—it was a living hell! —can't stand fucking bloody discos."

"You didn't do so bad did you?" said Stan. "Noise or no noise. What's more, you didn't seem to let Vic and Archie stop you either, well at least until the unfortunate incident in the lifeboat." He paused for effect. "Anyway, we're not at sea now are we, so you can whisk Catherine off to wherever you like this evening, and there'll be no bloody Welsh idiots, to spoil your fun. If it all works out the way I plan it, me and Michelle will go back to her place. Her parents are on holiday and we'll be free to do what we like. I'm sure there'll be plenty of bedrooms, so if you and Catherine feel like coming back, you'll have somewhere to, eh, renew your acquaintance, if you know what I mean." Stan gave an exaggerated wink to Turpin and started whistling.

"That's very kind of you Stan boy. I did think of bringing her back here, but it's a bit of a dump, and anyway, sneaking girls into hotel rooms can be a risky business," said Thrust.

"Yeah, remember those girls we met in Dublin on the Irish trip. Had to dress them up in our overcoats and rugby scarves to get them back to the room—like something out of *Mission Impossible*" said Stan with a chuckle.

"Thinking back, my knob would have self destructed if we hadn't got them into the room" said Thrust.

"Worked out alright in the end didn't it?" said Stan, "though listening to you having sex is a sound seared into my memory forever. You started off like a geriatric marathon runner, before switching to a passable imitation of a Japanese guard bayoneting someone in an out-take from the *Bridge over the River Kwai*, and you ended up sounding like Pavarotti having an enema. Casting my mind back to that famous evening, were you really trying to sing Nessun Dorma? It certainly sounded like it."

"Piss off, I just gave my all." Turpin reflected on one of his happier experiences. "She was a lovely girl, Siobhan. I still think of her now." Thrust was momentarily transported to a dodgy hotel north of the river Liffey.

"She's probably in a sanatorium after that experience Turpie boy. Apart from the noises you made, the sound of your belly flapping against hers was like someone hitting a wall of lard with a banjo. I just thank God the lights were off. Without that, the sight would have been terrible" said Stan winding Thrust up with vigour.

"Thank you Brad Pitt. I'm sure your girl was transported into ecstasy by your sterling efforts. How long did it last? My watch didn't do nano-seconds" countered Thrust with a wry sarcastic grin.

"All right. All right. Leave it there" said Stan, realising he was not occupying defensible territory. "I was just a bit, well, you know, excited. Anyway that was then, this is now. Let's get freshened up, give those two lunatics a shout, then get down to this bar they want us to go to, the Café Blue I think it's called, as soon as we can. I've got a feeling this is going to be a special night. May even stay here for a few days and let you modern day Burke and Hares get the bloody coffin yourselves" said Stan.

"Eh, come on—a deal's a deal," Turpin suddenly got serious. "You can always see Michelle on the way back, or come over for a special holiday. Don't back out on me now. Anyway, remember your country needs you. What's more, this is bigger than any of us, and will be our passport to fame, riches and will guarantee everlasting rugby success against England. And another thing, once we've turned Port Talbot into the entertainment metropolis we know it can and will be, with ourselves as it's very own Welsh Bugsy Segal's, we'll be ..."

"Who?" said Stan.

"The man who created Las Vagas stupid!" said Thrust. "Anyway it doesn't matter. With us as the main men, we can have any women we like, or, if you still persist in this romantic escapade with Michelle, you can fly her over and install her in a luxury mansion, or even live over here. It all makes sense, I've been through it with you in great detail, but you've got to help me see it through. Agreed?" Thrust felt he had made his point as forcibly as he could.

"Ok, ok, I'm sorry I said anything. I couldn't let you down. I'd never have a moments peace, but before we move on and dig up your hero, we've got a great night to complete, so let's give it our best shot. Right Turpie boy?" said Stan punching Thrust on the arm.

"Right, up guards and at 'em" said Thrust, trying not to wince, but glad that Stan was still going along with the scheme.

They left the hotel, knocked Vic's and Archie's door, and told them they were going to Café Blue, and then walked a few blocks to a typical trendy French café bar. It looked impressive. They went in, and grabbed a seat in the corner and were eventually served some beer by a waiter. A while later they were joined by Vic and Archie who, as usual, had been slow in getting ready.

They all sat quietly in the corner of the Café Blue and sipped on their lager. The bar was beginning to fill up with lots of young happy good looking French people, and this preyed on Vic's ingrained insecurities.

179

"Fancy Dan, frog poofs, poncing around in their trendy clothes and slick haircuts. Can't stand 'em. Why are they here anyway?" said Vic, his scarcely suppressed xenophobia bursting through his veneer of tolerance.

"Possibly because it's France" said Turpin, with a mild sneer, "and in any event they are entitled to have a good time like anyone else. Anyway just because someone is well dressed, looks after themselves and takes care of their appearance, doesn't mean they're poofs. In fact I'd say the opposite. Just look at those two" said Thrust laughing, referring to a young couple kissing passionately at the bar. The atmosphere in the café bar was relaxed, and was a marked contrast to the air of tension and macho posturing that hung around most bars or pubs in their home town.

"Balls, they're all nancy boys. They'd run a mile in the Penderyn. The French just don't have it when the chips are down. We British always give them a hammering—look at Agincourt" said Vic, returning to his favourite jingoistic theme.

"Fair point, but we won the battle, who won the war?" said Thrust, who had a pretty sound grasp of history.

"We did. Hammered them" said Vic, with an assertive bang of his fist on the table, that alarmed the couple on the next table.

"Not quite, if you recall the battle was part of the Hundred Years War—the French won that hands down. They kicked the British, or the English or whatever you want to call them, out of France for good. How did they do that if they were all poofs? And anyway, If they were such a pushover, why did we lose, and why did it last a fucking 100 years? Answers on a postcard please" said Thrust.

"Cos we were all knackered, it was a hundred years fucking war—stands to reason. We got fed up with hanging around and let them win. Obvious, except they won't say that in the history books" said Vic who hated losing any argument.

"Anyway, what about Waterloo?" said Archie weighing in, as usual on Vic's side.

"Well, you could say we only beat them because the Prussians arrived at the last moment and swung the battle 'our' way. Look it up good boy." Thrust was beginning to get on his historical high horse.

180

"I heard we only won because Napoleon had piles" said Stan, who had decided to lower the tone of the conversation.

"How did his piles stop them from fighting? Contagious were they? In the middle of a charge the entire French guards threw down their guns due to an infestation of Knobbies up their arses? What a load of crap" said Vic, steadfastly refusing to give the French, or any foreigners for that matter, any credit.

"It's true—he had an attack of piles. Napoleon had an attack of piles. Piles piles piles," Stan started to bang the table to emphasise the point he was making and they started to argue with gusto. A full scale punch up threatened to break out between the four of them over the role of Napoleon's arse in European history. A more bizarre argument would be difficult to envisage.

Suddenly a French voice interrupted their row.

"Excuse me, Turpin, Stan, Vic and Archie, these are Alain, Roland Veronique and Sophie my friends. You have all already met Catherine n'est pas?" said Michelle.

Catherine blushed slightly as she nodded to Vic and Archie, remembering the last time they'd met. The four lads stopped arguing and looked up at the group of slightly puzzled faced surrounding them. It was obvious they understood enough English to be aware that they had interrupted a raging discussion on piles. They were less clear as to what it had to do with Napoleon, battles or European history. Perhaps most pertinently of all the new arrivals wondered why these strange men were talking about such things on a weekend evening, when most of the young people around them were enjoying themselves.

"Ahh Catherine, delighted to see you. It's good to see you've brought some friends for us" said Stan suddenly losing all interest in Napoleon's piles. He decided to bullshit his way out of a potentially awkward situation.

"We were just having a quiet chat about the need to have piles of armaments and stores if you are to be successful in war. We often talk about military tactics in Wales—tonight it was the Napoleonic Wars. Tomorrow we could well be talking about Vietnam or the American War of Independence. We do it all the time." Stan's unconvincing smile failed to divert the

French students from feeling deep down that they were meeting some very odd individuals. The look that the three other Welsh boys gave Stan told him that they felt he'd be better just to continue talking about Napoleon's piles rather than tell such a pathetic blatant lie. However, they recognised that his infatuation with Michelle prevented any such candour on his part. They also knew he was a compulsive liar. Stan continued to smile unconvincingly.

The boys got up and were slightly taken about when the French group proceeded to parade around them with the males shaking hands with each of the Welshmen, and with the girls kissing them on each cheek. It took a fair amount of time but the consensus later was that it was refreshingly pleasant, and far better than the volley of 'alright but' and 'hiyas' that marked introductions back home.

The circle of chair's was widened and another French man appeared carrying a tray full of wine bottles and glasses.

"Bonjour, ca va. My name is Henri. Very pleased to meet you. Catherine has been telling us all about you and the great fun you had last night on the cross channel ferry. It sounded crazy" said the obviously well educated, good looking Frenchman.

Thrust glanced at Catherine. He couldn't tell from her face what she had told him or them—had she revealed about what happened in the lifeboat? Who was he anyway? Was he her boyfriend? Turpin was confused and disturbed by Henri's arrival.

"Catherine tells me that you, Turpin, are a lover of poetry and drama, and that you like the great Dylan Thomas. He is one of my favourite poets. What's the line 'Do not go gentle into that good night', yes that's it. He is brilliant. Although, as I'm sure you'll agree, we have some great French poets you know—do you like Rimbaud?" said Henri with an open grin.

"What the fuck 'as Sylvester Stallone got to do with poetry, or France?" whispered Vic to Archie.

"I don't know, perhaps Sly has got hidden depths, or maybe he made a big impression during *Escape to Victory*—wasn't that made in France?" said Archie shrugging his shoulders. He didn't know what the hell Henri was on about.

"Very good—yes excellent. In fact, I think Dylan Thomas described himself as the Rimbaud of Cwmdonkin Drive" said Thrust authoritatively. "I like poets of whatever nationality, though naturally I think our Welsh poets are among the best. I think it also helps you understand the poem if you share the poet's culture. Don't you agree?" He was adopting the tones and mannerisms of one of his University tutors. It was designed to convey intellectual superiority and indifference in equal measures.

"Yes indeed, though Dylan Thomas didn't speak Welsh did he?" countered Henri, totally unfazed, displaying a considerable degree of knowledge concerning Swansea's most famous son.

"That's correct, but he's still a great poet" said Thrust, a little on the back foot at Henri's demonstration of literary knowledge.

"Do you speak Welsh?" asked Henri, moving on to the attack.

"No, sadly not." Turpin was rattled, and realised that Henri had a hidden agenda. "It tends to be spoken in the West and North of Wales. The industrial South is mostly English speaking, though we're all very proud of being Welsh, as was Dylan Thomas." Thrust felt he was being probed, but couldn't tell whether it was out of hostility, curiosity, or merely in reaction to Thrust's own contrived posturing.

'It's unfortunate that you can't speak Welsh, perhaps you could learn? Most of us here have learned to speak English—it can't be hard, the language of your own country?" said Henri, beginning to push home the advantage.

"He can't speak English properly—especially after drink. In fact, if he drinks much more of this wine, and he won't be able to speak at all" joked Stan, sensing the edge between Turpin and Henri.

"Oh, you must not get too drunk. The night is young, and we will take you to our favourite nightclub later. LeZone, it is the best place in Dijon—it plays great music. House, garage, Techno, you'll love it, and there are plenty of beautiful French girls there as well. I've heard how good at dancing Vic and Archie are. They will have plenty of opportunity tonight

—but no ice tongs eh!" said Michelle with a mischievous giggle.

They all laughed out of politeness, though slightly uneasily for those whose collective memory of the previous night's events came back to haunt them.

"What kind of music do you like?" asked Alain to Thrust.

"Oh, rock, blues, bit of dance music, early progressive rock. A fairly wide range I suppose. I also play the guitar—I like all sorts of music" said Turpin, almost apologetically.

"Yeah, a wide range of crap music. Most of it's crap. In fact you could say he likes lots and lots of crap" slurred Vic who had by now nearly finished a bottle of wine himself.

"Yeah, he listens to crap, plays crap and talks crap. In fact you could say he is a crap artist." Archie fell back, giggling to himself over his fairly insipid pun.

"Yeah—the king of crap" said Vic.

"Of course I like crap, and obviously I talk crap—don't we all?" said Thrust flashing his most sarcastic smile.

Unfortunately Alain, who was struggling to follow Archie's strong Welsh accent misheard him and, not having come across the word crap in his traditional University English class, assumed he was referring to the music genre beloved of the local nightclub.

"Alors—you are also a rap artist Turpin! That is wonderful. LeZone is the premier venue for rapping in this part of France. Rappers from all around the world come to compete in competitions. There are big prizes—lots of money, and the girls go absolutely crazy for those guys. It is amazing. We will tell the owner, you should enter the competition" said Alain.

"Yes, there's one every Saturday night. Isn't that right Henri?" said Michelle.

"Mais oui."

Thrust failed to understand what was said next as Henri and Alain spoke French together for a while.

"You must do this rap act tonight" said Henri feigning admiration. "It will be a great honour for you, for your friends…, for Wales. Yes, you must enter the competition" said Henri with a look of earnest wonderment.

"Of course he will" said Stan slapping Thrust on the back,

sensing a wind up. "It's second nature to him—he is able to rap in his sleep. Even on the toilet." He winked at the other Welsh boys.

Vic, who was by now well into his second bottle, doubled up at this suggestion and hugged himself repeatedly saying 'He raps on the toilet', between giggling fits.

"Yes Turpin—your friends are overjoyed at the chance you've got. You must do this. You will be great" said Henri, obviously warming to the idea, and sensing Turpin's obvious discomfort.

Thrust looked around him nervously. He realised he was too far in to back out. The bloody wine had loosened his mouth, and he realised that rather than back down in front of Henri, he would have to see it through. He pulled himself together. No problem—there'll only be a few people there. He'd wait until last, then get up, pretend to fall, pull out the mike and put an end to the contest by standing on it or something radical like that. He knew he'd cope. Anyway, in the meantime he could bask in the glory of his bogus 'rapping career' and make some serious headway with Catherine. Simple he thought, couldn't be better.

He had a feeling that Henri knew that he was bullshitting, but decided to tough it out—he'd get out of it relatively easily, and possibly have a laugh on the way.

"Yeah sure" said Thrust, "we poets can turn our verbal dexterity to anything—if Shakespeare or Byron were alive today, I'm sure they'd be rappers. Of course I'll enter this competition, and win it by a mile—eh?" He looked around defiantly, "Oh, by the way, just checking out Alain—I don't have to rap in French do I?"

"Non, most of the rappers rap in English, usually with American accents. You can rap in whatever language you like" said Alain respectfully.

"Even Welsh eh" said Henri with a sly smile that implied that he was going to enjoy things later on. "Why don't we have some Champagne to loosen up our rapper" said Henri encouraging the others to drink up.

"Yeah, let's get some bubbly down you Turpie—you'll need some sparkle in your voice for this" said Vic equally eager to see how things would now work out.

Vic and Archie were delighted at the thought of Thrust making an idiot of himself in a crowded disco—it would give them even funnier stories, to add to the lifeboat saga, when they got home. They also both knew that the nearest Thrust had come to rapping was when he took over the bingo calling at the rugby club when old Gwilym was ill.

"Turpin's a really good rapper—especially at Christmas and birthdays" said Archie—his attempt at a feeble joke. "Rap... wrap... geddit!" No-one laughed. Catherine came and threw her arms around Turpin.

"Turpin, I didn't know you were a rap artist and a musician. You are so, so talented. I really adore a gifted man, and all that poetry last night—magnifique. Perhaps you could compose a rap poem for me and perform it on stage tonight. That would be really beautiful" she said.

Turpin couldn't work it out; either she was part of Henri's plot, or genuinely meant it. He decided to go with the flow.

"Yes, of course Catherine. I'm always inspired to compose poetry by a beautiful woman. It would be a privilege and a delight to compose a rap poem in your honour—and, with you there to support me, it will be easy. I'm sure I will win. In fact I can't wait for the first public performance—it will be, as you say, magnifique." Thrust decided to play the moment for all it was worth.

Catherine then passionately kissed Turpin, and murmured in his ear that she would look forward to finishing last night's unfinished business with him later.

Henri looked less than pleased, but Turpin didn't give a toss.

She then turned and blew him a lingering kiss before walking away. Turpin turned to pick up some of the freshly opened champagne with a broad grin of self satisfaction. He felt that things were on track again, and that the frustrating nightmare of the previous evening would soon be redressed.

"Are you fucking mad" hissed Stan into his ear. "You're going to get up on stage in front of hundreds, if not thousands of people, in a foreign country, and try to do something you've never done before in a contest with skilled performers. At best, you'll be laughed off, at worst, they'll bottle you to death."

"To add to that" continued Stan, "Catherine will see that you're a jumped up nonentity and will ditch you like a used condom. Even more importantly, the rest of us could be caught in the fallout. Michelle may even think I'm a bullshitting useless waster as well."

"She'll have to find out sooner or later" said Thrust with a self satisfied grin.

"Be serious, I think Alain and the rest believe you, but Henri's no fool—and it's obvious he's more than interested in Catherine. I'm sure there's more to that than meets the eye—he'd quite happily see you hung out to dry. Why don't you admit you've been the subject of a misunderstanding, and back off from this one, or else pretend you're too drunk to speak—or even as a last resort, just throw up over the mike—you're good at that" said Stan with sobering common sense.

"Look, I know I'm on a sticky wicket but I'll run with it for now—it's only a bit of a laugh. When I get to go up, I'll break the mike and it will be all over. In the confusion, I'll whisk Catherine off for a night of passion, and we'll be off to Switzerland in the morning. Stan, you know I can cope with it—remember when we had a free night in Pontardawe rugby club pretending to be Springbok Internationals— we carried that off didn't we? Come on you've got to have nerve and live life on the edge" said Thrust invoking previous joint escapades.

"Yeah, I remember it well" said Stan. "It went great until we met a retired miner who'd spent 15 years in Johannesburg. He soon rumbled us. In the end we were lucky to get out alive. You can't fool everyone—especially if, like Henri, they're on to you" said Stan knowingly.

"Shit," Thrust indeed remembered dodging the flying bottles as they left the club that time in Pontardawe, "I don't know, perhaps your right. I'll tell them it's all a mistake...."

Suddenly a familiar voice penetrated his brain.

"Turpin let's go to LeZone. I'm really excited at the thought of you performing just for me. It's so chic, it's so sexy" purred Catherine, who had unexpectedly returned. Thrust looked up at Catherine. "A man's got to do..." He mouthed to Stan. Stan turned to Vic and Archie and said with a resigned smile "Come on boys this should be entertaining."

When they got into the nightclub they realised that it was not a small compact venue. It was packed with hundreds, possibly thousands of madly dancing young people. Spotlights swept back and forth as the crowd thrashed like a basket of maggots. In the distance a huge DJ podium, looking down on the dancers like a modern day Aztec temple stood bathed in spotlights. The DJ stood in the middle of the podium like a high priest, manically moving back and forth mixing various sounds that made up the booming back drop to the human Serengeti that thronged in front of him.

Huge banners proclaimed in both French and English that tonight was the 'Grand Rap Contest', which had been sponsored by a well known drinks manufacturer, and that indeed the winner of the contest would win a large cash prize together with the fame of being 'Le Premier Rappeur de Dijon'.

"This way gentlemen" shouted Henri, leading them to the bar. "I will go and arrange for my friend Turpin to enter the competition. Have a few drinks here—it promises to be a very enjoyable evening."

The small group hovered by the bar and started drinking the fairly strong French bottled lager on sale.

"You're going to need plenty of those if you are going to get up there Turpie boy" said Stan with apprehension on behalf of his friend.

"I bloody well know. Shit—I didn't think there'd be this many people here. I'm thinking this is going to be a close call" said Thrust beginning to feel a bit uneasy at his predicament.

"What do you mean?" said Stan.

"Well, I'll probably have to go with this right up to getting up to the podium, then wreck the mike, and get out of doing this stupid rap con" said Thrust, pushing back his hair nervously.

"What if you can't damage the mike?" said Stan, ever practical.

Turpin paused and breathed hard. "I'll probably faint. Anyway, it won't be a problem—I'll drop the mike, then in the darkness, stamp on it and smash it to pieces. That'll nip this competition in the bud. They'll just have to go back to playing these moronic dance anthems. What a load of bollocks it all is" said Thrust, trying to detach himself from the reality of the situation he found himself in.

"Turpin, I will be so proud of you if you win. I've told all my friends that you will say a poem to me as part of your rap act. It will be such a fantastic occasion" said Catherine as she slipped her arm around Turpin's waist. She now felt she was going to complete their unfinished business, not only to get back at Henri, but also as she had begun to feel genuinely attracted to this strange, funny, yet vulnerable foreigner.

"Yes, yes of course. I will dedicate my entire act to you Catherine. Have no doubt that I will speak a wonderful poem to you when I am up there" said Thrust with all the fake sincerity he could muster.

Thrust caught Catherine's eye and gave a weak guilty smile and swigged on his lager. The situation was getting more desperate by the minute.

Suddenly there was a huge explosion and the compere came on to introduce the first of the evenings rap artists.

A huge black rap artist in a long leather jacket and an eye patch stepped up to the podium. The crowd went wild as the podium began to extend out over the crowd.

The rapper then began to rap over the backbeat and the crowd went berserk. He rapped in both English and French and used the mike and his arms to conduct and mesmerise the crowd. It was a powerful performance that set down a high benchmark for the others to follow. It would indeed be a long night thought Thrust, swigging more deeply from his beer.

As the event progressed, a host of aspiring rap stars came onto the stage. They were a mixture of black, white and Asian rappers, all of whom generally spoke in English or French, though one appeared to speak in Hebrew, whilst a Chinese one rapped, rather stiltedly but logically in Chinese. One rapper from Ireland rapped in Gaelic which certainly got marks for innovation.

The evening wore on and Thrust continued to drink more and French beers.

Stan decided to have a quiet word in Thrust's ear.

"Come on Turpin, for God's sake stop drinking—if your plan doesn't work you may have to actually go out there and rap—and if you drink much more you won't be able to belch, let alone rap."

"I know what I'm doing" slurred Thrust. "I've told you, I'll smash the mike and walk away from it—or else I'll dive into the crowd, and I need a few drinks to do that. So don't fucking worry." He continued to sing into the bottle he held in his hand.

Henri touched him on the shoulder. "Come on Turpin, allez, it is your turn next." A knot tightened in Thrust's stomach as they finished their drinks.

"Good luck—I love you" said Catherine as she embraced and kissed him. "Remember me when you're in front of the crowd. Forget all those pretty girls you'll see. I will wait for you 'ere'" she smiled and blew him a kiss.

Thrust was led through the thronging crowd in a state of shock. He must have been mad to agree to do this. Never mind, he convinced himself, he'd get out of it somehow.

Henri took him up to where the resident DJ console was and introduced him to the DJ.

"Ok. You are on next. Any request for the music you are going to rap to?" The DJ spoke excellent English.

"No—whatever you feel. I'll just go with the song" said Thrust feigning bravado.

"Song? I don't play songs. I play dance and rap. So you can forget about any songs. You're weird man" said the DJ in righteous indignation.

"Oh, I thought Run DMC's 'walk this way' with Aerosmith was really cool, and we'd do something similar" said Thrust, struggling to enter into the rap culture.

The DJ looked at him as if Thrust had farted in the Vatican. As far as he was concerned, Run DMC did not exist on his musical radar.

"I'll play Bitch Slap Whore by Jak Slak Ok," he said with a look of contemptuous pity.

"Yeah, ok, my favourite" said Thrust totally ignorant of every syllable uttered."Can I have a look at the mike?"

The DJ handed Thrust the mike.

Thrust looked at it expertly before dropping it at his feet. He then stamped down as hard as he could but felt nothing. He proceeded to stamp around madly, hoping to hit the mike. He looked like a demented flamenco dancer.

Luckily he hit the mike with one of his last stamps. He almost exploded with relief.

Henri, the DJ and his entourage looked on in amazement.

"Oh I am so sorry. I warm up by doing exercises and I appear to have stood on the microphone. What a pity. I'm so sorry that I won't be able to compete in the competition" said Thrust with a shrug, thanking every God that he knew.

"Don't worry, we have many spare microphones as we often get rap groups appearing here. They also often drop them onto the dance floor, so we also have back ups as well. You'll be okay to go on. Are you ready?" said the DJ, putting a new microphone into Turpin's by now sweaty hand.

Shit, thought Thrust. This is all going wrong. I'll just collapse or leap into the crowd. He looked down from the podium—it was a long way, and he was now less certain that the crowd would catch him if he jumped. His mind was reeling. What could he do next?

"Ok, ready to go? What's your stage name?" asked the DJ.

"Um" his mind went numb. "What?"

"Um, No good boyoooh!" he exclaimed as he was pushed into the rap podium which started to extend out into and over the crowd.

"Allo. Here is our last star tonight, all the way from the UK, Pays De Galles, No Good Boy!" shouted the DJ.

The crowd cheered as he looked around him. He still had a bottle of lager in his other hand, and he poured it over his head—partly to try to wake himself up, but also to wet his hair, which he ruffled up into a suitably dishevelled state. He pulled his sunglasses out and tore his shirt open. It was, to use the well known phrase, 'shit or bust'.

The music pounded around him as the extending podium carried him out above the crowd to the centre of the dance floor. The entire floor thronged below him. He thought he could see a banner in the background with Abertawe Nurses written on it held up by two blow up dolls. He could also see Catherine and the gang over by the bar. His heart was pounding like a jackhammer.

What the fuck was he going to say?

The keyboard melody play over seemed to die back and the music was pared back leaving only the pounding of the bass.

Boom, boom, boom, boom, boom, boom, boom, boom. The sound spun around in his head.

He'd heard a similar interlude in dozens of tracks played in discos back home. In some of their more drunken moments, he and the boys had sung old rugby and war songs to that beat. These songs had scanned perfectly, and dovetailed exactly with the rhythm and beat of the track being played around him.

Fuck it, shit or bust, here goes—he thought, I've just got to go for it.

He raised the mike to his mouth and gave it his best shot, speaking in what he felt was a fast Richard Burton meets Gangsta Rap accent.

"In a German Jail, where they hang you by the... nails and the damp comes running down the walls, two, four.... Where your hair grows thick from your belly to your dick and the mice play billiards with your balls!" Oh yeah!

He gulped and looked around—expecting to be booed off.

The boom, boom beat continued, the crowd danced. It seemed to be working. In fact they seemed to think he was the genuine thing.

He repeated the verse, with more of an inflected slurred rap edge, with a few grunts thrown in. What he said certainly scanned, and as it was said so quickly, and importantly in a strange tongue to a foreign audience, made it seem very natural and cool. In fact, like it or not, it seemed to work. In any event, he appeared to be proving his old saying—it's not what you say that's important, but the way that you say it.

The rhythm and bass pounding along led him to a bolder yet more melodic territory.

"It's a long way from Tipperary, it's a long way to go, it's a long way to Tipperary to the sweetest girl I know. Good bye Piccadilly, good bye Leicester Square, it's a long way to Tipperary, but my heart lies there" his words boomed out, seamlessly in time to the music, whilst in a time honoured rhythmic cadence of their own.

Fuck it, it seems to be working—let's go for it, he thought, as the crowd thrashed and swayed in front of him. They didn't seem to notice that he was, if not talking bollocks, certainly not talking rap.

"Oh, I haven't seen old Hitler for a hell of a time, I haven't seen old Hitler for a hell of a time, when I went to France to see what he was doing (the crowd cheered) when I got there the fucking place was ruined. Oh I haven't seen old Hitler for a hell of a time, he must have been blown up by a mine..." He jabbed the air with his microphone and laughed.

The crowd were now cheering as he launched into 'Sospan Fach' before returning to 'Tipperary'.

He had to laugh—the bawdy verses of decades of old rugby club songs were being effortlessly regurgitated as modern hip hop and rap.

However, over at the bar, the boys couldn't believe what they were hearing.

"Mince my balls in a blender—he's gone fucking stark raving mad—did anyone lace his drinks?" said Stan shaking his head in disbelief.

"No, don't think so. I think it's a combination of adrenalin, necessity and a deeply disturbed psyche—though I wouldn't put it past Henri to have laced them though" said Archie.

"We can't let him go on like this—apart from the embarrassment, God knows what he's going to do next. Come on boys, let's stop him before it ends in a riot" said Vic.

Stan and Vic pushed their way through the crowd up to the podium. Archie just laughed and kept on drinking. Thrust was still reciting in his bizarre 'rap meets Max Boyce' fashion extracts from rugby and war songs. In his excitement he'd now moved on via 'Hitler's only got one ball' to 'Goodby Dolly Gray' and then on to 'Up and Under here we go'. Against all the odds his words seemed to scan, and the crowd appeared to be oblivious to his words and were dancing happily.

"Henri, for God's sake, stop this. You've had your fun. Get him back here" said Stan, grabbing Henri by the arm.

"Non, he is doing very well," Henri smirked, seemingly knowing the true situation, though amazingly most of the people around him seemed to be either indifferent to Thrust's 'act' or actually taken in by it, and enjoying themselves.

"Ok, if you won't, I will" said Stan, leaning down and

pulling the large electric cable that led to the DJ's console and deck.

Thrust had just finished his rendition of 'Roll me over in the Clover', when the entire sound system suddenly went dead. He stood, in total silence above the crowd.

There was a pause that seemed to stretch for an eternity. Shit! he thought.

What was he going to do now?

He had to say something!— not just anything—he knew deep down he had to recite poetry! In his panic, he briefly toyed with the idea of reciting 'Eskimo Nell', though he soon dismissed that idea as being a rap too far.

He suddenly remembered his promise to Catherine—it had to be a poem, and it had to be Dylan Thomas! A surge of adrenalin welled up within him. It just had to be. He hoped he could remember the lines. What's more, it's what Burton would have done.

Summoning up his most resonant Burton accent, he projected his words far over the still anticipating crowd.

"To begin, at the beginning…" he paused for effect, "it was spring, moonless night in the sleepy town, starless and Bible-black" he paused again, then continued with the opening lines of *Under Milk Wood* by Dylan Thomas.

The crowd continued to look up at him, spellbound by his, or rather Dylan Thomas' words.

He felt as if everything he'd ever done, read, dreamed about, was coming together. He was on a roll—it was his moment—he was doing this not only for the need of keeping the audience from rioting, but also because it seemed bizarrely, the right thing to do. What's more, he couldn't stop now. With scarcely a pause he moved on to recite *Fern Hill*.

"Oh as I was young and easy at the mercy of his means, time held me green and dying, though I sang in my chains like the sea."

He rolled the words out with weight and emphasis—he was enjoying every minute of this. The crowd were still standing silently. They either thought he was mad, or were actually listening to what he had to say. Whether they understood a word was another matter. He decided to bring his poetry recitation to an end on a high note. He knew, instinctively what he had to say.

It had to be 'do not go gentle into that good night'.

Behind him the DJ and Henri had located the cable that Stan had pulled out, and were struggling to reconnect the electricity.

Turpin's voice boomed out over the crowd.

"And you, my father, there on that great height, do not go gentle into that good night, rage, rage against the dying of the light." He repeated the last line with power and emphasis. The last word echoed around the still silent nightclub. The crowd seemed genuinely mesmerised and consumed by the words of the poem.

There was what seemed an eternity of silence following his last words, before in an explosion of sound, the music came booming back.

The crowd erupted, and roared their approval, and began to dance and leap about like life prisoners suddenly released. Whoops of joy and appreciation shot out from the crowd as the spotlights roamed back and forth. The upsurge of energy was almost physical.

He momentarily worried that their joy was at the music returning to drown out his words. However, looking down as the sea of upstretched arms and beaming faces, he knew he'd won the day.

Thrust suddenly felt the gantry being retracted and realised his moment of glory was coming to an end. The final surge of adrenalin and the heady concoction of the roars of the crowd, coupled with the blinding light and booming music made him lose control totally.

He began to rap / shout through the mike, "Catherine—for you … I love you …Wales, Wales, Vivre Pay de Galles, Dylan Thomas, Barry John, Lloyd George, Richard Burton…" he was by now punching the air in time with the music… "up the Wizards, come on Bravon…" With a final jolt, he found himself being yanked back from the gantry by numerous grasping hands.

"Bravo mon ami—magnifique—c'est magnifique" said the DJ reverting into French. "You are the winner—no doubt about it. Such fluency, such passion. The poetry—superb. It was an honour to be 'ere tonight. I salute you," he grabbed

Turpin and hugged him vigorously.

"Hey, well done man, you were great" said Henri slapping him on the back. "I didn't think you were so talented." Thrust couldn't work out whether he was taking the piss or whether Dylan's words had indeed won him over.

"Turp, you are fucking mad. Truly, madly, deeply. What the hell were you doing out there! You seemed to think you were the poet fucking laureate or something. I've heard you talk some bilge before, but that took the biscuit. You were lucky you weren't bottled to death" said Stan, shaking his head in bemused admiration.

"Well, I wasn't! I wasn't intending to go out there, but when it happened I just had to do something, and everything just went from there. It all just seemed to make sense though I'm sure no-one understood a word" gasped Thrust, still intoxicated by his brush with stardom.

Catherine came hurtling out of the throng of people around him and threw her arms around him.

"Turpin, that was brilliant—all for me! You held everyone spellbound—it was magnifique." She kissed him passionately. Henri turned swiftly and unnoticed, moved off into the crowd.

"Yeah, they couldn't believe what they were seeing" said Vic, ever the cynic.

Thrust looked over Catherine's shoulder and noticed Henri moving away as she embraced him wildly. His look declared that whatever you might think, I'm the one holding the girl, so go chew on a stick. I've talked the talk.... now I'm going to walk the walk.

Henri turned with a look of disgust, and disappeared into the throng.

"Tonight we will do everything we didn't do on the ferry, and... more" whispered Catherine in between passionate kisses. She now was certain that she would spend the night with Turpin, and sort Henri out on her terms later.

Thank you God, thought Thrust. That old Burton magic sure worked tonight. All the more reason to bring him back safely to his homeland. The nearer we get to him, the greater the magic! He now knew that whatever happened between himself and Catherine, he had to complete his mission.

CHAPTER SIXTEEN

'Lost in France'

Thrust awoke with a throbbing headache—he'd certainly had a lot to drink last night. Vague memories of floating on air above a large crowd came seeping back. He seemed to recollect singing and talking to them. It was all very confusing. It couldn't really have happened.

He then realised he was lying next to a firm, beautiful female body—suddenly more memories of the night before came back. It was almost a ying and yang counterpoint to that terrible night he'd spent in Port Talbot with the 'Last Chance'—everything that was wrong with that night had been put right last night. No lined puffy face, no dirty stained sheets, no forced violent sex, no contrasting images of the Pontypool front row and nubile starlets, no leering extortionate brats and mange ridden pets, no embarrassing painful naked sprint through rain soaked streets to get away from a hideous repetition of the night before. Everything had changed now, it was like being in heaven. He didn't ever want to move from where he was, here, safe and warm in Catherine's arms, and here he would happily stay for ever.

She awoke and kissed him delicately but warmly.

"Turpin that was a wonderful night. You were fantastique," she said in a slightly husky, enchanting French/Swiss accent.

Thrust blushed slightly and recalled his sexual endeavours of a few hours ago. "You weren't so bad yourself Catherine. We had a really beautiful night together." He smiled in smug satisfaction.

"No Turpin. I mean what you did in the rap concert. It was superb—your courage in reciting such raw poetry before all those people, and all for me—it was remarkable. I will never forget that night" said Catherine, puncturing his fragile illusion of being a wonder lover.

"Oh thanks—it was nothing" said Thrust, putting on a brave face despite being considerably deflated by the realisation that his love making had seemed to make no impression upon Catherine at all. He slowly began to recall the details of the nightclub, the rap contest, his lunatic decision to embark upon a rap recitation of rugby and war songs—the Dylan Thomas poetry in a Richard Burton voice. The whole fucking shebang.

A cold hand gripped his pounding heart. What the hell had he done! He would never live it down. Panic seized him. He then calmed slightly. Thankfully no-one would know about this back in Port Talbot, it was miles away. Bollocks! Panic came flying back—unless those bastards Vic, Archie and Stan talked! They'd be bound to! He'd be the laughing stock of the Rugby club. Owen Jones would be bound to put him on a disciplinary. He could see it now, 'bringing the council into disrepute'. The first in 50 years. The shame, the shame. Shit, he must have lost his senses. He'd done some stupid things, but what he did last night topped them all. He stopped and took some deep breaths.

He'd just have to tough it out, or... or... why not stay here? His fertile mind started to wander into fantasy, and he began to calm down. He'd always liked France. He'd got a wonderful girl, Dijon seemed a nice place—he could get by, perhaps as a resident DJ in a club—LeZone? He could appear as 'Le Good Boy' or whatever he'd been introduced as... his mind began to run away from reality. Visions of him driving in an open topped sports car in the French countryside with Catherine, playing rugby for Grenoble, or whoever the local side was, drinking the best wine, rapping and singing to hordes of adoring females. They could turn Port Talbot and the bloody council into an open air abattoir for all he cared. He could quite happily stay here forever. What a life—all sorted. A warm glow enveloped him. Catherine rolled from his embrace and then got up and made coffee together with some toasted French bread.

She placed a breakfast tray next to the bed, then slid in next to him.

Yes, he was in heaven. He was certain of that. They then lay in the bed and chatted nonchalantly.

This is where I want to be, forever, he thought admiring her beauty, bathing in the warm, comfortable sunlight.

"Catherine," he said, summoning up every shred of sophistication and sincerity he could muster, "I'd really like to stay with you—I think we've really got something special between us" he said, ruining the effect by suddenly covering her with crumbs.

"Oh Turpin—I didn't realise you felt that way. I thought it was... what you say 'in the moment we seized'. it was beautiful, but I didn't think you thought so much of me. I really like you but I really need to think much more about this. Anyway, we can't stay here, my home is in Switzerland. We have no reason to stay here." She paused and looked out of the window.

"Anyway, I must go back to my family today. I'm not saying I don't want you or to see you again, but I need time" said Catherine.

He didn't realise his hopes could be dashed so quickly or so woundingly.

"Ok, I'm happy for you to think about things. I just felt that I had to tell you what I'd been feeling." He said, putting a brave, debonair face on things. "My friends and I are going to Switzerland anyway. That'll give you time to think. Give me your telephone number and I'll phone you—perhaps we can meet up, and see what you feel once you've had time to think." Thrust tried to mask his feelings, but this was definitely not what he wanted, or thought would happen. He felt like packing things in and going home. His pathetic fantasies of a life in France melted like the butter on his toast. He still felt he had to try to keep things going with Catherine. He couldn't let her go so easily.

"Yes of course, here, I'll write it for you," she said. "Phone me when you get to Switzerland—I will meet you and tell you my thoughts. I need time to think, but remember whatever happens, we had a very special time last night. It will live with me for ever" said Catherine smiling sweetly.

They kissed again, but something had gone out of the embrace, and part of Thrust wanted to break away from

Catherine, but the memory of the previous night and the hope of nights to come made him hold on for some time in a kind of limbo. He recalled the stolen looks she'd seen her exchange with Henri. What if...?

The silence was shattered by a knock on the door.

"Turpie, are you awake? What are we going to do? We'd better get a move on. Michelle's parents will be home soon and they won't take kindly to a pair of Welsh yobs lounging around their Louis XIV furniture," said a voice with a Welsh accent.

They both looked at the door.

"Are you there Turpin? Say something." He knew the voice was Stan's.

"Ok, ok, I'll be there now. Can't I have any peace to say goodbye?" replied Thrust, realising that reality was about to re-enter his life and shatter his dreams irrevocably.

He and Catherine dressed in silence. Thrust then kissed Catherine goodbye and with some considerable effort turned and walked out of the room and went down the stairs and met Stan outside in the warm sunlight.

"You had a bloody good night. Tell me all about it. First things first though. What are we going to fucking do next?" said Stan.

"We press on to Switzerland like we planned, got to see it through" Thrust lied. He now only wanted to go to Switzerland to hopefully meet Catherine again. He'd all but forgotten about the mission to retrieve Burton in the excitement of his night of passion with Catherine.

"Good boy Turpie—I thought you'd done something daft like falling in love. You were really funny last night, it should be on TV. Richard Burton would've been proud of you. You really nailed your colours to the mast. They'll certainly all remember you—and Wales! They'll all want to find out where it is now. It's all part of the legend—you've got to see this through" said Stan, slapping Thrust on the back.

"Yeah, all systems go for Switzerland" said Thrust trying to ignore the pain in his back. "We've got to get to Celigny by tonight. First though, we've got to go back to the van and see if those lunatics are still alive. If they are, we'll get moving straight away. If they're not there—we'll get moving anyway.

They're next to useless, and we haven't got the time to hang around for them. They could've been neutered by the busload of nurses for all I know. Anyway you and I could complete the mission. No time to lose. Right Stan?"

"Fair enough, but Turp, I've been thinking. I don't' know if you and I can dig the grave out, lift the coffin, then replace it with empty bottles and fill it in. We'd be knackered" said Stan injecting some realism into the moment. "In fact, do we really want to go through with this anyway? The girls are really nice."

"Show some dog Stan. Adrenalin and commitment boy — remember the Tonmawr game — we'd been up all night clubbing in Swansea. Your dog had been run over, and the Indian we'd ate that night was rancid. But did we give up? No — last minute try. They were gutted — adrenalin and commitment. We did it then, we can do it NOW. Let's get going" said Thrust trying to get Stan back into the right frame of mind.

"You're right Turp — we go back a long way. We've been through a lot. Yeah, plenty of dog. I'm still with you on this. Let's go for it" said Stan as their stride quickened.

They soon got back to the van, and found Vic and Archie sleeping inside amongst the mound of consumed beer cans and wine bottles.

It was not a pretty sight — they looked like a montage of crash test dummies, and their snoring sounded like a dozen hacksaws cutting through steel rods.

A few kicks and shakes of the van soon awoke them from their catatonic postures.

"Oy, who's kicking our van you foreign bastards!?" rasped Vic, oblivious to the fact that the foreign bastards might not understand what he'd said.

"Shut it, Boutros Boutros Ghali, the voice of the United Nations! It's only us — wake up!" said Stan.

The door slid open, and Stan and Turpin got into the front seat. They peered into the noxious hell behind them.

Archie's voice croaked from the fetid can festooned swamp that was now the back of the van.

"Jeezus — what a night. Thrust you were epic. I couldn't make up something like that. It was the funniest thing I've seen since Caradog Owen Jones got his dick stuck in a hair dryer and security short circuited the council's electricity supply trying to free him. We'll never have to buy another drink in the Club. It'll be 'have one on us boys, and tell us again about Turpin and the French night club'" said Archie, grinning like a lottery winner.

"Ey—and he had a shag after" said Stan with an emphasised wink.

"Jammy bastard—but for once, he deserved it" said Vic grudgingly.

"Yeah, reward for that terrible night he suffered with the 'Last Chance" said Archie.

"Ok—we can all talk about it on the way. We're off to Switzerland. We've got to get the show back on the road. Let's show some bloody dog" said Thrust.

Archie and Vic groaned, cleared some space amongst the cans, and then suddenly the van spluttered into life. As the van chugged through the streets and moved out of Dijon, Stan asked the others what had happened on the night before.

"Well, after the exploits of that lunatic kicked off and you two sped off with your other halves, we tried to get off with some French girls, but they didn't want to know about us. The fact that we couldn't speak French, or any language at that stage of the night, were dripping in beer and kept trying to recite poetry didn't go down too well with them" said Vic.

"Anyway" continued Archie, "we were finishing off a few beers in the corner of the club when the bouncers asked us to leave. We found ourselves standing outside the club when a melee of demented women came boiling down the street, singing, shouting, snogging men, women, postboxes— anything. Somehow it penetrated my brain that a few of them were speaking some bizarre language, when the penny dropped—all those boring lessons in the 3rd year were worth it—they were speaking Welsh, and I realised that it was some of those bloody mad nurses from Swansea!"

"Anyway, we were able to stop a few of them and explain who we were—started chatting like—turns out one of them is Full Kit Gloria's sister, now living in Swansea" said Vic. "Amazing."

"Of course" said Thrust, stroking his chin, "she had mentioned it."

"They were off to some medics sport festival in Switzerland—full of pumped up doctors playing rugby—athletes, body builders, the lot—from all over Europe. Apparently, they go every year—it's like an Alpine Sodom and Gomorrah—sport, drink, sex, dancing—like the Olympics without the drug tests" continued Vic.

"They love it—save up every year" said Archie. "They never miss it."

"Well, it seems that they normally like a good night out" said Stan, recalling the bus, and the ferry with a mixture of awe, envy and fear.

"Stands to reason, they're nurses. But they really go mad on this trip" said Vic.

"They have twosomes, threesomes, tensomes—it's amazing. They said that they keep scores—marks out of ten—bit like his (pointing at Vic) wanking Olympics only more natural. The winner gets a matching yellow T shirt and a years supply of condoms—very prestigious they said. Some of them meet doctors from other parts of the world and never come back. It's the ultimate nurse fantasy!" said Archie.

"However, the hard core" went on Archie,

"No pun intended" interjected Vic.

"Come back, and nurture a new group for next year. It's a legend in the medical world. They'll probably make a film out of it one day" said Archie, looking out the window.

"Very demanding though—no three humps and 'goodnight girl'—if you don't shag your weight it's a syringe up your arse and you wake up an open sewer somewhere. If they're in a really playful mood they drug you into total limb paralysis then experiment on your nether regions with any implements they can get their hands on—remember that bloke on the bus?" said Vic, squinting like a Gurning champion with his balls in a gintrap.

"Yeah, he didn't deliver the goods—he's still probably trying to get a Petrie Dish from his arse. Brutal they are, if the mood takes them" said Archie.

"Anyway—full kit Gloria's sister, Beryl—mad as fuck—

say's that… are you ready for this Turpie boy? That Gloria is mad for you. Can't stand that wanker Finlay Quench, dying to knock him on the head. She also can't stand Owen bloody Jones, she only stays in the council to see you. Can you believe it? And yes—she does live up to her name—wears a full kit everywhere—even ironing or in the gym. Solid commitment that" said Vic with a look of envious wonderment.

"So when you get back—tell Gloria what you think of her—you'll be doing yourself a big favour!" said Archie.

Thrust couldn't believe what he was hearing.

"When he gets back? If he gets back" said Stan. "He's in love with that Swiss girl. Had a good result last night, must've been all that poetry and rap. Swept her off her feet—I didn't know you had it in you," he said punching Turpin playfully.

"Neither did she!" said Vic.

They all laughed at Thrust's expense, but were secretly slightly jealous at his good fortune.

"Nothing to do with his physical prowess. Bullshit and crap more like—very funny though. Turpie, you came up trumps—you could have been killed, that Henri wanted to see you fail big time. I think he fancied your girl—you really pissed him off with your Burton poetry routine—he really didn't expect to meet a quick talking educated Welshman" said Stan.

"Nobody ever does" said Thrust.

"Mmm—anyway—what finally happened to you two?" said Stan, anxious to piece together the strands of the previous night.

"Well, we didn't feel we were up to the standard the nurses wanted. We wished them all the best, and left them pursuing some Ukrainian weight lifters" said Archie.

"We wandered off, and met two Algerian girls—told us they were rat catchers, but I'm sure we lost something in the translation" said Vic.

"Yeah—we struggled a bit—none of us could speak any language that the other understood, apart from er, very basic sign language. We tried to snog them but they insisted on us buying them some drinks and a meal first" said Archie.

"Can't blame them" said Stan.

"We ended up in a Chinese restaurant and they drank, and

ate everything we got for them, and went on to eat what we had ordered for ourselves. In fact they ate quite a lot of what was on the table next to us as well. I think most of the people in the restaurant were quite frightened" said Vic, ignoring Stan's attempt to interrupt the story.

"Yeah, these girls were both well over 6 foot, and big to match. We were both frightened as well. In fact, there was a lot of fear swilling around in that restaurant" said Archie, looking increasingly uncomfortable.

"Well, one of them then borrowed quite a lot of money from us to make a phone call. I should have worried when she took all the money we offered, but they seemed ok. Anyway, when she didn't come back her friend went to look for her, and that's the last we saw of them. The bastards" said Vic.

"Borrowed money to phone? That's a new one" said Stan with as much irony as he could muster, winking at Thrust.

"Our last bit of money went on paying for the meal" said Archie.

"That we'd never had" said Vic. "The bloody robbing bastards."

"Basically a crap night, with a bit of poop on top" said Thrust, nodding to Stan.

"Well, I'm so sorry I could gargle the piss of a dying hyena in sympathy. A sad story boys" said Stan. "I thought you might have had a result, but no doubt you'll learn from the experience."

"Nah, our luck's out on this trip—not like you two. What's happening with your two girlies then?" said Vic ruefully.

"Well, I'm seeing Michelle on the way back," said Stan smugly, "or if not, we'll meet up in the UK when she goes back to college. Nice girl. But nothing too serious. Got to keep my options open. Never know who I might meet in Switzerland" concluded Stan with a flourish, clearly on the crest of a wave, but mindful of his rarely mentioned commitments at home.

"Well, you may get off with a few corpses, or a vampire or two—Celigny graveyard is a real happening place" said Vic, with his usual added sarcasm.

"Nah, won't be five minutes digging the boy up—hide

him in the booze cans—we'll need to stop for some soon—then out for the night, must look on the bright side eh. Of course, we won't be able to stay in the van—no room, plus kipping with a corpse, even if it is Richard Burton, isn't my idea of a good night" said Thrust in his most conciliatory tone.

"In any event, we'll have plenty of time to nip into town" said Archie. "I don't know Geneva but we're on a roll, and we may even find the busload of nurses—that should be an excellent way to round off the trip—rumpy pumpy all round" he added, on what he hoped was a high note.

"Could be the end of us all" said Stan.

"What about you Turp—what about your girl?" said Vic. "Catherine isn't it?"

Thrust cast his mind back to the morning's parting from Catherine. He suddenly felt very sad. However, he decided to put a brave face on things.

"I hope to see her in Celigny. Her parents live close by. We may see a lot more of each other—I think she really likes me, and I really like her. We've been talking about living over here you know" said Thrust, hoping that things could go back to the way they were in Dijon.

"Aw, that's nice" said Archie.

"Woah! Like her—OK, but could you really live over here? You must be mad. You'll never leave Port Talbot, or at least Wales. You cannot be serious" said Vic.

"Bloody right I am" said Turpin, rising to defend his idyllic dream of living in France, or even Switzerland with Catherine, still hoping against hope that it would one day come true. "What's wrong with living over here? It's everything Port Talbot and Wales is not—it's clean, it's rich, it's full of beautiful countryside and historic buildings. It's got brilliant food and world famous wine. The weather is hot in the summer, you can ski in the winter, and it doesn't rain all year. The people aren't mad and they don't throw pies at you if you read a book in a bar. What's bloody wrong with it here?" He posed the question again for effect. "It's a damn sight better than back home if you ask me" said Thrust, summing up over 30 years of resentment at living in the gloom, grime and despair of Port Talbot.

"Nah – love has robbed you of your senses", said Vic, ever

ready for an argument, especially if it wound Turpin up. "There's no better place in the world than Wales, and Port Talbot's situated in the best part of it (even Vic felt he was on stickly ground on that one)—anyway—it's not just the place – it's the people, the atmosphere, the history, everything. What's more, you'd miss the rugby club, the verbal abuse, the draft Bass, the strippers on Sunday, the Indian and Chinese Restaurants, the cockles, the lavabread, dewberry tart, Evans' pies, the pall of smoke that's always over the town, the gnawing, pregnant hope that Aberavon will one day beat Neath, or for that matter Wales beat England, or that you'll meet a decent woman in the nightclub. You'll miss the sun on the sea and the wind in the hills. Let's face it, you'll never leave Turpie boy, because if you do, you won't be you – you might have a nice house, car, wife, whatever, but if you leave you'll cease being you. You'll be an evolutionary dead end. Your kids will speak French, won't know what a 'wew' is, they won't have the hairs on the back of their necks stick up when they hear Calon Lan. Basically you just can't fucking leave—and even if you do, your body might not live there, but you—you will always be a part of it. Accept it—put those daft ideas behind you and face reality. You're too old to change and what you've got can't be worth changing anyway. So let's do what we've got to do, get pissed, then bugger off home" said Vic.

Thrust looked at Vic and thought that those were the first sensible words that had come out of his mouth for decades. Moreover, what he'd said profoundly disturbed Thrust, probably because they were true, and rooted in every fibre of his being.

"Yeah, of course I'll go back—you can't really compare Dijon to Port Talbot" said Thrust injecting as much irony into his voice as he could muster, in a desperate attempt to shake off the deep doubts that had entered into his soul.

"Well, if you're really going to stay out here, why the fuck are we driving to Switzerland in a van, to dig up Richard Burton's coffin and bring it back to Wales? Why not leave it where it is, and appoint you as it's very own on site guardian?" said Stan, pointing to the foothills and mountains rising before them. "Make your mind up good boy."

"Fair point Turp, you always go on about the decline of Wales, and how Richard Burton wouldn't have put up with it, and how most Welsh people who really make it sell out and live abroad and here's you, the great 'I love Wales patriot' selling out and moving out even before you've made it—that's a turn up for the books. In fact it makes you not only look like a dick, but also, which is worse, turns you into a hypocrite—just like all those 'I'm a Welshman, but I live in Richmond, LA wherever, no good fucking boyo's" said Vic with a grim flourish, sensing that he was pushing Turpin into a tight corner.

Thrust felt he was on a loser, and could feel his own flimsy construction of reality collapsing in on him. They were right. If he really felt like living out here, what the hell were they doing? Why didn't they just turn around now? Didn't all his fine words and impassioned arguments just look like meaningless, clichéd empty posturing? What Vic and Stan had said to him forced him to re-evaluate what he'd always stood for. His mind swirled, as he looked out at the mountains in the distance. Should they stop, and go back, or look for the girls? He wavered for what he felt was an age. He suddenly decided a way forward. He couldn't back down now. He had to go with the plan. He could think about what it all meant on the way to Celigny. What they'd said had shaken him though. He knew he had some difficult decisions ahead. However he knew he had to keep going.

"Ah, leave it out. I'm just a bit besotted. It was a great night. Such a contrast to the 'Last Chance'. My mind's not right. We've got a job to do. Let's keep going. We'll stop at the next supermarket and get some more booze in—we'll need a lot to cover the coffin. I also need to get some tarpaulin and shovels, plus a few lamps. We're going to be busy tonight boys" said Thrust, with renewed confidence and vigour.

"Well—we want a good drink after all that digging, and I'm not hanging around to swap stories with Richard. Once it's done, I'm off to the nearest club" said Stan.

"So let's make sure we get plenty of drinks in. There's a 'Le Clerc' up there on the right. We need to get some food in as well, I'm so hungry I could eat a road kill goulash" said Vic.

"With added hedgehog" said Archie. "I'm fucking starving."

"Aye, and tramp's scab pickings" added Thrust as they pulled into the supermarket.

His mind was in turmoil. Should they go on, do what they'd planned and remain true to their roots, or pack it in and do whatever they felt was easiest? He knew he had to make his decision soon.

CHAPTER SEVENTEEN

'Some Corner of a Foreign Field'

The van, piled high with lager and wine, pulled into a small lay-by near to the church in Celigny.

"Right boys, this is the place. We'll have a quick recce of the churchyard, see what's what, then try and get some kip before we start digging, probably around midnight. We'll need to get some rest though—it could be hard digging, the ground looks pretty hard. I'll just check that we've got everything we need. Picks, shovels, tarpaulin, bin liners, torches and cassette player. Ok?" said Thrust, casting an eye around the van.

"What the fuck do you want the cassette player for?" said Stan.

"Stands to reason," said Thrust. "It's a religious occasion— we can't just dig him up—I'll have to say a few words, perhaps read from the Bible, then some hymns. I know you lot can't sing very well, so I've taped some traditional Welsh hymns." The others looked at each other in amazement. "In any event, it adds to the moment, and anyway it's what he would have wanted. I'm told they had a Welsh choir here when they buried him, so it's only right we do the same when we dig him up—in our own way of course—we couldn't get a bloody choir could we?" said Thrust, slightly defensively.

"You're fucking mad. I can't believe I'm really going to dig up Richard Burton's body in order to try to smuggle it back to Wales, let alone to do it being serenaded by taped Welsh hymns. Anyway, you couldn't make this up. What if someone hears or sees us?" said Stan.

"We'll be ok—there are no houses nearby, and anyway I think it's their annual holiday so they'll all be celebrating down the pub" said Thrust.

"I still think we should call it off. If we get caught, we'll all go to jail and what's more probably be branded as necrophiliacs or whatever. Can you imagine the headlines in the *Western Mail*—it'll be a national outrage. We'll bring shame on Wales. It's bad enough being called sheep shaggers. This is worse! We'll never be able to go back to the rugby club again" said Archie shaking his head.

Vic thought of starting an argument about whether sheep shagging was worse than necrophilia, but decided to let things go.

Thrust decided to nip this embryonic mutiny in the bud. "If we don't do it, that'll be a national outrage—we've come all this way—it would be madness to turn back now. We owe it to ourselves, but more importantly we owe it to him in there, and to Wales! Stop being plastic, posturing Welshmen—content to cheer at rugby and sing a few bars of the National Anthem—do this, make a bloody difference, start the ball rolling, we've been through all this before, so don't back out now. We've got to do it—no if's and no but's. One in, all in. I'll do it on my own if I have to, but I know you won't let that happen. Come on, one day we'll look back at this, laugh yes, but also be glad. We had the guts and wherewithal to come over here didn't we? Let's not waste everything... it's our chance to grab our place in history." He banged the dashboard, immediately regretting it as it hurt his hand. However once Thrust had made up his mind, he was going to carry out the plan.

"It's hardly the fucking Alamo, or storming the Bastile, Turp" said Stan, "so calm down."

"Yeah, but it's something, and at least you won't get killed doing it. What's more we can do it, here and now. So let's get moving" said Thrust with frightening conviction.

"Come on boys, let's humour him, we've come this far. It's got to be worth having a go. We can't let him down" said Vic.

"All right, but once we've done it, I'm off to the nearest nightclub to get as pissed as I can—and I'm not coming back til dawn. What's more, I don't care if he was a Hollywood legend — I'm not sleeping in the same van as a corpse. Understood?" said Archie, being unusually assertive.

"Ok, once you've done it" said Thrust, "you can sleep where you like."

"Right we've agreed. Lets's go and have a look at the grave" said Stan.

They walked through the small graveyard, alongside the steep ravine filled with fast flowing stream. The small church seemed to give off an aura of serenity that made it a fitting place for a person to seek the calm of a final resting place.

"Nice here innit" said Vic.

"Yeah, bit like Pontryhdyfen really. I can see why he wanted to live here, and be buried here. It gives you a real sense of calm. Do we really want to disturb it?" said Stan, looking around him in wonderment.

"Look, shut up," said Thrust. "It's nice ok, but it's not bloody Wales — and that's where he should be buried. I'm certain there was a plot by the government to stop him being buried in Wales — they were frightened that it would become a magnet for Welsh Nationalists — a national shrine if you like. MI6 probably brainwashed him, or forged his will, or something like that. So, we are just righting an historical injustice — like returning the Elgin Marbles, yeah that's it, an act of national repatriation. Look, we're not only helping Wales in doing this — it's really a blow for small, dispossessed nations throughout the world. Think of yourselves boys, not just as good Welsh patriots, but also crusading internationalists, fighting for the basic human rights of all mankind" said Thrust, on a roll. He'd thought about the reason for the journey deeply, virtually all through the journey from Dijon, and he now knew he had to see it though.

The other three just looked at him in a puzzled yet benign way. They all thought that to push him on this just wouldn't be worth it.

"Where's the grave then Turpin?" said Archie, realising that he had to now get his hand's dirty.

"Over there — I recognise it from the books" said Thrust, calming down.

They wandered over to the simple gravestone. It read 'Richard Burton 1925—1984'.

"So that's it eh?" said Archie, slightly crestfallen.

"I thought they'd have put a bit more on it than that" said Vic.

"Like what?" said Stan.

"Well—a quote from his best film or a line from Shakespeare, you know, 'To be or not to be' or something like that" said Vic.

"What about that line from *War of the Worlds*, 'Who would have believed in the last years of the 19th Century...'" said Vic.

"I'd have the bit in *Zulu*, 'In the hundred and twenty five years since the inception of the Victoria Cross...'" said Archie.

"What's the fucking, oops, sorry Rich—what's the point? They're other people's words—they don't signify anything of his," said Thrust, irritated that they were taking the piss out of him and, even worse, Burton.

"Perhaps they could have a photo sensitive tape recording of his greatest lines—anyone visiting could then listen to him whilst standing by the grave" said Vic, half joking.

"Yeah, ok, why not a video hologram of him in his favourite roles. That would really be something" said Thrust sarcastically.

"Yeah, good idea. That could catch on. Celebrity graveyards, you could get thousands of people visiting. It would certainly add to the experience. They've got the technology these days. Perhaps we'll install it when we bring him back to Wales?" said Stan, ever the opportunist, warming to the suggestion.

"Leave it out, I was only winding you up" said Thrust. "It's exactly right as it is—simple, dignified, effective—it's what you'd expect—nothing gaudy. People know the legend—just give them the name—history will do the rest" said Thrust, bringing the conversation back to what he considered to be reality.

"Ok, we've seen what we've got to do," said Stan. "I'm busting for a beer and a kip, so let's get back to the van, then come back here later and do it—we're wasting time here talking about holograms and crap like that. If you want to stay, that's up to you. But I'm going to go back to the van. It'll soon be dark and I don't want to stay here, Burton or no Burton, longer than I have to."

"Yeah, come on. Nice as it is now—this place will give me the creeps after dark and anyway, I need a drink before I dig him up, it's not exactly going to be a bag of laughs is it?" said Vic.

They went back to the van and opened a few cans of lager and talked about the trip so far and the girls.

"I've arranged to meet Catherine afterwards at a nightclub in Geneva. I don't know if you boys are going to come along. She said she'd bring some friends along. Anyway—I think we'll need a few drinks after this" said Thrust, trying to cheer them all up.

"You'll need a bloody good wash first! It's going to be a dirty smelly messy business—we won't have a hope in hell of romancing any women, apart from itinerant abattoir workers, if we don't get a shower after this," said Stan. "I'm happy to join you for a drink though. We'll need something to raise our spirits! Ha bloody ha—spirits—graveyard—get it? Anyway, especially as we'll be fully qualified graveyard diggers. That'll impress the girls in Geneva."

They pulled their sleeping bags around them and tried to grab some sleep in the gathering gloom.

Thrust awoke around midnight. He'd fallen asleep in the driver's seat, and saw that Stan was also sleeping next to him in the front passenger seat. He looked in the back and in amongst a mound of cans and bottles saw two pairs of smelly trainers sticking out at odd angles in the gloom. He heard loud rasping snores and realised that both Vic and Archie were also sleeping. The light clanking of the bottles and cans told him that they had made considerable inroads into the store of booze.

He clanked a few of the bottles loudly together.

"Wakey wakey, rise and shine. We've got some digging to do!" said Thrust in his best Windsor Davies voice.

The chorus of abuse and flying cans told him that his intervention was not warmly received.

"Come on, the quicker we do this, the quicker we get to the

nightclub" said Thrust, trying to inject some urgency into things.

Eventually, the motley gang tumbled out of the van, and gathered picks and shovels in from the back, and wandered onto the path to the graveyard. Thrust carried a portable cassette player and a lantern torch.

"Hi, ho, hi, ho, it's off to work we go, with a shovel and a stick and twelve inch dick, hi, ho …" sang Stan.

"Shut up. This is serious. No messing about. We go in, dig him up. Say a few respectful words, put him into the tarpaulin, fill in the grave with some of those cans and bottles, cover it all over, bring him back to the van, cover the tarpaulin with the rest of the cans, have a quick wash in the stream—then drive down to Geneva for a well deserved drink. OK" said Thrust.

"Ok." They all muttered their grudging agreement.

They trudged over to the gravestone. The only sound was that of the stream rushing past. It was pitch black apart from the lantern. If they could have stopped and looked in on the scene they would have laughed, but they were too far gone for such rational thought. Thrust was driven by his long held ambitions, Stan driven by general loyalty to Thrust, and Vic and Archie purely by alcohol and the need to complete the task in order to consume more alcohol. They gathered silently around the grave. Thrust solemnly placed the lantern on the gravestone, with the cassette beside it. He coughed and then spoke in hushed tones.

"Richard, we mean you no disrespect in what we do. We are only doing it because we know that you really want to come home and, this is perhaps what's most important, Wales needs you back home. They should have done this back in 1984, we know that, but they didn't know what they were doing burying you here. We've come to take you home. It's all for the best. God bless you. Amen. Archie—you and Vic dig first. Right boys—let's get digging" said Thrust reverentially.

Thrust pushed the 'on' button on the cassette and the sound of the Treorchy male voice choir singing 'Calon Lan' drifted over the graveyard. Archie and Vic giggled. The spades crunched into the grass and the first sod of earth was thrown to the side of the grave as Vic and Archie started the excavation of the soil.

After about ten minutes digging, Vic and Archie threw the spades to one side.

"This is hard fucking…"

"Ssshh, show some respect" said Thrust.

"Sorry, hard blooming work. We need a rest, and a drink. It's over to you boys for a while" said Archie, visibly stressed by his exertions.

Thrust grimaced, and then nodded to Stan. "Ok Archie—we'll take over."

Vic and Archie trotted off to the van, whilst Stan and Thrust took over digging.

"I can't believe I'm doing this" said Stan. "Apart from the total insanity of it—what if we're caught?"

"We plead diplomatic immunity, or if that fails, insanity. Anyway, we're nearly there now so keep digging and stop talking. This is your, our, key to a better future" said Thrust, "and anyway, we're on a national project."

"More like a key to a better sleep, and that's all we're hoping for. Anyway, what if the coffin has crumbled and he's been all eaten up by worms or even worse, not been eaten and is now a mass of decomposing flesh?" said Stan with genuine distaste.

"Don't worry. He was a millionaire—they'd have used the best wood, and probably a fully lined coffin. It wasn't that long ago anyway—it'll be all intact. We're bound to be able to lift it up, with just a bit of effort" said Thrust putting a brave face on things.

"Effort? What if it's a lead lined coffin. We could rupture ourselves" said Stan.

"Nah, we're four big blokes, and he wasn't that tall," said Turpin. "Anyway I'm certain it's not lead lined. I saw them on TV., his brothers, all elderly, lowered him down in 1984. I know it was a good coffin, it was in one of the books I read—they said he was buried in coffin of finest Welsh oak, dressed from head to toe in red, with a Welsh rugby jersey on him, together with the family Bible, and a special message from Elizabeth Taylor."

"Seems daft to me. What's the bloody point?" said Stan.

"Of what?" said Thrust.

216

"Of any of it—why in red? Why the rugby jersey? Why the message? It's a load of crap" said Stan.

"'Cos it made him feel better. I don't fucking—ooops, sorry Rich—know. Just keep digging, we'll soon find out" said Thrust, plunging the spade deeper into the earth, with a loud tut.

Thrust and Stan kept on digging. Soon Vic and Archie came back to join them with some bottles.

"That's better" said Vic. "Thirsty work this grave digging. Any luck yet?"

"No, still digging down" said Thrust.

"All quiet back there?" said Stan. "Yeah, not too bad, but I'm sure I saw the busload of nurses driving past on the main road."

"Are you serious? What the fu… hell would they be doing up here?" said Thrust.

"Probably on their way to Geneva and they got lost" said Stan.

"Or maybe they are looking for us?" said Archie.

"Or maybe they've come to exhume Richard Burton—wouldn't be surprised, these medics will do anything—probably a rag stunt" said Vic, starting to wind things up.

"Yeah, someone told me Cardiff Medicals had Lloyd George's knob pickled in a jar in their common room" said Archie.

"It's a wonder there was anything left of it—he shagged half of Europe didn't he" said Stan.

"I don't bloody know! Anyway, they could be on the same mission as us" said Vic.

"Just forget it—no-one else would be mad enough to do this. What's more the chances of anyone trying to do it at the same time as us are longer then Archie's chance of being picked to play for Wales next season. They are probably lost, or even more likely, figments of your alcohol riddled imagination. Grab this—it's your turn to get digging." Thrust threw a spade to Vic.

"Ok, ok, keep your hair on—want a drink to cool you down?" said Vic.

"Yeah, it is thirsty work, and we need some reward for all our labours" said Stan.

They swapped places, and Vic and Archie resumed digging, though not as vigorously as Turpin and Stan.

Stan and Turpin stood by the graveside and quickly drank the beer they'd been given. Thrust changed the tape, and the lament of 'Tyddi a Rhoddaist' swirled through the night air.

"I'm saving the National Anthem for when we open the coffin" said Thrust.

"Why don't we just take the coffin back without opening it?" said Archie.

"Well, we need to open it to check that everything is in order. Anyway, I want to see if the stories about the rugby jersey are true" said Thrust.

"Bloody mad" said Vic.

They kept on digging. After a while Vic and Archie started to moan and groan and their rate of digging slacked noticeably.

"Right. It's our turn" said Thrust. "A bit more effort and we'll be talking to Dickie 'in the flesh' so to speak" said Thrust.

"Bloody marvellous thought. I just hope he doesn't start to speak back!" said Stan in an attempt to lighten the situation.

"Yeah, what if he says 'What the fucking hell are you doing? Leave me here—I don't want to go back to Wales" asked Archie.

"Watch your language" said Thrust. "Why don't you get some more drinks, and start loading the empties into black sacks so that we can fill the grave up when we've got him out, and leave the philosophising to me."

"Right. Will do, and if we see the busload of nurses this time we flag them down and ask them what they're doing" said Archie, wandering back to the van.

"Yeah, you do that, but don't tell them what we're doing. I need to concentrate on this digging and the nurses might get in the way" said Stan.

"I never thought I'd ever hear you say that" said Vic.

"Nor me, but just get on with it" said Thrust.

Thrust and Stan continued digging. They instinctively knew they were getting closer to the coffin. They dug more quickly.

Suddenly there was a thud of metal on wood.

"We're there. We've hit the coffin. We've done it!"

"Sshh Stan—you'll wake the dead," said Turpin.

Vic and Archie came running back.

Stan and Thrust dug more furiously, whilst even Vic and Archie threw down their drinks and helped dig. Soon the whole lid of the coffin was exposed.

Thrust unscrewed the brass screws and tied thin ropes onto the handles on the lid. He climbed out, and brushed himself down.

"One final thing" said Thrust.

He put the last cassette in, and the strains of 'Mae hen wlad fy nhadau' rang out.

"Right boys, it's time to meet Mr Burton" said Thrust.

The four of them pulled on the ropes and the coffin slowly rose up. They pulled steadily and inch by inch the coffin rocked slowly upwards, discharging small pieces of earth from the surrounding sides of the grave.

"It's lighter than I thought," said Vic.

"Well, he was quite old and small when he died," said Turpin, authoritatively.

Soon, the coffin was at the top of the shaft.

The tension was unbearable. They were all sweating profusely, but not solely due to the exertion.

"Ok, let's move it over" said Thrust.

The coffin was moved over to one side on the ground next to the grave. They gathered around the coffin, in the blackness.

The strains of the Welsh National Anthem continued to ring out over the otherwise silent graveyard.

"Let's see him then" said Archie. "Open the bloody thing."

"Ok, ok. Stan, bring the lamp over. Steel yourselves boys, it might not be a pretty sight, but you will be looking at what's left of the greatest Welshman ever—it's something to tell your children. Right swing the lamp over and let's see him" said Thrust, undoing the screws of the coffin.

The unscrewing seemed to take an eternity. Eventually he slid the lid from the top of the coffin.

The light shone down into the open coffin. The four of them peered over the edge into the large wooden box.

No-one spoke. The shock was almost physical.

CHAPTER EIGHTEEN

'The Whole Truth'

"He's not fucking there!" said Archie.

"There's nothing there!" said Stan in disbelief.

"I don't believe it, the bloody coffin is empty" said Vic, shaking his head.

Thrust's own head was reeling. He couldn't believe it. There was nothing in the coffin. Sweet F.A. They'd come all this way, sweated and toiled, for nothing.

All his dreams, his schemes—had been shattered. He felt like being sick. They stood for minutes staring down. The Welsh National Athem suddenly ended.

"Er, have we got the right grave?" said Vic, breaking the silence.

"Well there's a big rock here with 'Richard fucking Burton' written on it. So I think it's probably the right grave" said Stan.

"If it isn't, what do you want us to do, dig the rest up in rotation to see if he's been buried under a nom de fucking plume? Or dig those with vaguely British sounding names? Or those dug in the 1980s. Bollocks. He's not there. We've got the right grave. I can't believe it but there it is—sodding bloody empty." Thrust's voice erupted in frustration.

They continued to stare down into the empty coffin. Suddenly Stan pointed at the coffin.

"Look, its not empty. There's a piece of paper or something in the corner.

Stan leant into the coffin and reached into it.

"Yes, it's an envelope. It's sealed" he spoke softly.

"What's in it?" Thrust asked.

"Hang on, I'll open it now" said Stan.

Stan picked the envelope up and moved under the lamp and started to pull the envelope open. In it was a small piece of paper. Stan opened it and read out the words written on it. 'Mae 'di mynd adre nawr'.

Stan folded it back and stared into the darkness.

"Well, what does it mean?" asked Archie.

Stan started to laugh. The others looked on in amazement. Stan stopped laughing.

"He's gone home now, it's written in Welsh—it merely says 'he's gone home now'" said Stan, continuing to chuckle to himself.

"Jeezus bloody H!" said Thrust. "Someone's beaten us to it! Someone else has nicked his body. The bastards! It's probably on it's way to a theme park in Orlando as we speak. Shit—I can see it now—'Come and see the remains of Dickie Burton, the famous English actor, who married Elizabeth Taylor'. Arghhh... I'm absolutely gutted" said Thrust punching the gravestone. "Ouch, that fucking hurt, aaarrhhh—sorry Richard." Thrust rubbed his hand, whilst wincing in pain and despair.

"I doubt it" said Stan. "I'm no Sherlock Holmes, but firstly this is an old envelope, it's browned and crinkled with age. It hasn't been put in here recently. Secondly I doubt whether any grave robbing theme park operatives from Florida would write 'He's gone home now' in Welsh on an envelope and leave it behind. They might write 'Have a nice day' or even 'Sue me motherfucker' but I don't think they'd write such a simple honest statement in a language they've probably never heard of." Stan's clear logical words cut through the silence.

"No, whoever took him, if they ever did take him, took him a long time ago, he may never have been buried here in the first place. I'm fairly certain of that. Remember how corroded the screws were? I think he was either taken soon after burial, or that he was simply never buried here at all," said Stan with resonant clarity.

"Stan, that makes sense. I never knew you were a detective. Well done," said Vic.

"Bloody hell—what a turn up for the books. What a

monumental, huge, twelve inch dick of a waste of time—coming over here to dig up an empty grave. This is more far fetched than the plot of Dallas. Nevermind, it'll be a great story for the *Western Mail*—no not just them—this'll be international—*Times, New York Times, Sun*, you name it, they'll all want a piece of this. We'll be able to sell it for tens of thousands—we'll all be rich, ha ha no pun intended—not such a wasted journey, eh, Turpie boy." Archie started to laugh and hug Vic.

"No, not a wasted journey, and no, we're not going to sell the story," said Thrust. "In fact, we're going to fill the grave in and leave it just as it was. We can't betray a man's greatest secret—and a secret it is—and shall remain, just for money. If we're worth anything, and by that I mean if our self worth means anything, we won't sell this story, and we'll keep this secret. It's what he would have wanted and also what whoever took him wanted. We can't break this story—it's too important for that. We must respect this whole situation. It's only right."

"Come on Turp, I've got a camera in the van. Just a few snaps, we can remain anonymous. We'll be rolling in money, you can give up that shite job in the council—get a decent car, whisk Full Kit Gloria off to the Caribbean, the works. We've just got to sell the story" said Vic.

"Everything's got a price hasn't it?" said Thrust angrily. "Every nympho who has shagged a politician, every alcoholic footballer, every talentless wannabee who has done more gobbling than a 100 year old turkey—they all sell out don't they? Are we the same? Think about it. We were brought up in communities with values—yes—you'd work hard—yes you'd use your talents, and if they were great enough, like the bloke who was buried here, that hard work and that talent could make you a millionaire. That's the way to make money, not selling out. We don't want to sell out our birthright, our honour, to some two bit tabloid that'll make a joke out of it to demean him, his family, his town, his country—for a couple of grand? Leave it out." Thrust felt tears welling up in his eyes.

"But, didn't you come here to dig him up to turn him into a circus? To publicise his name further and to use it to create a Burton industry in south Wales? You've changed your tune

Turpin" said Archie.

"Maybe I did want to use him," said Thrust, "but..." he paused "...I thought about this a lot earlier, and that was why I wanted to see this through—yes—in order to rejuvenate a dying town—to give people something to do—proper jobs, dignity whatever and possibly something more. To use him as an example of achievement—of being the youngest of thirteen children, brought up in the depression yet having the talent, the guts, the 'star quality' to break out of all that and to do something with your life. That's what I wanted to do, and would probably still do it if he was here, but I certainly won't put my name to betraying this last great secret, it's a cheap trick, and you know it" said Thrust, firmly occupying the moral high ground.

"Yeah, Archie, think about it for a moment. Whoever did this won't be best pleased. They might expose us, or come after us?" said Stan, injecting a note of caution.

"Bollocks—if it's his family, they're all dead or too old to do anything. We needn't be worried about that" said Archie, with a sneer of bravado.

"What if it's not his family? What if it's some shadowy organisation, some sort of secret society—half Masonic, half Druid? I read a book once that claims there are these secret societies that exert tremendous power over the generations—they go around collecting relics and artefacts, and if you cross them, it's goodnight and God bless!" said Vic, ever the coward.

"Yeah—like the Knight Templar's, or that skull and cross bones society in America. I've read about them. Gives me the creeps. We could be in deep shit for betraying their secrets" said Stan.

"Yeah, perhaps there is some ancient secret Welsh society, a sort of 'Meibion Glyndwr with knobs on' who go around protecting and conserving the Welsh heritage—who knows, perhaps they've taken him to some Welsh Valhalla in the depths of mid Wales, where he is laid to rest alongside all the great Welsh heroes... Caractacus, King Arthur, Merlin, Owain Glyndwr, the lot—they have never found any of their graves have they?" said Vic, carried along with the rolling tide of conspiracy theory.

"Yeah even Lloyd George—without his knob," said Stan.

"Shit. You might be right. All right, all right, I'll go along with you boys. Forget the money, forget selling the story. Let's fill the grave in, have a wash, then get pissed. I've had enough of this—it's spooky enough here as it is, without some secret society coming to kill me. Let's just get out of here" said Archie.

"Right boys—are you all agreed on this?" said Thrust, not wishing to develop any more dubious theories.

"We fill the grave in, and make it look as if nothing has happened, and then we swear, on everything we hold dear, never, never to utter a word of this to anyone. Agreed?"

"I agree" said Stan.

"Yes" said Vic.

"And me" said Archie.

"Right, let's fill in the grave" said Thrust, "and put things back exactly as they were."

They filled the grave in in silence in double quick time, anxious that their activities would be spotted.

They finally laid the cut turf back over the grave and stamped it down with their feet.

"If anyone sees the grave tomorrow and inspected it closely, they would assume that a group of well wishers had stood around it. Other than a few muddy footprints, nothing would indicate that the grave had been dug up the night before" said Thrust wiping the sweat from his forehead.

They stood around the grave, then on Thrust's insistence reached over it and placed their right hands one over another and swore, on everything they held sacred, never to reveal what had happened. As far as anyone back home would know, they'd had an eventful booze trip to the continent and had plenty of tales to keep everyone entertained. But of the true nature of their trip, not a word would be spoken. No-one would ever know that they had 'gone for a Burton', and returned empty handed.

CHAPTER NINETEEN

'He's All Around Us'

The trip back proved much less eventful that the journey out. After they put the coffin back into the grave, they managed to freshen up and drove down into Geneva, and park up the van in a back street. They then lost little time in moving on into one of Geneva's trendy night clubs where, as usual they drank too much and totally failed to make any inroads with the local females. They had arranged to meet Michelle and Catherine there. Turpin was pleased to find that Catherine was indeed there, but she was accompanied by Henri who, it transpired, was her long standing boyfriend, whom she revealed was an aspiring politician studying at the Sorbonne and who proved to have an open mind and a taste for unusual excapades. Catherine had indeed confronted Henri with his infidelities, and trumped them all, as Henri was painfully made aware of the truth about her and Turpin. This had shaken Henri's ego to it's core, and he realised he could no longer treat Catherine so lightly. Her plan had seemed to work, and bizarrely Turpin's night of passion had the opposite effect to what he had hoped and intended. Instead of luring Catherine away from Henri, their night of passion had ironically brought them closer together. However, Catherine felt she had to put Turpin straight on her future plans. They had a deep and quite touching conversation at the club, where she told Turpin everything, and where she reluctantly explained that whilst she really felt a lot for Turpin, in particular his voice and what he said, nevertheless their brief relationship was merely a fleeting dalliance and that she saw her future with Henri. Thrust was upset that Henri had been

225

involved with Catherine but he felt perhaps it was for the best and that at least she'd been straight with him in the end!

Turpin comforted himself with the thought that he'd really pissed Henri off by taking Catherine from him for one brilliant night and that that had not only knocked the smile from his smug, handsome face, but also perhaps, had taught Henri to value Catherine. He was also comforted by the growing certainty that he really wouldn't have settled in Switzerland or France, and that Wales was really where he wanted to live. He also concluded that anyway, Welshmen living in the Geneva area tended not to have a long life expectancy, especially if it involved repeated exposure to the vigorous sexual activity he'd experienced with Catherine in Dijon.

They drove back through France in a relatively subdued mood, playing their traditional bizarre rugby team's game, or just talking about the trip.

On the ferry they'd finally met up with the legendary busload of nurses, who by their own riotous standards, had had a quiet crossing—the only incident of note was when they'd had to throw a life vest after a naked man they'd been chasing had jumped overboard. The boys noted that the tally of sexual conquests marked on the side of the bus was very impressive and intimidating, but Thrust benignly put it down to girlish high spirits, and hoped that he'd be able to track them down on their return to Wales. Sadly as time went by, that never came about, though many a pub conversation, and indeed many a visit to another pub, in time honoured fashion, was prompted and enhanced by the very mention of their name. In fact, the busload of nurses were never seen again, though their exploits grew into legend, and, like some South Walian version of 'The Flying Dutchman', phantom sightings of the busload of nurses were often reported on dark and foggy nights in the Valleys.

On the journey back from the ferry, Thrust became heartened by the unexpected news that Full Kit Gloria was madly in love with him, and that he was, for possibly for the first time in his life, eager to go to work on Monday to see her and finally tell her of his feelings for her. He also admitted to himself that perhaps his nights in the Bryns, especially after his experience with the 'Last Chance' ought to be brought to an end, and certainly knew that the thought of sharing his life with Gloria, and only to a slightly lesser extent, her ubiquitous 'full kit' seemed a much more attractive option than trawling seedy nightclubs searching for the 'Last Chance' and her ilk.

He thought about the 'Last Chance' and as he reflected on how their lives had come together, concluded that perhaps he'd been unfair on her. Ok, she was no Angel, but he didn't know what she'd had to put up with, and what had turned her into what she was. Thrust certainly didn't have any moral high ground in these matters, and decided to be less judgmental about the girls in Bryns in future.

He also thought about what he really wanted to do in the future. He knew whatever happened, he had to get out of the council—he couldn't go on just writing down what other people said—he wanted to write down what he said, or at least do something, rather than watch other people do it.

Whether he'd leave Port Talbot was another matter. Since the trip to Switzerland he'd thought a lot about his home town, and whilst it would never be described as rustic or quaint, there were nice parts of it, and he had a genuine love for it's people and their traditions, their sense of humour. They were some of the finest people he'd come across—straight, rough, funny— steel people from a steel town. It and they were part of him, and he was part of it, as had been his family for generations. He doubted whether he could ever leave. Perhaps if things worked out with Gloria they'd bring up a family, just like his parents and their parents before them, in the town, which had made them, and him, the people that they were.

As their van, piled high with booze, though lacking any coffins or corpses (apart from Vic and Archie who were passed out in the back) sped over the Severn bridge into Wales, Thrust reflected on what had happened on the trip and what it meant to him.

Did they really waste their time going on a crazy journey to get Richard Burton's body? Would it, did it, make any difference that they hadn't found it? Did it really take a body, or person, real or otherwise buried in the soul of a Nation to make that Nation great, or proud of itself?

Of course not, he concluded. It would, at best, only have been a symbol—a symbol of what things once were, and which he was certain could also be again.

In Thrust's mind, Burton didn't need a grave of a long lost hero to inspire or enable him to do what he did—neither did Owain Glyndwr or the other heroes in the past. Ok, they may or may not have needed inspiration—but that came, not from a grave, or even a statue (though he still thought a statue to Richard Burton would look nice in the town square) but from what that person did—and that he was sure, lived on irrespective of any physical remains, through word of mouth or great deeds—or nowadays, like Burton's case through sound recordings and films.

It was all there, he reasoned, all around them, if only people looked, or were shown, and that's where, to Thrust's way of thinking, things had gone wrong. No one told the stories anymore, or read the books, or showed the films that revealed the deeds and talents of generations that had gone before. They were left mouldering in libraries and cupboards. In his view, the task for Thrust and people who thought like him, who wanted a vibrant, proud, rejuvenated Wales, was not to bring back relics, or mindlessly bemoan the failings of the present, but instead to use the past, not so much to tell people today what other people before them had done (though that was undoubtedly important) but to use it to tell them what they could do today. If that message caught on—then it would rejuvenate the town or village, or the whole bloody country, even England, or why not, the whole world! and enable it to turn out more Richard Burtons—in a hundred different fields of life. He also considered the question, had Wales itself 'gone for a Burton'? that mindless, inane phrase that had earlier been thrown at him by the hooray henry rugby player, that after what he had gone through, had some ironic resonance for him at this time.

The answer, he was sure, was no. He was confident that there were countless potential Burtons already there waiting to emerge, all they needed was a catalyst, a spark to ignite their talent, and he resolved that he was one of the people who was going to do something about it.

Interestingly, as he passed through Cardiff, he noticed a large billboard proclaiming the Manic Street Preachers headlining at a sell out concert supported by the Stereophonics. As he looked out, there came over a news item revealing that a crop of young Welsh actors including Catherine Zeta Jones and Ioan Gruffudd were now being tipped as Hollywood superstars. Perhaps the Burtons had already started to emerge? He didn't really know, but felt sure that something was happening.

He took a day off before going back to work and went up to the Cemetery in Jerusalem Chapel in Pontrhydyfen near Port Talbot, where, in an interview in the 1970s Richard Burton had said that he'd reserved a plot for himself and Elizabeth Taylor. Thrust went there to check it out, intrigued by what he'd seen in Switzerland. Thrust didn't see any grave marked Richard Burton, but he did see a small unmarked plot in the corner of the graveyard.

He thought to himself, 'Had Burton's last wish been granted? Was he now safely buried back in Wales in his birthplace Pontrhydyfen? Could someone really have brought him back? Had he in fact been buried here all along?'

He looked around him and felt there was something unseen, yet strangely tangible which led him to believe that Burton was there. But he thought, perhaps that was the lesson he'd learned from the trip. You didn't need physical things to make a village, town or nation, it was the people and their spirit that really embodied these things, and irrespective of Burton's final resting place, that spirit was still and always had been in that village, and in the country itself. He thought of the cliched old saying 'he is all around you, but you just can't see him'. A cliché it undoubtedly was, but he certainly felt that more than ever in that small sleepy chapel graveyard in the heart of the Afan valley.

As he sat at his desk in the council on his first day back at work and stared at the piece of paper in front of him, he decided that he still needed to do something to get out of the endless tedium of his job and in so doing hopefully enrich the literary life of the nation, or at least he thought, make people laugh.

Thankfully, Owen-Jones was off with chronic piles, and

there were no committee meetings for a week. He resolved to tell Gloria what his true feelings were, and he was sure she would confirm that she'd loved him for ages and that Finlay Quench would be expelled from her life forever. He would then take Gloria out for a meal to celebrate where he would invite her to share his des res in downtown Port Talbot. He hoped that Stan was happily back with his girlfriend and child, and in a flush of bonhomie, that Vic and Archie would arrange a joint date with the two nubile strippers from Clydach they'd seen in the Rugby Club. First though, he needed to start that bloody book.

He picked up his pen, and poised to write the first words of his novel. His previous efforts, jotted in a worn notepad, were not much more than a few hastily cobbled together lines of old jokes and personal observations. He needed to start again, especially if he was going to live up to his aspiration to release the Burton in himself, and hopefully later in his literary career to encourage others to do the same.

To inspire him to write, he ran through the routine in his mind once again, for old times sake. He couldn't act, couldn't sing, and his guitar playing was sub garage band level. Yes, it was the only option. The only thing he could ever hope to do was write. He knew it was his destiny. He resolved to get on with his novel whatever the cost.

He revisited the opening lines he'd previously written. He thought an out and out sex and romping novel really wasn't what he wanted to do—the market was pretty saturated. Anyway, he had a degree in English Literature—shouldn't he write something a bit more ambitious? He considered whether he could write a novel about the sexual and physical abuse of a poor farm worker in a country mansion at the turn of the 19th Century which would stand as a metaphor for the oppression, of the subject nations of the British Empire. He thought of utilising sado masochism as a symbol of mercantile imperialism. He thought perhaps the novel could juxtapose these historical themes with the psychological conflicts sparked by main character's intertwining relationships in order to give it a refreshing modern relevance. The entire novel would be built up layer by layer and chapter by chapter and would stand as a true literary masterpiece. He'd probably have to dig out his old University lecture notes to give it some added gravitas, he thought, with one eye on the Booker prize.

He stopped suddenly and laughed out loud. Turp—don't be a dick he thought. Better to leave such pretentious bilge to people who live and breathe it, and who are better equipped to write about it. It didn't sit well with him, his life, where he lived, or what he thought. Do what you feel is right, he told himself, not what you think might impress others. Be yourself, be true to your roots and they were for good or for bad, Wales and Port Talbot.

He thought he'd just stick to what he wanted to do in the first place. Write a funny book about the often weird and entertaining lives of ordinary people, their friendships, loves (both real and imagined), their humour, what made them laugh—in short their and his stories. It might not be high literature, but it would at least be true (well, part of it!) and it may eventually prove to be a best seller.

Even if it didn't, at least he'd have some fun writing it. He didn't really know what exactly to do, but he knew he had to start somewhere, and anyway, he already knew he had the opening line ...

"Finbar O'Driscolls' pert young buttocks quivered in nervous anticipation at the sight of m'lady's riding crop."